Glum and Mighty Pagans

By

Eve Ottenberg

ISBN: 1-4140-4792-4 (e-book)
ISBN: 1-4140-4791-6 (Paperback)

This book is printed on acid free paper.

1stBooks – rev. 01/15/04

I

One afternoon in the late 1970s, in a small, exquisitely kept town on the west coast of Florida, a girl in a red bathing suit, blue flip-flop sandals and white cut-off shorts, carrying a little, striped, canvas bag, was walking north along the beach, away from the bathers. She had no discernible destination, for the white shoreline stretched before her, seemingly endlessly. The beautifully tended houses and condominiums whose pastel colored walls, wrought-iron balconies and clusters of palm trees faced the beach had already given way to scrubby, brown and yellow half-cleared lots, amid which rose the skeletons of soon to be posh high-rises. Beyond the construction loomed a greenish tangle of undergrowth, and nothing else, as far as the eye could see. This undergrowth, bordered on one side by the beach, extended, on the other, to a black strip of boulevard, beneath whose Royal Palms occasionally passed a Rolls Royce or a shining new Mercedes. The heat shimmered up from the soft asphalt. And through the gold and silver waves of heat the brownish, ribbed palm trunks rippled and swayed and appeared like chocolate, to be melting from the sun. Even by the water's edge, the heat was intense. Every now and then the girl would dart into the aquamarine gulf, up to her knees, splashing her face and arms. Though seventeen, she looked slightly younger because of her slenderness and her deep tan. Nonetheless, from time to time, over the continuous plash of the waves, a distant whistle could be heard as one of the construction workers paused from his drilling or hammering on the tenth or eleventh floor of some gigantic, windowless structure to note her passing.

There was no sea breeze whatsoever. The waves, which were quite low, looked rather like lumps in an otherwise smooth sheet of turquoise edged only by the bone-white swatch of sand and, at the horizon, the pure blue of a still and cloudless sky. The girl, who had been walking for over an hour and was now the only figure on the shore, seemed to be tiring. She more frequently shifted her bag from shoulder to shoulder, and less often swung it at her side, She had stopped bending over when she came upon a scarce or lovely shell. Instead, she now gazed listlessly out at the gulf, or over at the boulevard beyond the vacant lots, but rarely directly ahead. Now and then her lips moved as she breathed out, or rather sighed the words, "Oh well. That's that."

The last empty lot before the wildness of undeveloped land began was marked off on either side by half-completed luxury high rises and had a white gravel path down the middle, leading to the boulevard. Here and there "No Trespassing" signs stood out. Half of the lot, evidently intended to be a tropical park, already sported Bayonne trees, coconut palms, flowering bushes, benches and an occasional piece of soapstone sculpture. Though there was something almost forbidding about the incompletion of these deserted two acres, it was here that the girl turned away from the gulf and headed inland. By the time she reached the gravel path, the sun had moved into the far western quadrant of the sky. But the heat did not abate. If anything, it had become more suffocating. She did not slow her pace, however, nor did she hurry, but continued as before, the only person visible in that vast, well-groomed landscape. Now and then a piece of gravel

4

would flip through one of her sandals, and she would jump as if it were a live coal. Often she raised one hand to the back of her head, protecting her short, reddish brown hair, which seemed to burn as if it were on fire, from further contact with the sun. And she continued occasionally to move her lips, uttering the same four words, until she reached the deserted boulevard. There she stopped and watched a Bentley, black as a hearse, approach and pass. Briefly, through its shut windows, she glimpsed the occupants of its air-conditioned interior — an elderly woman in gray silk and bejeweled and a young man, probably her grandson, suited and smoking. She watched the automobile for some time, and, long after it had disappeared in the direction of the town, stood there, gazing almost mournfully after it, as though it had carried off forever the only person she cared about in the world. After some time, she proceeded down the boulevard through the unrelenting afternoon heat.

At last the girl stopped before a pink and tan apartment house at the back of which could be seen the motionless and dolphin-filled bay. Like many of the others, this building had screened-in, elaborate, wrought-iron balconies and lush tropical gardens on all sides. Over the flowering hedge on her left, the girl could see orange and lemon groves, while on the spotless sidewalk before her, small green lizards darted into the bushes for protection from the sun. Beyond the hedge, a uniformed chauffeur, mopping his face with a handkerchief, walked slowly toward the indoor parking lot. Otherwise, all was hot and listless under the brutal, scorching sun.

The girl looked up, her hazel eyes searching out a particular balcony on the tenth floor. But she was distracted for a moment by the pelican perched on the sign by the fountain that, gurgling, splashing and gleaming heralded the driveway's entrance. Then her clear eyes focused on the sign which read, "Le Chateau, A Private Residential Club." She sighed, put her bag over her shoulder and trudged up the driveway. "Yes, it always was private," she said aloud, to no one in particular.

As usual, the lobby was empty.The Spanish tiles on the floor and walls shone from lights discreetly placed above the teak trellis that hid the ceiling. The girl passed the indoor fountain, to the calm of the club room with its empty, elegant, leather chairs, to see who was at the pool out back. A blond, fortyish woman, well-bronzed from the sun, lay in a lounge chair, flipping through a copy of <u>Vogue </u>magazine. When the girl slid the glass doors open, the woman looked up.

"Clara, you poor thing," she said to the girl, putting aside her magazine. "I wondered where you were."

"Just to the beach," Clara replied, sitting down in a lawn chair.

"You have to be careful of that riff raff down by the pier," the woman laughed. "I hope no one tried to pick you up."

Clara shook her head and gazed out at the bay. A yacht was heading toward the ocean, its multi-colored pennants limp in the windless air. After a few minutes of silence, during which the woman gazed at her with unconcealed curiosity, Clara spoke up. "Did you see any dolphins today?"

"A whole school of them. Leaping and playing, just at the water's surface."

"I like them," Clara remarked in an absent-minded way, as if she were talking to herself and somehow also savoring some secret bit of enjoyment. Her response seemed to have a meaning remote, interior, and accessible only to herself. Her words seemed somewhat to remove her from the present, from the sparkling blue pool, the paradisical harmony of palms, lawns, flowers, bay and sky, from the smothering, late afternoon heat. And this seemed to afford her some pleasure. Clara smiled at the silence that followed her remark. "Oh, well," she said at length. "That's that."

"Don't be glum," the woman, sitting up now, went on. "It's exciting to start a new life, though I guess you've done that before. Think of me, I've got to sell your grandmother's apartment. Your aunt left no question about that. It's worth about 300,000 dollars on the open market, but it'll get snapped up. They go like hot cakes, then life returns to normal. I liked it better, when I had just gotten into real estate. Now it seems like all I do is managerial chores." The woman paused to light a cigarette with her gold lighter which made such a sharp, definitive snap when it shut. "I think it'll be great, living with someone like your aunt. She'll send you to college. You mathematical wizards!

I never could do a thing with numbers — advanced math, I mean. You must have gotten that from your father."

"Will you drive me to the plane?" the girl asked in a suddenly tired voice.

"Of course, dear. Now go change."

Clara rose, went back to the lobby and took the elevator to the tenth floor. When she got off, three girls her own age, all sun-burned and carrying tennis racquets, stepped into the elevator. "Boy, are you tan!" one of them exclaimed.

"Is it <u>really</u> hot out there?" asked another.

Clara paused, her round, prettyish face suddenly solemn as if from the effort of recollecting what the weather had been like; but then, just as she was about to reply that yes, it was quite hot, painfully hot, that the very air seemed to scorch one's lungs, that it was hard to walk and besides, the ground was too hot to touch with bare feet, that it was the sort of heat that could kill, that she had been out in it for too long, longer than she knew even, and that it had made her dizzy and sick clear through to her bones so that she hardly knew where she was and certainly didn't care, because all it made you want to do was dive into cool water and drown — just then the elevator door slammed shut.

***

The late afternoon light streamed across the park, through the thin, white and very modern Venetian blinds, causing the middle-aged woman who stood at the living room window of the twelfth floor duplex to squint. Even this expression did not disturb the implacable serenity of her face. In an unkind mood, one might have called it horsy; but there, with the sun glowing on her white, silken skin, the bones in her face seemed light, as if they had just floated to the surface of a still and translucent pond. Her designer-made dress of yellow silk with brown stripes radiating irregularly from the left shoulder and left hip, accentuated a grace that ordinarily might not have been discernible in her tall, thick body. But despite this evident sartorial care to soften and lighten her appearance, there was nonetheless a harshness, even a hardness in her presence, above all, and most irrepressibly, in her voice.

"Chimes," she said, poking up one of the blinds to get a better view of the street below. A cab had stopped opposite the building to unload a passenger. "Really," she continued, gazing steadily and critically at the gleaming yellow roof of the taxi. "What kind of a name is that?"

Behind her, on the vast and also quite modern blue and white couch that stretched away along the wall, sat a large, still athletic but now rather thick than muscular, gray-haired man in a gray, three-piece suit, holding a gray London Fog raincoat over his arm. His blue eyes gazed without focus upon the enormous blue, white and yellow oriental rug that covered the parquet floor. Now and then he would tap his big hand against his knee for a few beats, in time with the grandfather clock which stood in a corner diagonally opposite him. By some trick of interior decorating, the clock fit in perfectly with the room's other, newer appointments. Since the woman at the window continued to stare critically down at the street and did not turn around, the man, who looked very distracted, or tired, or both, did not answer. Once, when he tapped his knee, he said, as though still intent upon some previous conversation, "Two hundred units, at 150,000 dollars apiece."

"Come on," the woman continued after a moment. "You're my expert."

"Anglicized," he promptly replied.

The silence, except for the ticking of the clock, resumed. In the distance the faint rumble of Manhattan traffic could be heard, and somewhere a church bell was ringing. But these noises scarcely penetrated the luxurious quiet of the apartment. Instead, they seemed only to heighten it.

"Two hundred units, at 150,000 dollars apiece," the man repeated, and his blue eyes looked incongruously tired in his wide, ruddy face which, with its prominent cheekbones and round, rather tanned nose, otherwise bespoke health and vigor.

"Marilyn would do that," the woman finally said, still addressing her remarks to the window with its view of the park and the West Side beyond.

"I doubt she had anything to do with it. His grandparents would have been the ones —"

"No, silly, not the last name. Clara — calling the kid Clara Chimes. It's ludicrous, like calling

someone 'bats-in-the-belfry.' You know, I could
have predicted she'd miss her plane." The
woman paused and in the harsh streaks of
sunlight, the blond of her light brown hair
glittered like gold. "That'll get ironed out
though. You've got to be punctual in real estate.
Not missing planes and weeping for days and
having a ludicrous name. Maybe she should
change it."

"No more ludicrous than Libby, nee
Elizabeth Anne Darlinger, I wouldn't think,"
said the man on the couch. "Nor, I might add,
than Marilyn Vaughn Darlinger."

At last the woman at the window turned.
Her pink lipstick and hazel eyes made her look
younger than forty-seven. "Nor, I might add,
than Ward Fairless," she retorted and for a
moment looked almost playful. But then, as she
strode over to the antique, walnut and glass
cabinet at the other end of the room, the old
hardness of manner returned. She removed a

gold and crystal cigarette lighter from the cabinet, along with a matching cigarette case and began methodically attaching a filter to a cigarette. On the gold of both lighter and case were etched the entwined letters E, A, D, F. After exhaling a long plume of smoke, she turned and coldly regarded the man on the couch. He seemed conscious of her scrutiny but continued to stare at the rug.

"How much, by the way for that Florida apartment?"

"Oh," he answered, "300,000 and change, I would say. Unless of course, the girl objects."

"She won't. She doesn't know she can."

"Just as well," the man went on. "I'll put the money into those buildings on East 21st street. We've got almost all the tenants out of there now, and we'll be selling at at least triple what we paid, even with the renovations. I'd just as soon not borrow any more," he paused and tapped his knee with his big, strangely formless hand. "And she'll be an asset, that Clara. Her mother was telling me they'd had her tested and she was a mathematical genius. IQ went straight off the chart. Of course that was years ago, before Marilyn died, and for all we know, the girl's bored with arithmetic. She probably likes higher math, quantum mechanics, logic, things like that."

"Too bad," the woman matter of factly replied, while flicking an ash off her dress. "I'm not spending a penny to send her to college. It's a waste anyway. All those kids getting out, and they can't get jobs. I went to college and, let me tell you, it was a waste."

"Indeed," was all Mr. Fairless said.

By now the sun had begun to set. Its blood-red rays poured into the room, tainted the white walls, streamed across the blue and white carpet and settled in a hot, glowing pool upon the face and form of the woman who leaned against the walnut cabinet casually, even languidly, smoking. Her hand, as she raised the cigarette to her mouth and then drew it away, had a reddish shine and so did her eyes, while her hair looked like a crown of flames.

To her companion there must have been something especially disconcerting in the sight of her, for when at last Mr. Fairless looked up, he stared. "Sometimes," he said, "you don't look at all like the woman I married."

"And divorced," she replied.

"It was you who," he began, but was interrupted by the sound of the buzzer.

For a moment they just looked at each other, and there, the brilliant light of the setting sun seemed to highlight a certain helplessness in the man's face, and in hers an annoyed, harsh boredom. They remained thus, gazing at each other for a second or two. "The child is here," she said at last.

***

"He was a mobster, from what I understand," aunt Libby remarked that night over dinner on the subject of Clara's paternal grandfather. "I always thought that gave him a certain flare. Of course, mother was horrified."

"She only associated herself with clean businesses," Mr. Fairless smiled, while carving the roast beef, "like her husband's real estate empire." He passed Clara a plate of rare meat. "Your parents were quite the young idealists, didn't want anything to do with either family. Stupid. That's how Marilyn got herself disinherited."

Clara's aunt offered her a glass of wine. "No thanks, Mrs. Fairless," the girl replied. The man and the woman looked at each other, and he cleared his throat.

"You aunt," he explained, "has resumed her maiden name."

They were seated at a long polished table of cherry wood, at the far end of the large high-ceilinged, yet dark dining room. Opposite Clara was an extra place setting, with the chair pulled back, as if awaiting its occupant, and beyond that a view of the park and of the lights twinkling in the buildings on the West Side. For a while they ate in silence, which was only interrupted by Mrs. Darlinger's praise for the way Clara's black and white striped, summer jersey dress fit her. At length, however, there came the sound of the front door lock turning. The diners turned to see the tall form of a young man on the threshold of the dim room, silhouetted against the light of the vestibule.

"Better late than never," was all anyone said. It was Mr. Fairless, and there was irritation in the tone in which he addressed his son.

"Sorry," the young man answered, placing his briefcase on an uncomfortable little chair, covered with nineteenth century needlework in the hall. "The market closed way down today, so I stayed late at the office."

"Paul," Mrs. Darlinger said, "you know Clara Chimes, Marilyn's daughter."

Clara turned and extended a hand to the man in the gray suit with the brown hair and blue eyes who had stepped up next to her chair. "Last time we met I think you were playing tag with the kids in the park," he smiled and then took his place opposite her.

At first Clara did not like him at all. He seemed rarely to acknowledge his father's presence, addressing his remarks about bonds and the market and points to his former step-mother, whom he appeared to hold in a rather cool and wary awe. She, in turn, accepted this homage with apparent reservation, as though she perhaps suspected, while offering advice on buying and selling and making money make money, that there was something very wrong

21

with the young man. But, though as aloof and hard as ever, it seemed a topic that truly animated her. Meanwhile, on Clara's right, Mr. Fairless ate in silence, gazing occasionally from his son to his ex-wife and then back to his Wedgewood plate. He downed several glasses of red wine.

"And what," Clara asked at length out of politeness, "do you do, Mr. Fairless?"

The conversation at the other corner of the table, on the auspiciousness of taking over the stock of a steel company in Pennsylvania, came to an abrupt halt.

Mr. Fairless looked up and, for the first time that day, his blue eyes settled on Clara's hazel ones. "I do what you will be doing," he said in his deep, tired voice, that somehow made Clara long to go to sleep. "I buy, develop and sell real estate. It's a fairly large firm, though my only partner is your aunt. We do rather well. In fact, it is a very small, infinitesimal percentage of companies that makes such profits as we do with so few employees. And since we'll be spending a lot of time together, you might as well call me Ward."

His old blue eyes were still on her, when Clara looked away questioningly at her aunt. But Mrs. Darlinger was gazing across the brightly cluttered dining room table at her former husband with frank annoyance.

"Of course it's up to you, Clara," she said in a hard tone, still looking at Mr. Fairless. "Ward has an unfortunate way of saying everything as if it's destiny." Thereupon she turned and smiled at her niece. Paul Fairless was smiling at her also, but differently. There was something chilly about his smile.

"But for someone with your particular abilities," Mrs. Darlinger went on, still smiling warmly. "I do think you'd find the work interesting. At least I would urge you to give it a try this summer." She paused and reached for a cigarette, which her stepson hurried to light. "I noticed," she went on, exhaling a stream of smoke that rose over the table, then curved down and crept, stealthily it seemed, to the open window and out of the room into the lively, twinkling, urban night, "that book under your arm when you arrived this evening. What was it called?"

"The Structure of Scientific Revolutions," Clara replied.

Mrs. Darlinger nodded. "Yes, the title caught my eye. You see, you will have a chance, if you work with Ward, to learn about financial revolutions. That's what we'll soon be in, in real estate, and above all in this city. The only thing I remember from college was a little bit from a course on economics." Here Paul Fairless smiled and lit a cigarette. "It was something," she went on, "about convulsions in value. That's what's starting in New York. Give it a few years. Soon enough it'll be in full swing here and then happening all over the country. But we're getting in at the beginning, or rather, we've been in all along. For three generations and in other cities, we've been waiting for exactly this to happen. We're very lucky, <u>you're</u> very lucky, to be around for it. There was a time in this town, just a few years ago, when you could buy a building, renovate it and not be able to unload it for love or money, if it was in the wrong neighborhood. So we stuck to luxury buildings in luxury neighborhoods and commercial real estate. But now, Clara, if you have the money, or even just the credit, and we have more of that than we know what to do with, you can pick up a useless, dilapidated building in Chelsea, worth nothing, fix it up, and sell it for a fortune. And you can do it all without spending a cent."

Mrs. Darlinger had grown very animated in the course of her talk, and for the first time Clara had warmed to her, or rather, to her animation. She had scarcely grasped the meaning of her aunt's words, but the life, or what she took for the life, behind them, made her want to share in its intensity. Mrs. Darlinger observed the enraptured glow on her listener's young face and reached out and clasped her hand.

"And there is no reason," Mrs. Darlinger went on very firmly and slowly and softly and with a strangely repressed energy that Clara detected not only in the voice but also in the hand that held hers, "why the doors of this world of money and power should be closed to a woman."

***

That night Clara unpacked her few possessions, mainly clothes and books, in her room on the second floor of the duplex. Aside from the bed placed next to the window with its wonderful view of the park, Clara also had a

---

Chippendale desk and dresser, a comfortable wing back armchair covered in green silk and an immense walk-in closet. Her aunt had thoughtfully placed a vase of irises beside the elegant, blue, glass lamp that stood on the night table. The carpet, green and blue, with its repeating pattern of peacocks and temples, had a vaguely Oriental look. The curtains had a similar pattern. There was no bookcase, so Clara stored her little library on the closet floor.

After putting a framed photograph of her father and mother on the night table, she undressed and curled up on the bed with the book that had caught her aunt's eye. "History even suggests that the scientific enterprise has developed a uniquely powerful technique for producing surprises of this sort," she read. "If this characteristic of science is to be reconciled with what has already been said, then research under a paradigm must be a particularly

effective way of inducing paradigm change."
Clara put the book down, to ponder these
words. She tried to fit them to what she had
learned in her senior year of advanced high
school physics. "I probably won't really be able
to see what it means," she thought, "until I've
had some college courses." But then she
remembered the remark of her aunt indicating
that she might not be going to college, and as
she contemplated this possibility, she began to
grow uneasy and alarmed. There was no other
way, she knew, for her to learn more physics
and math. And in even so brief an absence from
these subjects as a summer, she always forgot
something which had to be relearned in the fall.
She closed the book and gazed anxiously out
the window at the lights of the city, which
danced like molecules in the darkness. Perhaps,
she thought, combing her short chestnut hair
with her fingers, she could save enough money
working for her uncle in the summer to pay for

her education in September. Her grandmother's illness had prevented her from applying to college and even if she had, she would not have bothered to apply for scholarships — a girl with such a wealthy aunt and grandmother as she could hardly expect to get one. If only grandmother Darlinger had not died. She, at least, had left Clara alone in her pursuits. She had not understood the science that so fascinated her precocious granddaughter and had even called Clara's interest in it "unwomanly," but the thought that Clara might spend her life working with an electron microscope was no more offensive to her than that of any other occupation the girl might have aside from raising a family. Grandmother Darlinger was a woman, as she liked to say, of the old school — fiercely provincial, anti-cosmopolitan, sternly religious, distrustful of education, and vigorously opposed to any non-Christian religion, Democrats, anyone who was not rich and the income tax. These were the subjects on which she liked to her her preacher expand and on which she would elaborate during the intermissions of Billy Graham's evangelical TV show.Clara had learned years ago just not to listen. If she had, it would have offended and then bored her, and her grandmother never intended and would never have wanted to do either. On the one occasion when Clara had become upset with these occasional rants, it had made old Mrs. Darlinger cry. "Oh, but Clara," she had said as the tears settled on her wrinkled cheeks, "I love you so much. I love you even more than I loved your mother."

This had not been something Clara particularly wanted to know, though she had, on the occasions when her grandmother recriminated against Marilyn Chimes, suspected it. Marilyn had been willful and unloving, Mrs. Darlinger observed, she had done rash foolish things. It was no surprise that she and her husband had gone through the windshield. They had been drinking and were undoubtedly speeding. It was a miracle they had had the good sense not to take their five-year-old daughter along with them. Nonetheless old Mrs. Darlinger was sure that in her first five years of life Clara had suffered irreparable exposure to the unwholesome company of jazz musicians, actors of questionable masculinity, alcoholics, kept women, communists, frequenters of race tracks and fights, and other such unspeakable low life. Perhaps she was right. Clara did have an unaccountable liking for what she read about such people but never, much to her grandmother's relief, enough to distract her for very long from mathematics. Her interest in this discipline had withdrawn her, to a great extent, from the social world. Not habituated to the company of others, Clara had become shy and had the rather distracted air of one whose mind is not on the people and things before her and who, therefore, tends always to by surprised by them. On the whole, Mrs. Darlinger had thought this awkwardness rather a good thing. It would, she correctly judged, keep the girl out of trouble with sex, something which, Mrs. Darlinger was wont to exclaim, there seemed so much more of than in the past. It was all over television, filled the magazines, and in the warm weather the young women went about so scantily clad that half the time it seemed to her they might as well be stark naked.

It had been a difficult time to raise a child, especially for a widow in her seventies. The kids, as Mrs. Darlinger called them, who were five to ten years older than Clara had demonstrated against the government in the streets, taken drugs, refused their military service and in general behaved like barbarians.

The youth of the nation was still confused. And for this Mrs. Darlinger, unlike most of her Republican friends, did not blame the kids but their diet and their parents. The wrong food, Mrs. Darlinger was convinced, cold lead to the most unpredictable behavior. Too much Coca Cola could make anyone jumpy. Clara was never allowed to drink it after lunch, and she was as calm and uninterested in politics as could be. And though Mrs. Darlinger herself was addicted to sweets, these too, she knew, could imbalance a person. All those kids had undoubtedly gone off to college and eaten nothing but sweets, Coca Cola and, worst of all, pizza. This Mrs. Darlinger had long regarded as a dangerous foreign food, liable to cause indigestion, pimples and an addled mind. Mrs. Darlinger thought it no accident that in one of those shots on TV of an angry crowd converging on Washington, several teenage girls were eating slices of pizza. Clara was warned never to touch the stuff.

Twelve years under the gastronomical tyranny of her grandmother had left Clara utterly indifferent to food. She could not cook and indeed hardly ever noticed what she ate. What she did notice was that at certain times of the day she was hungry, at which points she just opened the refrigerator and ate whatever was there. If she was outside the house she would get a cheeseburger and a Seven Up, which she usually ate while walking wherever she had to go. Fortunately she had never had to worry about her weight. As a child she was skinny, as a teenager slender. Her grandmother, very proud of Clara's figure and seeing in it a confirmation of her own dietary beliefs, lavished clothes upon her, to which Clara, in her mathematical preoccupation, was also indifferent. This did not bother old Mrs. Darlinger, who chose to see in Clara's attitude a healthy Christian unconcern for the things of this world. In short, Mrs. Darlinger was convinced that she had raised a perfect child, and done it much better than her inept daughter Marilyn ever could have; and if on occasion the thought strayed across her mind that Clara's complete innocence could more accurately be attributed to her total absorption in an abstract world than to her rigorous upbringing, Mrs. Darlinger never really believed it.

The only real danger for Clara, the only one that had actually caused Mrs. Darlinger to fret, was the thought of who she might marry. The old woman spent hours pondering this matter. She was fond of imagining Clara married to a Congregationalist. Anything else somewhat disturbed her happy picture of Clara's future. But when such thoughts did beset her, she would quickly succumb to the most extreme pessimism, telling herself, "like mother, like daughter. "At such moments, she invariably began to think that perhaps it would be better for Clara not to get married after all. Fortunately Clara was too preoccupied and too beleaguered by her watchful old grandmother, to be very interested in anyone. Her parents, had they been alive, might have worried that she was so solitary. Old Mrs. Darlinger, however, had less and less energy to supervise Clara as she approached adulthood and therefore regarded her relative isolation with relief.

That isolation, as Clara saw it however, was more accidental than anything else. Because she undertook a heavy curriculum of advanced physics and math throughout high school, the students she spent most of her time with were all brainy whiz-kids, or, in the deadly accurate vocabulary of adolescence, nerds. In her spare time Clara liked to imagine herself falling in love at once and forever, like in the movies. The problems with this delightful fantasy were twofold. Every time she considered this scene of dramatic, romantic recognition, her mind, straying ironically around, could not picture this wonderful, Hollywood embrace without also envisioning her knocking over some glass beaker of hydrogen chloride in the process. To make matters worse, the only near approximation that she had ever encountered in the flesh to the man of her dreams was Stanley Katz, a student a few years older than her and very unlikely ever to be found anywhere in the vicinity of a laboratory. Stanley, whose father owned a race track outside of Miami, had all but flunked out of school. Stanley's interests, she could not help but observe, were extremely limited. They extended mainly to lying on his surfboard in the gulf as much of the time as possible, not even riding it because there was no surf, and to trying to trick her into going to bed with him.

This Clara was just too nervous to do. She was afraid of getting pregnant, afraid she might get a disease, afraid of her grandmother finding out, and afraid that if she did this he might lose interest in her, because then, after all, there would be no point to his second most favorite pastime.

Further removing Stanley from her dreams of romance was the fact that he did things like drink ketchup out of the bottle at the local Burger King, fall asleep at all but the goriest drive-in movies, read comic books, make bets on everything from the World Series to how long it would take to walk to the corner and call Clara a JAP — half a JAP to be sure, but one nevertheless. Lying on his stomach, his blond hair flopping over the edge of his surfboard, he would try to entice her to go up to Boca Raton for the weekend or to Miami for a boxing match. He would watch her eyes widen with interest at his detailed descriptions of the fighters and the fights, as she lay on her surfboard next to his, not surfing. Then when he judged his listener sufficiently interested, he would commence a recitation of great boxing catastrophes, blindings and the like. Clara would invariably begin to chicken out and start making excuses. These sessions usually ended with Clara paddling away and Stanley paddling after her, shouting out detailed descriptions of the blood and gore of the ring.

He had ultimately gone of to Tallahassee State University, to the utter amazement of his family, Clara, and anyone who knew him. Once or twice he had driven down in his noisy red Chevy to pick Clara up, then driven her north to the race track, the radio blaring all the way and trying to get her to bet against him on which hit singles were were in the Top Forty. Her fondest and indeed most vivid memory of him was looking for a place to park one find afternoon after a rainout beyond the horse stalls. "You smell something?" he asked, stopping the car in what looked to be the middle of nowhere. Clara, gagging on one of his cigarettes, could not smell a thing. Ahead of them, on a little rise just off the highway, a man was gesturing frantically. "P-U, I don't know if I want to park here," Stanley said, stepped out of the car, sank and then tripped into a whitish mush. Clara gasped from the overpowering stench of sour milk and held her nose. Several thousand gallons of it from a truck overturned hours before had soaked into the mud. They did not go to the races that day. Stanley, glowering, cursing and, to tell the truth, stinking, spent the rest of the afternoon disinfecting himself and his vehicle and accusing Clara of giggling at him. "I'm not giggling," she had lied. "I just bet you five dollars we go into McDonald's and everyone in the place starts sniffing."

That had been ten months ago, before Mrs. Darlinger's illness took a turn for the worse and before Clara had ever dreamed that she would live in New York. After her grandmother's death, Stanley had phoned to announce that he was driving down. But Clara had explained that there was no time — she had to hurry and pack and move. And as she stood in Mrs. Darling's large, quiet apartment, filled with costly antiques and told him to stay in Tallahassee, she imagined him there at the other end of the line, listening, tall and blond and handsome like the eternal beach boy and wondering if he should just drive down in his noisy red Chevy anyway. In the end, he did, despite her protests, and she missed her plane to New York.

***

"She's an insufferable little egghead," Paul Fairless was telling an acquaintance over their one martini lunch in the financial district. His acquaintance, a medium height, blondish fellow with a nose that seemed entirely too short for his face and a distinctly unctuous air, also worked at an investment firm, and the pair had, by long habit, met once a week for lunch.

"There are worse things than that," his friend rejoined, chewing a stalk of celery with his mouth open. "Good looking?" he asked while swallowing.

"So, so," Paul replied, fishing for the onion in his martini with a finger. "Not like that one," and he nodded his head to the left. The friend needed no further indication to know who, amid that vast crowd of eaters in the semi-darkness, Paul meant. He gazed off in the direction of the voluptuous blond English businesswoman they had both fruitlessly pursued.

"Not many are," his friend said. "You're unreasonable. Always were."

"She reads science books, she's probably a virgin, she's nearly flat-chested and she's half-Jewish, which makes her the worst kind of JAP. And that, Drew, is the end of it. Besides, I don't like her eyes."

His friend pulled the sleeves of his suit straight with exaggerated efficiency and asked what was wrong with Clara's eyes.

"Hazel, like Libby's. And you can't tell anything from them.Whether she's smart or just a ditz, likes you or doesn't. They make me uncomfortable."

"Maybe she's judging you," his friend suggested.

"Stupid little snob."

"Smart stupid little snob."

The conversation, such as it was, turned to other women, boats and baseball. After each of these had been properly dissected, they moved on to the more fertile ground of who was making more money than whom. This lasted into and all the way through the main course. But Drew could not help noticing that his friend seemed bored with the talk, even distracted. Finally they rose to leave but, passing the bar, encountered some acquaintances and decided to stay for another drink — in Paul's case a cola. In a matter of minutes Drew had turned the subject back to Clara, whom he wanted to meet.

"Don't be ridiculous. She's seventeen."

"That makes her nine years younger than you," Drew retorted, lighting a cigarette. "I think you're interested in her."

"Don't count on it," Paul replied, leaning up against the polished wood of the bar. Thereupon his friend launched into a lament over the fun they were missing by working so hard. He had been going out with a college student who did nothing except demonstrate for what was left of the women's movement, sleep, he said, with anything that walked, and take

44

drugs. That was the life. She made fun of him for going to work every day, and for all he knew, she was right. What really did he care about pension funds and municipal bonds? He liked the money he made, but what with rents starting to go up so fast and with the cost of entertainment, he was always broke.

Paul paid little attention to this threnody. He had, after all, heard it many times before. But he was preoccupied with trying to pinpoint, through a slight alcoholic haze, exactly what he did not like about his step-cousin. This took longer than he thought. As he gazed from his image in the smoked mirror behind the bar to the bottles that lined the shelf in glimmering rows, he realized that she annoyed him. There was something about such self-possession in someone so young that he disliked. He watched the fat, ruddy bartender in his red vest clink some coins into the shiny cash register. It seemed to him that Clara had "a side to her," that she was not to be trusted. "Science," he snorted to himself. "That's all we need, a little Albert Einstein in a halter top."

The two men strolled out of the restaurant into the hot, June afternoon. They walked side by side in silence, Paul in a tan suit, Drew in a gray one, along the old gray streets that at times were so narrow it seemed as if the sidewalk traversed the bottom of a ravine. Finally they came to a halt, on the spot where they always parted, in front of the stock exchange.

"So I take it you're not going to introduce me to the beautiful Miss Chimes," Drew remarked, tilting his head to one side and shielding his eyes with his hand from the harsh glare of the dusty, slanting sunlight. "And I know she's beautiful, because your stepmother has that picture of her on the beach. Reading a book, as I recall."

"You really are insistent."

"Uh hunh," his friend smiled, and when he did, his short nose looked shorter than ever. "You would be too. It's just that you don't have to, because you can see her anytime."

And there in the ugly afternoon light, in that busy gray district so famous for its pecuniary obsession, they stood for a moment, the one smiling, the other not, and then parted.

***

To Clara's surprise her aunt, unlike her grandmother, seemed completely unconcerned with how she spent her time and in fact told her that she could go wherever she pleased, do whatever she wanted, meet whomever she liked and that, in short, she was on her own. "I'm too old to be responsible for a teenage girl. You're an adult; you can take care of yourself," Elizabeth Darlinger observed on their way into Saks. This, Clara thought, was quite opposite of her grandmother's attitude. With a sudden surge of excitement she realized that now she could have some fun; but then with an equally sudden surge of disappointment she saw that she did not know anyone to have fun with. Aunt Darlinger's conception of her responsibility was apparently limited to making sure that Clara was very well dressed. They spent the entire day in one couturier's shop and department store after another. Clara was bought summer suits and winter suits, sandals and a variety of high heels, makeup, perfume, pants dresses, stockings, bathing suits, what Stanley Katz would have called "the works." She was marched into her aunt's beauty salon and her short, straight chestnut hair was cut and restyled. She resisted but was overcome and given a manicure. Then she was told she was going to have an emulsion. Clara had no idea what this meant and was busy pondering the meaning of the word as it was used in chemistry when the first swatch of hot wax touched her legs, whereupon she let out a scream and accidentally kicked the brush out of the hand of the beautician, who was so startled by these acrobatics that, if not for the alert Mrs. Darlinger, she would have fallen over. "You're like a little wild animal," Mrs. Darlinger remonstrated. "Behave yourself."

"As I said, you can do whatever you want," Elizabeth went on, dragging her exhausted niece into Tiffany's. "I'm not exactly naive about people your age. I assume you smoke."

Clara stared.

"I mean <u>cigarettes</u>."

Clara confessed that once or twice on the front seat of a red Chevy she had managed to inhale.

"Well it's just lousy for your health," Elizabeth went on in her hardest tone, lighting a cigarette herself. "But I suppose you'll do it no matter what I say." Later that day she bought Clara a fifty dollar lighter.

In the course of an afternoon, a great deal of grandmother Darlinger's careful work to shelter her precious girl from the world was undone. The absolute capper came on Park Avenue and Seventy Seventh street, when Elizabeth, with alarming efficiency, tried to direct Clara into a doctor's office. "I'm not about to have you getting pregnant in my house," Elizabeth declared. "I know my mother. You've probably never even been examined. She wasn't either. Some quack once told her that it would upset the alkaline balance in her body, and she believed him."

Clara, though at first embarrassed, quickly decided that her aunt was the most wonderful woman in the world. She would undoubtedly let her eat anything from hot green peppers to pizza in the house. However, she speedily informed her that so far, in the gynecological department anyway, there was nothing to worry about.Elizabeth regarded her skeptically.

I

"I've read an awful lot of articles, young lady, about what's going on with people your age. Unless you're terribly shy, or unless my mother terrorized you — which is not impossible —" Clara assured her that this had been the case.

"Frankly, you're not missing much," Elizabeth uttered her final, imperious pronouncement of the subject while stepping off the curb to hail a cab. "I always found sex somewhat overrated."

When they got home Clara, exhausted, collapsed on the long blue and white couch in the living room. Elizabeth, however, seemed to have just got going. "Why don't you go change into those nice shorts we bought and the matching top," she called out from the kitchen, where she was mixing a gin and tonic. "Then come back down and fix yourself some pizza. It's in the freezer." Clara hurried into the kitchen to see her big, tall aunt in her green and white print Ladybug dress, leaning up

51

against the counter and belting down her drink. "I know what that old sparkplug did to you," Elizabeth answered the surprised look on Clara's face. "There were only five things you were allowed to eat, and rice pudding," she fairly spat out the word, "was one of them. It drove Marilyn and me crazy. On top of that she was a complete teetotaler, and she probably made you take Geritol. The woman was out of her mind, and century. And you didn't know him, but Daddy was made of the same stuff. An absolute tyrant — convinced there was a communist conspiracy to take over America and twice nearly joined the John Birch Society. They thought the reds were going to get us through our food and water, among other things. You undoubtedly got the lecture of fluoridation turning us all into mongoloid idiots."

Clara nodded.

"More than once."

Clara nodded again. "And you undoubtedly had to drink that purified stuff she bought in plastic bottles, and brush your teeth with baking soda. She did all that years before the fluoridation hubbub. I'll never forget the time your mother, she was the bad seed you know, flushed the baking soda down the toilet and filled the box with salt and flour. My sister got into more trouble when she was a kid — and when she was an adult, I might add. That marriage, boy, it blew the top off of everything — a socialist, Jewish, a TV reporter, and with that unspeakable, that criminal family in the background. You probably don't remember the legal battle over who got custody of you, but it was not pretty." Elizabeth paused to take another swallow of her drink. "Ironically enough, years later, through real estate, I got to know the other side of your family. I liked them, did some business with them, in fact. They asked about you a lot. I told them you were getting a fine American upbringing from the wicked old witch of the west. I can show you their graves if you like, out on Long Island. They were mainly in entertainment and communications. You'll get the stock when you're twenty one."

Clara lugged her packages upstairs, changed into the clothes Elizabeth had suggested, and then decamped to the living room to find her aunt seated in a Mies Van der Rohe chair, reading the real estate section of <u>The New York Times</u>. The blinds had been pulled up, and sunlight streamed through the huge picture windows, lending the room a brief and deceptive aura of calm. Clara asked for and was given a cigarette, which she lit with her new lighter. "We'll have to get it engraved," Mrs. Darlinger remarked, glancing critically at the lighter over the top of her newspaper. "Remind me." Feeling bold, Clara asked why her aunt had reverted to her maiden name. "I always liked it better," was the reply. "And I also liked being called Mrs., so I kept that. What do you think of your step-cousin, or whatever you call him?"

"I think he's icky," Clara answered, at last inhaling a lungfull of smoke with no trouble.

Mrs. Darlinger nodded. "A cold fish." The case of Paul Fairless thus settled, she proceeded to read aloud to Clara from the real estate section of the <u>Times</u>. Reading aloud to a captive audience was, apparently, Elizabeth's one unlikely passion. And it was a tyrannical passion, in which Clara discerned more than a trace of her grandmother's character. "Now listen to this!" she would exclaim, before launching into the droning recitation of some stupefying paragraph on the value of an empty lot on the East Side. Clara felt her eyes glaze over. Indeed once or twice, when certain that she was not observed, she allowed them to cross. <u>The Structure of Scientific Revolutions</u>

lay unopened beside her on the couch. Clearly she would not have a chance to read it today.

When Elizabeth's voice at long last and mercifully began to grown hoarse, she folded up the paper and dropped it on the coffee table. "Play cards?" Clara shook her head. "Want a drink?" Clara said she didn't think so. "What about a walk? You can see the park. "Before Clara could answer that she was too tired to move, Elizabeth was up and heading for the door.

"Athletic?" she asked, as they strolled past a group of young men playing baseball. Clara replied that she liked to swim and water ski.

"Well, not much of that around here, though when you visit me up in Maine you can do it to your heart's content. I'll have to sign you up at the health club. Remind me." At his point Mrs. Darlinger broke off, to pick up the baseball which had rolled to her feet, and pitch it back to the players. "I used to love sports, but once I got married that was that. Ward was rather a drip, but then, husbands usually are. I suppose you'll want to get married one of these days."

"I don't think about it very much," Clara said. "Besides, the though of being pregnant sort of makes me sick."

Mrs. Darlinger nodded. "The thing to watch out for when you get married is your money. You don't want to go giving it to your husband.Next thing you know he'll be divorcing you and taking it with him. I was <u>very</u> careful about that. Keep it in the family." Elizabeth's hazel eyes flickered over Clara's face for a moment to make sure she had taken this in. "I'll bet you five dollars that's something <u>she</u> never told you."

"She had that refrain about a woman fitting herself to her husband's life," Clara meditatively replied. "Which makes some sense. After all — keeping it in the family. Who's family, if your husband isn't?"

Mrs. Darlinger stopped walking, and there in the light and shade from the bright afternoon sun that filtered through the leaves and boughs above them, her hair and eyes now and then flashed like amber. "I am your family," she answered softly but with distinct firmness. "The way mother thought is the old way, part of a world that's gone. Things are different now. They got worse. People are more alone. All you ever really have is the people you're related to by blood and your money." She smiled distantly, as though she were turning her remark over in her mind and had just discovered something in it that she had not seen before. "Blood and money. That's what it's about."

"It?" Clara asked, gazing curiously and with some awe at the tall woman who stood under the changing, gentle light and shade. "What's it?"

"Oh, why — life, my dear. That's what life's about." With that she broke the peculiar charm of the moment and resumed walking.

At length, after they had circled the field, they stopped at a bench beneath a maple tree. Elizabeth said she was going to have a cigarette and "be vacant" for a while on the bench. Clara sprawled on the grass and wondered whether perhaps her aunt wasn't just a little cracked. "I am your family" — the sentence had, she thought, a slight tinge of megalomania.But then, at present at any rate, it was accurate. What she shuddered at, though, was the notion it had somehow suggested that it would always be accurate. Clara had never thought very much about marriage. That had simply been one of the inevitables assumed to be looming hazily in her future, along with a Ph.D in physics and eventual happiness. Until that very week she had always located that future in some sandy, coastal Southern town. And as she closed her eyes and felt the sun on her face, she seemed to hear the ocean breeze. Right now, had she been at home with old Mrs. Darlinger, she would be lying out on the balcony, finishing the book on scientific revolutions and rising from the chaise longue to go down to the beach. She would pass under the swaying palms on the boulevard and walk along the gravel path that wound through the gardens of Surfside Towers to the shore. The sun would be very hot, and there would be no place to hide from it. The sand would scorch her feet as she kicked off her sandals and raced to the water which waited for her as always in the green and blue serenity of certain perfect gems. Farther out, the porpoises would leap and flash and play, and Clara, floating on her back, would wish she were one of them.

She began to doze, dreaming of the lonely paradise in which she had been raised. When at last her eyes opened, she saw her aunt, sitting on a bench in Central Park and waving a bee away in annoyance. There, she observed, nothing delicate about Elizabeth. Her sturdy legs and arms suggested that she had been a strapping girl. She had the grossness of movement of a hoyden, yet was not bad looking and had, in her face, a lot of character.The slight hollows under her eyes, her unlined forehead and firm chin seemed to reveal that she had lived but not been worn down by living, that she had suffered a bit, but always been quick to do something about it, that she thought and perhaps deeply, but had never abandoned herself to it, and that her soul, in its experienced naivete, was essentially unknown to her. Her face was that of someone capable of hurting people and not caring unless she herself had undergone exactly the pain she inflicted. She did not appear, nor was there any trace in her speech or manner, of the imagination to penetrate the thoughts or feelings of people very different from her. But when she did perceive an experience similar to her own, she appropriated it entirely — there was no question, in her sympathy for Clara's penned-in childhood with old Mrs. Darlinger, of Clara having a different view of it. Clara, in fact, understood enough to know that she herself had <u>no</u> view of it, that it had been stifling but certainly not crushing and that, at times, it had been melancholically wonderful. But it was clear that to Elizabeth they had undergone the same thing, that the only other person in the world who had shared in this uniquely bizarre, painful and ridiculous experience was Marilyn. And Marilyn was gone.Which left Clara, and the certainty that because they had both grown up under the same iron rule of old Mrs. Darlinger, not only would they have the same view of it, but, in a sense, Clara's experience of it and, perhaps, Clara herself, would belong to Elizabeth.

The one thing, Clara knew at once and instinctively, that did not and could never belong to her aunt and which Elizabeth therefore drew away from, was her background. The fact that Clara was only half a Gentile could, it seemed, separate her from Elizabeth's fierce ownership. But this was neither given nor absolute. It was a matter of choice; and it was something that could change. It could vanish or become more pronounced — whatever it was. In fact, she did not know what it was, merely that it existed, that there was a difference that she could act on or ignore.But even here her aunt had already made an inroad. Elizabeth had referred to knowing Clara's other family. She had liked them, seen them as her kind, done business with the, understood them in a way that Clara never could because she had never met them. The message was clear: this other family belonged not to Clara but to Elizabeth, and to know them, Clara would have to go through her aunt's world, in her aunt's way. But as she lay on the grass and gazed away from the woman in the green and white print dress on the bench, she did not believe her.

The message, however, was sincere. Elizabeth, a person of money who believed in money, had known the Chimeses as people of money who also believed in money. Clara knew nothing about money. She knew that certain things could not be done without it, but she had no idea of the scope of things that could be done with it. And although she perceived her own ignorance and her aunt's sincerity, she still refused to believe that somehow because of money her other family belonged more to Elizabeth than to her.

"What an ass," Mrs. Darlinger suddenly declared in response to the news, blared from a passing transistor radio, of the president's latest doings.

"You mean Carter?" Clara asked, pulling her body into a jack-knife position and then stretching out.

"He's almost as bad as Nixon. Now that was a bungler, and a bad looking bungler. How we could make a man with that nose president I'll never understand. I mean, have you ever seen a honker like that on television?" Mrs. Darlinger pointed her own aquiline and rather prominent olfactory organ in the air. "It gives me the heebe jeebees every time I remember him muttering into a microphone."

"But you voted for him of course."

"Of course. I always vote a straight Republican ticket. It's very simple.The Democrats want to take my money away and give it to underprivileged drug addicts, homicidal recidivists and a variety of other unsavory loafers of whom I entirely disapprove. The Republicans want to leave me and my money alone, put the addicts in jail, kill the recidivists and force the loafers to work.The only thing the Democrats have ever been right about is abortion, which, aside from war and capital punishment, is the only solution anyone's come up with to the problem of the population explosion on the one hand and life on the other. Otherwise they're a bunch of incompetents and always have been. Adlai Stevenson! A bad joke. Complete boobs. Incapable of doing anything but spend other people's money in such vast quantities that in another decade we'll all be in the poorhouse. Watch out, you'll get grass stains on your shorts."

Clara had been doing leg raises and abruptly stopped. "You sound just like grandma. Every time she'd hear a plane go by she'd say 'Oh good! I hope that's the FBI or the CIA going to bomb those Cubans to smithereens.'"

Mrs. Darlinger wrinkled her nose. "My mother lived a rich fantasy life."

Clara sat up cross-legged. "I don't think so," she said very seriously. "I don't think she dreamed about anything. She just wasn't the type. I think that's why she was so content with her life."

Visibly startled by this reply, Elizabeth, with uncharacteristic attention tilted her head slightly to one side. Her hazel eyes sparkled down at the girl on the grass with curiosity. "No dreams," she said quietly after a moment, still gazing intently at Clara. "You think that was her secret."

It seemed to Clara that her own mind was suddenly very clear on the subject, and she nodded. "Not for money, power, love, certainly not for art or science. I don't know why this was, but you're right, no dreams. Ever."

They stared at each other. It was as if Clara had uttered something she should not have and had tried with the words "you're right" to shunt part of the responsibility onto Elizabeth. But from the moment it had been said, they had both believed it to be true, to be the words that expressed what had long hidden in their minds about old Mrs. Darlinger. Yet it was awful to hear it so publicly; as though Clara, impelled by some strange power, had in one leap dived to the bottom of someone else's being and come back up to the surface, all in a second, waving a precious truth in her hand that she had no right to hold. And there in the silence between them that seemed to shut out all the noises of that lovely spring day in the park, that trophy glittering in Clara's hand, seemed to have been obtained at some great cost to the old woman. "No dreams" was something that, once said, could not be unsaid and, once said, seemed to kill old Mrs. Darlinger once again.

Clara seemed to shiver.

"Come on kiddo," Elizabeth said, rising and at the same time reaching out and pulling Clara up by the arm, "Let's go over and watch those jerks try to hit a ball with a bat."

***

In the weeks that followed, Clara and Elizabeth became very close. Clara admired her aunt and began imitating her dress, her abrupt manner, her harshness of speech. Elizabeth admired her niece, seeing in her the mirror image of her own youth, to which she responded with a determination that Clara would make none of her mistakes, would have no bad marriage, no miscarriages, no divorce, but would, instead, follow a straight, unbroken and upward line of success. This Elizabeth considered, was not unreasonable to hope for. After all, she discerned many of her own traits incipient in Clara — a certain toughness, independence, self-possession and an ability coldly to distance herself from any social situation in which she might find herself in order to judge it. Clara had a fine, healthy, competitive spirit. But the kid, as Elizabeth had taken to calling her, had something else as well, something she herself did not have, because she lacked those unexpected flashes of brilliance on which it depended, but which she was glad to have at her disposal and which delighted her in and of itself. The kid had what Elizabeth rather dramatically described to her ex-husband as a killer instinct.

"It could make her a good, maybe even a great scientist," was all Ward Fairless had replied, his old blue eyes gazing tiredly at Mrs. Darlinger's rather tense and excited face. But Elizabeth hardly heard him. "And it could make her a femme fatale too, but it won't," was her harsh reply. She dwelt instead on those sudden insights that made Clara's assessments of people and things so often devastating. "That

I

kid really has a tongue on her," Elizabeth exclaimed. "If words could kill, the Pentagon would be after us to add her to its arsenal." To this Mr. Fairless had said nothing, concluding that Elizabeth's enthusiasm for her own projects had led her once again to exaggerate. After all, he had seen no trace of this supposed killer instinct in the shy, quiet girl who came to his office every day and bent her head over the papers he gave her. He felt sorry for Clara. She had no interest in speculation, development, renovation, zoning laws and zoning variances. He had observed how she entered the office every morning with that book on science under her arm and how she placed it on the far corner of her desk to read during her lunch break. It lay there rather incongruously amid the memos, contracts, papers and charts. And he had noticed that the mark in the beginning of the book where a corner of a page was turned down seemed hardly to have advanced to the

71

middle in the passing weeks. Once, toward evening, he had stopped by her desk and flipped it open. "What I have been opposing in this book is therefore the attempt, traditional since Descartes but not before, to analyze perception as an interpretive process, as an unconscious version of what we do after we have perceived," he had read and then let the book flip shut. The girl had looked up, and, with those startlingly clear eyes of hers, was staring at him through the failing light after sunset. And he, his back to the Venetian blinds and to the huge buildings that loomed in the shaded dimness of twilight beyond, had felt called upon to explain this passing gesture. "What's it about?" he had asked. "It's about how people have made great scientific breakthroughs," she had answered at once. "It suggests that scientific communities spring up at a certain point, when a revolution is achieved by general acceptance of certain methods and theories. But that later, when these theories are digested and new scientists no longer need to justify their every assumption, their research accelerates, but eventually becomes so esoteric that it's almost secret knowledge." He had not known exactly what to say to that and so had just stood there for a while, noticing how red, how beautifully red her hair was in the little, remaining light and then, finally, had simply said "Oh."

She had looked somewhat disappointed, as if she had expected more from him; and as he gazed down at her, he became conscious that it was getting dark and late, and that it was odd of him to want to prolong his conversation with this diffident and unusual girl, and that it was even odder for him to want to find out what he wanted to find out. "I suppose you don't like it very much here," he had said. "Nor at your aunt's, nor in New York."

She looked up in the fading light at the man whose face seemed young but whose eyes seemed old. "Why do you say that?" she had asked, looking from his broad countenance to the book he had just opened and then pulling it away from his corner of the desk to hers.

"Because you're very, very young to be in the midst of all this," he had replied, conscious that his voice sounded tired but also unaccountably sure that he did not have to explain that what "all this" meant was his life, and Elizabeth's and their money and their discord that continued, married or divorced, to unite them with the force of what he had often called destiny. She would understand, he knew, that what he meant was that she should not be caught up in two adult destinies, when hers had not yet been forged, that it could harm her, that he saw something unfair in it, regretted it, and that although he would not help, he sympathized.

Clara had nodded and set her mouth rather grimly. He thought that made her look younger than ever, practically like a child. Indeed the thought occurred to him that had he and Elizabeth had a daughter, she might have looked very much like this. "I suppose I am young for it all," Clara had said, and then, after a pause, "Oh well, that's that." She did not seem to want to continue the discussion.

If only she had not caught on to the work so fast.Then he could have told Elizabeth that it was hopeless, the girl had her head in the clouds, send her to school where she belonged. Even if that had been the case, Elizabeth would not have believed him. As it was, he considered it useless even to try to deceive her. Instead he tried to keep Clara from getting bored by bringing her more and more into the business, and indeed even after a few weeks had begun to wonder how he had managed so well without her. But still, he did not like this bit about a killer instinct. Maybe Clara had it and maybe she didn't. If she did, that was her affair. Elizabeth had no business singling it out and distorting the poor child's personality. At least Clara was a girl — she would eventually get married and then, Ward Fairless liked to tell himself, whatever harm her aunt had done would be undone.

Clara did not, he was relieved to see, appear too unhappy. She hardly had time to. She had been drawn into the whirlwind of her new life. The pace at the office was quick, the work constant. She took papers home with her every night. When she ever had time to look at them, Ward could not even guess, for like in the East Side duplex was not exactly conducive to concentration. Elizabeth's frantically busy social life was in such full swing that whenever the girl was not actually at work, she was swept along in a relentless round of cocktail parties, dinner parties, opera, theater, restaurant and movie going, openings, fashion shows, trips to the country, lunches, brunches and joint shopping expeditions with Elizabeth's friends, all of whom thought Clara was "the most exquisite thing." Though at times Ward noticed that she looked haggard and, on one morning, distinctly dizzy, she had nonetheless begun to develop a taste of her own in clothes, cigarettes, magazines and alcohol, although she still remained utterly ignorant of and indifferent to food.

"It's hopeless. She has the most repressed palate I've ever seen. It comes from the traumatic experience, early in life, of my mother's kitchen," Elizabeth exclaimed to a friend one night in a staggeringly expensive French restaurant of whose famed escargots Clara had just, as always, said, "it's okay, but you know me, I'll eat anything." The remark precipitated on of Mrs. Darlinger's acid commentaries on her mother's culinary beliefs, culminating in a disquisition on halitosis. "Marilyn and I were especially fond of her homey little speeches on the futility of mouthwash," Elizabeth concluded. "She seemed somehow to have got it lodged in her head that mouthwash was a French invention, and since she regarded the French as a nation of alcoholics and perverts, she would have none of it. For some reason her mania fixed itself upon Listerine. I don't know why, but that was the brand she always railed against. She probably thought Listerine sounded French."

Clara, who had continued chewing throughout this discourse, listened avidly, as she always did at the least mention of the infamous Marilyn. Over the past few weeks she had gleaned quite a bit about her mother from Elizabeth's casual conversation. From time to time portions of her father's life — the equally infamous Frank Chimes — had also flared into sudden illumination. Everything about them sounded wonderful.

They had, apparently, eloped. Though whether or not they had first, to use Elizabeth's phrase, shacked up together, was an open question. Aside from sports and Frank, but mostly Frank, Marilyn's complete lack of interest in anything had been her most notable trait. She had been a most unusual being, Clara concluded. She had had no career and had nearly flunked out of school and college, because, Elizabeth said, she had never in her life read an entire book. She had liked introductions. Sometimes, if an author appended a postscript she would read that. But reading had given Marilyn headaches. In fact anything aside from being outdoors or with Frank had made her wicked. Old Mrs. Darlinger, needless to say, had been convinced that her youngest daughter was loading up on pizza and anchovies at every opportunity on the sly. Since Mrs. Darlinger had never believed in psychology, Marilyn was instead whisked off to her minister for regular lectures. But they didn't take, nothing did; the girl, Elizabeth said, had been wild from the start. Her marriage threw Mr. and Mrs. Darlinger into a year-long funk, from which they emerged with a most peculiar view of how to handle the situation. Marilyn had been cut off, which made little difference to her — she and Frank, living in California, could have had plenty of money from old Mr. Chimes, but they seemed to prefer to live on credit. Oddest of all, however, was the line of communication that the Darlingers established with their renegade daughter. They never telephoned. Instead old Mrs. Darlinger wrote letters — to Frank Chimes. He could hardly have been interested in the goings on at her country club or in her minister's sermons, yet he received, and replied to, reams of correspondence on such subjects. After Clara was born, these epistles, which had previously arrived at the Chimes' Los Angeles residence weekly, began to arrive daily. From the first, old Mrs. Darlinger had objected to the name Clara. For some reason, she and her husband were convinced that the girl ought to be named Emily and were quite put out when Marilyn had not seen fit to take their suggestion. And of course it was Marilyn they blamed, not Frank, who after all had wanted to name her Rachel — "and you see," old Mrs. Darlinger had exclaimed to Elizabeth, waving one of Frank's letters in her face, "that pigheaded girl won't even listen to her own husband! Though to tell the truth I think Rachel is even worse than Clara. But that," she had concluded triumphantly, "is not the point." Thereafter, she had not only written every day, but had taken to having her maid telephone the Chimes in Los Angeles. She would never pick up the phone until she was sure it was Frank she would be speaking to. And she would never ask about Marilyn. After a few perfunctory questions about his TV work, she would demand to know what they were feeding "that child," how much she weighed, did she wake up at night and other such questions pertinent to the baby's health. She had let it be known that the will, changed once to exclude Marilyn, had been changed again to pass her portion directly on to Marilyn's daughter. Eventually, not satisfied with Frank's descriptions of Clara or with the gurgles and coos that came over the wires when he held the baby up to the receiver, she had been unable to hold out any longer and had sojourned to California, despite the fierce disapproval of her husband. She returned with a glowing description of a child that looked nothing like Marilyn and nothing like Frank but entirely like her side of the family. Her daughter and son-in-law, she reported, might just as well be residents of Sodom or Gomorrah.

They kept liquor in the house, were out late every night and often went to Las Vegas with friends to gamble.And their friends — "Well," Elizabeth said, "that subject kept old motor-mouth going for months." The only really startling news from California, startling enough to make the Darlingers revise drastically their view of Frank Chimes, was that he had been decorated for heroism in the American landing at Anzio and wounded and decorated again on the road to Berlin. They had never known of his military history before, and indeed old Mr. Darlinger, a veteran himself, suggested that Marilyn had deliberately suppressed the fact just to deny them their pleasure in it, knowing that there was nothing they respected so much as someone who had fought for his country.

"How was he wounded?" Clara asked, sipping lemonade one balmy Sunday afternoon, as she and Elizabeth sat in the living room with the windows open. Prior to her aunt's reminiscences, Clara had been reading <u>The New Yorker</u>, which now lay open on the couch beside her. Elizabeth in in a rather unique outfit of white shorts, white knee socks, sneakers and a print blouse, was as usual draped with portions of the <u>Times</u> real estate section. Her gin and tonic stood, half finished, in a glass on the coffee table. "A shell exploded, or something or other, very near him," Mrs. Darlinger explained. "Hit him in the upper body. But they sewed him up. And except for a big scar, and I mean big, across his neck and shoulder, he was okay. Which was more than you could say for almost everyone else in that company. He was very lucky, at least that's what he always said. Frankly I don't see what's so lucky about having several inches of metal explode through your neck, but soldiers have a different way of viewing things. Hey!" Elizabeth exclaimed, jumping to her feet. "We're missing the Yankees!" Once the color TV, perched in a corner on a thing — for Clara could find no other word for this piece of modernity — of wood, stainless steel and glass, was blaring away noisily, Elizabeth, an ardent fan, went off in search of her baseball hat. She returned wearing it and looking more incongruous than ever, especially since it was a Mets hat. She also brought a bowl of peanuts and in no time was chomping happily and yelling, "Go, go, go!"

Clara remarked, as she often and fruitlessly did in an attempt to get the volume turned down, that she really failed to see the appeal of a sport that consisted mainly of a bunch of men loafing around a field, looking as though they had nothing to do and no good reason to be there.

"Don't be such an intellectual," was Elizabeth's reply. "Always poking your nose in a book."

Clara snorted contemptuously — a mannerism she had picked up from her aunt — and returned to her magazine. But what with the noise from the TV set and Elizabeth's incessant howls of disappointment or shrieks of encouragement, Clara was unable to concentrate on what was, to tell the truth, a rather incomprehensible report on the state of affairs in Taiwan. "Nuts!" Elizabeth exclaimed, stomping her foot, and before she could expand upon the athletic crimes committed before her very eyes, Clara could not help remarking, "Next thing you know I'll be hearing the rebel yell."

Clara retired to her room, muttering "a bunch of crackers. A bunch of cracked crackers, that's my family," under her breath. It didn't matter that they had originally come from New England, Clara thought, lying down on her bed, they had probably been bonkers up there too. She wondered vaguely what her father had

I

made of all this, but could not come up with anything because, very quickly, she began to doze. When she awoke from a dream in which Frank Chimes and Stanley Katz had been, all too obviously, mixed into one person lying on a surfboard and shooting a machine gun at a tank that for some reason was rolling through the waves on the Florida coast, it had already grown dark. The lights in her room were off, and at first as she lay gazing out the open window, she did not know where she was. She sat up and stared out at the darkened trees, swaying gently in the deep shadow of the park below. In the distance she discerned a glimmering — it was the surface of the lake, she thought — and here and there the high beams of automobiles shot through the evening air. Below her there was movement amid the trees, and at length the dark forms of birds rose in a flock through the gloaming, circled up and then curved in a long arc over the park toward

87

the west, like a streak of black paint on the dim air, and for no reason in particular, while she watched them she realized that she was lonely, lonelier than she had ever been; that her aloneness seemed to go right down to the bone. The birds soon merged with the general darkness, but the aloneness remained. And Clara, rubbing her eyes to wake up and then regarding the black wall of buildings that lined the opposite side of the park and the dots of yellow and white that flickered here and there in their large forms, wondered why she was here and not somewhere else, and what she had to do here and what, all in all, the purpose of living here could possibly be. She thought the magazines she had been reading were rather silly, and the more she considered it, the more she wondered why they were even printed. The clothes were nice and so were the various social expeditions with Elizabeth, but in the end they bored her profoundly. So did her work with

Ward Fairless. Elizabeth and Ward, she thought, had an active fascination with money. That fascination drove them; and most of what they did, they did because of it. Hence most of what they did interested them greatly. But Clara did not share that fascination. She had begun to understand it, and with that understanding came the knowledge that at most, she could only ever share that fascination passively. As long as she remained who she was, unless she changed, she could never pursue what they pursued. She could become competent in their business, she could become effective, but if she devoted her life to it, it would, she thought, be only half a life. If she pursued the secret of matter, that would be more than a life, it would be her real life. But she had already begun to see that there was a social world with which she would have to contend and with which she was most unfortunately unprepared to contend, in order to insist upon her own real life. Her mother, it seemed, had grown up fighting, had learned to do it young and had married someone even more skilled in saying yes and no to what he did and didn't want. Marilyn had married someone who, once and for all, took her away from the fight and who, thereafter, fought for her whenever necessary. For Clara, on the other hand, old Mrs. Darlinger's world had had the magical atmosphere of a perfect dream, a lonely dream, but one in which she was free to do exactly what she wanted. Indeed, had she grown up with Elizabeth, she probably never even would have discovered what she wanted. But then again, had she grown up with Elizabeth, she might have learned to fight like Marilyn.

Downstairs Clara found a note to the effect that Elizabeth had gone to the Longhill's cocktail party which a number of real-estate moguls were expected to attend, that Clara was a lazy bones for sleeping in the afternoon and that pizza could be found in the freezer. While the pizza unfroze in the microwave, Clara, once again gulping down lemonade, wandered through the quiet apartment. Elizabeth had done very well with the decorating, in blending her inherited antiques with her own taste, which tended naturally to the hypermodern. From the long kitchen, all wood, tile and stainless steel, Clara meandered past the round glass table in the breakfast nook through the little, corner, triangular bathroom to the pantry. There was of course a more direct entrance from kitchen to pantry in the form of a door, but Clara was in a mood to take unusual routes — of which the apartment only afforded a few. The first floor of the apartment, after all, with its two long halls, three bathrooms, living room, kitchen, dining room and Elizabeth's room had a fairly uncomplicated rectangular layout, except for the pantry, which cut aslant from the kitchen to the south wall. On the other side of the pantry was the dining room. Clara did not need to turn on lights as she went, since her aunt, who thought it absurd to economize on electricity, habitually left all of them blazing through the night. This made the pantry rather dazzling, for it was entirely white, with a long white porcelain sink, and, built onto the walls, wood cabinets, painted white, behind whose little square glass panes the crystal and crockery twinkled. White linoleum covered the floor, and the walls, tiled up to about shoulder height, were also white. Though Elizabeth did not much care for plants, a welter of them nonetheless crowded the pantry window, most prominent among them and enormous rubber tree in a huge, beaten bronze bucket. A transistor radio gleamed beside the sink, above which sparkled a round, brass-framed and evidently turn-of-the-century mirror. And for the first time, Clara observed in a corner, amid the luxurious fronds of Elizabeth's mundane and exotic plants a lovely, high, and delicate table, topped by a shiny oval slab of white marble. It stood on one long, slender, mahogany stalk and a round base. When she approached it, Clara observed at the front end of the carving that decorated the marble's edge an ornamental, flowing script which read, Josiah Vaughn Darlinger. Passing her fingers over the raised letters, she realized that she had never heard of him before.

She quickly traversed the dining room which she did not like. It was after all only used for social occasions. Even when they had a meal at home together — which was rare enough since Clara rose and ate breakfast three hours before Elizabeth, and dinner, as far as her aunt was concerned, meant a restaurant — they ate in the kitchen. And then the dining room, with its wood and drapes, was gloomy. It reminded her of her first night in New York and of Paul

Fairless, whose admirer she was not, smiling icily at Elizabeth's version of her future. The living room, however, with its unexpectedly harmonious mix of old and new seemed much more welcoming. The walnut cabinet, fireplace and grandfather clock seemed to converse together in their own quiet and old-fashioned corner. They had created their own aura of antiquity to which every detail in the vicinity contributed, but most of all, the large framed photograph of Elizabeth that had been taken twenty-five years ago and stood on the mantelpiece. The eyes of the twenty-two year old bride who had married a divorced businessman eleven years her senior twinkled out from beneath the coiffed hair and white veil with such evident hypocrisy, such false submission, that Clara smiled every time she saw it. Somehow the photographer had captured the true Elizabeth, and it seemed quite fitting that she should remain there, young and utterly revealed, amid her mother's antiques, forever.

The thick, blue oriental rug muffled her footsteps as she passed between the constellation of leather and chrome chairs and the long, very modern, blue and white couch. Along the opposite wall was another couch, a white with some blue, tweedy, L-shaped thing that curved to fit in the corner, its short end stopping just where the windows began. For some reason no one except guests ever sat on this couch, perhaps because it was less comfortable the the other and afforded no view of the TV. Covering most of the wall above it and curving with it to cover a section of the wall was an enormous, dramatic, black and white mounted photograph of the New York City skyline. Ten feet long, four and a half feet high, this urban vista wrapped that infrequently used end of the room in a hard and awesome atmosphere of modernity. Whenever

Clara gazed at this image "of gold," Elizabeth called it, "the real city, nothing but real estate," the ticking of the grandfather clock seemed always to come from afar, as if it were in another room altogether. Once when she had been told Ward was visiting, she had walked into the living room and been unable at first to find him. Then she had noticed the brown suited legs on the couch. The rest of him seemed to have disappeared into the photograph of the buildings, or to have been so dwarfed by it, that for a moment he had become so insignificant, it had been impossible to tell he was there.

The windows afforded the same view as from Clara's room directly upstairs. By now night had fallen.The park was a stretch of impenetrable blackness, set off, along Fifth Avenue, by street lamps which illuminated little more than the occasional benches by the east wall of the park. Now and then a passerby

slipped from the shadows into the artificial
light and then hurried along into the darkness
again. In the distance she discerned the lonely
clip clop of the mounted police. It had grown
cooler, which, she was relieved to think, made
it unlikely that Mrs. Darlinger would act on the
threat, made earlier that afternoon, to turn on
the air conditioning. Although Clara had grown
up with less air conditioning than many of the
people she knew in Florida, since her
grandmother seemed to prefer the heat as she
aged, it had still been in constant use for at
least five months of the year. In this Clara
benefited by coming to New York. She did not
know whether she was happier to have escaped
the electrically chilled air or the suffocating
heat of the Florida summers that had always
made her feel like she was roasting in a kiln.

Walking into the apartment's entrance way,
Clara gazed sharply to her right, into the
dining room. Less sharply to the right, where

the pantry and kitchen walls met in an angle, was the staircase to the second floor and its three rooms, while directly before her was the door to the kitchen and, a little to the left of that, the vestibule. She wandered in this direction, stopping by the front door. She rested her hand on the door knob, considering whether or not she wanted to go for a walk. But then she looked from her left, down the long hall that ran parallel to the living room, to her right, down the corridor between the kitchen and Elizabeth's room, and then before her. There, and closed, was the door to Elizabeth's room. Clara opened it and went in. This was the only room in the apartment that could be described as completely and starkly modern. Even the mauve chase longue had something of the twenty first century about it. Once, in a book on modern painting, Clara had seen a number of reproductions of DeChirico's work. The first time she had ever set eyes on Elizabeth's room, those pictures, with their sharp lines sweeping away from the viewer, with their deliberate emptiness that made the human figure appear so alien and insignificant, had come vividly to mind. She always passed through this room or approached its objects gingerly, and she had always wondered why her aunt chose a style for her bedroom that could only make her feel that she didn't belong there. The room seemed to exist solely and entirely for itself. It had no need of any person. To Clara it was one of those rooms one stumbled upon in a dream, where everything, until its discovery, had been reassuringly familiar. And then, in the house one had lived in for years, whose every room and corner was well known, one opened a door and found a room of ominous beauty that had never been there before. Every time she entered this room, it seemed she was walking into that dream-room in, that room whose very existence made her an outsider in her own familiar world and which put everything she had taken for granted, everything she had trusted, in question. And every time she stood there, alone, without her aunt, a silence only analogous to the silence of dreams descended upon her and everything in view. In that silence she trusted nothing and believed that anything, no matter how awful, could happen. It was a room that, in short, filled her with fear.

Sometimes at night as she lay in bed, she imagined Mrs. Darlinger's room downstairs. And she always imagined it empty, with all the lights blazing. Once, to reassure herself, she had stolen down the staircase and peeked in. "What's wrong kiddo, bad dreams?" Elizabeth had asked upon Clara's appearance in her white nightgown on the threshold. Clara nodded and was directed by her aunt to make herself comfortable on the chaise longue until the mood passed. Elizabeth, who lay on her bed in her full-length pink velour bathrobe, reading a spy novel, had not been talkative. From time to time she reached over to the night table and popped a hard candy into her mouth. Her finger and toe nails, recently manicured and painted an orangey vermilion, clashed somewhat with the robe. In the harsh white light, her face had not appeared tired at all, and Clara had imagined her lying there, wakeful and reading, until dawn. At length her sense of unease had subsided.

It had not, however, gone away. And as she stood in the room alone, it seemed that she, in her blue jeans, sneakers and red and white striped sailor shirt, was a trespasser in an unfriendly place. But the feeling also annoyed her and, determined to conquer it, she passed across the room to the bed. She sat down on the blue quilted bedspread by the night table and immediately noticed a photograph of her grandmother's Florida apartment house lying by the lamp. Shot from the front drive, the picture took in the entire building and the tiny, but still discernible sign, "Le Chateau, A Private Residential Club." Clara's eyes at once sought out the tenth floor balcony, but she could make out no figure, neither her grandmother nor herself, behind the screen. "Funny," she thought, "we would have been there." The picture was dated 1974.

When she moved to replace it, she observed the sheet of paper upon which it had lain. Thinking that it might be a letter from old Mrs. Darlinger, she had no compunction about picking it up and reading it. It <u>was</u> a letter, but not from her grandmother. She immediately recognized the names of the attorneys who managed old Mrs. Darlinger's estate. The legal jargon was fairly incomprehensible, but she got the point. Elizabeth was her guardian and had control of her money until she turned 18, which would happen in two months. However, the money could be kept in trust for Clara until she married, at her guardian's discretion. That was just like old Mrs. Darlinger. If the girl was turning out badly, the only cure would be marriage, and the money would be an incentive to marry. The only thing her grandmother had not counted on was that she and her daughter might have very different ideas about what turning out badly meant.

Clara replaced the letter, with the photograph on top of it, exactly as they had lain before. She rose, walked once around the bed, and then, without realizing it, began to pace, back and forth around the bed. At length she stopped and realized that for a few minutes she had been so angry she had not known where she was. Elizabeth's speech on marriage and the fact that Elizabeth had never told her any of this had, for a moment, appeared in a very ugly light. Yet that light had already begun to fade into sorrow, loneliness and general incomprehension. At least the Chimeses, of whom she had not the slightest memory, had trusted her enough to put her in charge of her own affairs at age twenty-one. But by then, she thought, it would be too late for science, too late for the secrets of the universe. "Oh well. That's that," Clara said aloud and walked out of the room.

"You've got to be more of a fighter. Don't give up so easily," Elizabeth exclaimed later that evening over the telephone, when Clara said she was too tired and depressed to take a cab down to the theater district to meet Mrs. Darlinger and her friends for a Broadway show. "I used to get fits of depressions," Elizabeth went on. "You've just got to fight it off. It's probably your period anyway. By the way, is it?" "No. I'm too depressed to have my period," Clara replied rather absentmindedly.

"Well that's a first," Elizabeth snapped. "Now you just get in a cab. Rita's got me fixed up with some Wall Street type who's an excruciating bore. You've got to save me. If I have to listen to this pompous droning on for one more minute, you'll be reading about me in tomorrow's newspapers. Heiress murders banker with dinner knife in East Side restaurant. All my friends will get the wrong impression. They'll think I was having an affair with this numskull. I've told Rita a thousand times not to do this to me. It's always a disaster. And it's humiliating. As if I wanted to get remarried. You're really not going to come?"

Clara replied that she was going to bed.

"Okay. Ordinarily I'd say you're a wet blanket, but you really do sound down in the dumps. Get some rest."

In the weeks that followed, Clara gradually thought less and less about what she had learned in Elizabeth's room. At first, it had constrained her somewhat around her aunt, but she never mentioned it, and Elizabeth, alarmed at her sudden taciturness, had hied her off to a doctor who pronounced her health perfect. Then, growing suspicious, Elizabeth had taken her to a gynecologist whose conclusion, "everything's in perfect working order, but she's not pregnant," did at last set her mind at ease. By then Clara had become cheerful again anyway, and Elizabeth chalked her niece's sudden spate of ill-humor up to hormones. Over time Clara grew accustomed to the thought that she was Elizabeth's dependent, solely because that was what Elizabeth wanted her to be and had the power to make her be. It was not, after all, such a horrible state of affairs. Clara thought her aunt was terrific and saw that Elizabeth, in turn, had grown to depend on her — on her companionship, her admiration, her mere presence as someone who conceivably needed to be taken care of, and, most notably, on her judgment. Elizabeth trusted Clara and came not only to rely on her insights into the motivations of social acquaintances but on her business acumen as well. More and more she turned to Clara in real estate matters, and more and more she turned to Clara to double-check the decisions and transactions of her ex-husband.

After all, Clara often told herself about that day in the park, Elizabeth had not said, don't marry. She had merely said, keep your money for yourself. So clearly she was not advancing an argument for spinsterhood in order to control Clara's money. Besides, she had more of her own than she knew what to do with. No, Elizabeth had been advancing an argument in order to control Clara, not Clara's money. And the thought that it was so important to a person to be in control of her, was not entirely unpleasant. She took it as a sign of love.

But still she could not bring herself to mention that she knew what power her aunt was exercising. More than once of an evening at the office Ward Fairless seemed on the verge of betraying his ex-wife and telling Clara what she already knew. All he needed was a push, or even a question as simple as "what do you mean?" But Clara always greeted these tentative sallies with silence or apparent incomprehension. She gave him no encouragement because she was afraid to discuss what Elizabeth was doing with anyone except Elizabeth. And she did not want to discuss it with Elizabeth. Yet Mr. Fairless, in his own persistent yet timorous style, did not give up. All through the summer, he was dropping hints.

As her eighteenth birthday drew near, Clara began to hope that perhaps her aunt intended to surprise her. That would clear up so many things and would be so convenient with regard to going to college, that she convinced herself it was the case. In her excitement, she forgot to be lonely and went through her daily routine with uncharacteristic cheerfulness and vigor. Clara rose at seven thirty every morning, showered and had begun fixing breakfast down in the kitchen by eight. She had taken to singing by the end of July and on more than one occasion Mrs. Darlinger, lying in her darkened room with the shades drawn, heard the girlish tunes through her drowsiness and muttered, "what's that child so damn happy about?" before sticking her head under the pillow to get back to sleep. On these weekday mornings when Clara set out to work, she looked very professional in her skirt, jacket, man-tailored shirt and high heels. But to the melancholy Ward Fairless, there was something sad in the sight of someone so young in the dreary attire of the adult workaday world. "She should be out at the beach," he could not help thinking. Of course she did go to the beach on weekends to Elizabeth's beach house on Long Island, but then had Elizabeth not decided to stay in the city to be with Clara, she would have had a chance to go to Maine. Mr. Fairless had delightful memories of the house on Deer Island and from time to time regaled Clara with descriptions of the gloomy, even sinister beauty of the New England coast.

The day came; Clara turned eighteen; Elizabeth and some friends took her to a baseball game then back to a party at home. That evening after everyone had left, they sat in the living room, and Elizabeth read aloud from an article on real estate. "Oh drat!" she exclaimed at last, throwing the paper onto the coffee table. Having had a bit too much to drink, she could focus her eyes on the newsprint only with difficulty. And then, after finishing her last gin and tonic, she yawned and staggered off to bed. Clara stayed up for a while longer, sitting on the blue and white couch that for some reason had begun to remind her of old Mrs. Darlinger's beach umbrella and stared at the imposing photograph of the New York City skyline. At last she rose to go upstairs but as she passed through the hall, the telephone rang. It was her aunt's stepson, Paul, whom she had avoided at the party that afternoon. He wanted to take her out for a drink. She declined, and they chatted for a while. He was about to hang up, when he seemed to recall something he had meant to say earlier.

"So real estate's the way to go. You've decided that's the point of being independently wealthy at the ripe old age of eighteen?"

Clara held the receiver away from her head and looked at it for a moment, before returning it and saying, "I really wouldn't know. You'll have to ask my aunt. Good night."

***

Early one hot summer evening in August a young man was sitting in a window booth of a coffee shop on an uptown avenue, drinking his second glass of iced tea, much to the annoyance of the proprietor, who wanted the booth free for bigger spenders. The customer drank steadily but slowly, from time to time glancing over at the revolving door of an office building across the street. He was tallish and not at all bad looking, except for a certain haggardness and rumpledness which bespoke an evident desire to get out of his suit. His tie, askew when he had walked into the coffee shop, was now undone, and he was clearly considering taking it off altogether when something across the street caught his eye. He rose, dropped a few coins on the table, paid and walked out onto the avenue. He went along in that brisk manner — not even stopping when he bumped or was jostled by someone else — for which New Yorkers are so well known and loved. Indeed his pace, which was somewhat quicker than that of the passersby going in his direction, bespoke the grim determination of someone who has elbowed his way through the thicket of narrow, crowded streets in the financial district, year in and year out.

After a block or two he crossed the street and in a moment had reached his objective. "Clara," he said, tapping the arm of the young woman in the blue and white striped skirt and jacket, who had been racing along faster than was probably safe given her high heels and preoccupied air. "Oh, hello," she said, stopping. "What a coincidence."

"Hardly," came the reply. "I was uptown on business."

"You should have dropped by," she said rather uninvitingly. She had not smiled when she greeted him.

"I didn't know if I was welcome."

"Why shouldn't you be," she said rather than asked. "It's your father's firm."

He stared at her curiously and then said, "You're going uptown." And since he began to stroll in that direction, she fell into stride beside him. "What I meant," he resumed after a moment, "and what I think you know I meant was that I didn't know if I would be welcomed by you."

Clara could come up with nothing to say to this that was neither rude nor a lie and so fell back on the transparently false "what makes you say that?"

Paul Fairless looked at her with frank annoyance. "Nice weather we're having," he went on after a moment with his tongue in his cheek.

Clara rolled her eyes in the manner she had adopted from her aunt and quickened her pace. Not too surprisingly she found out that he could walk just as fast as she could. So they went along like that for a while and in silence until Clara began to grow tired and slackened her pace. She had not spoken to Paul in two weeks, and it was irksome, she thought, to have run

I

into him. If he walked with her all the way home, he would undoubtedly expect to be invited up for something to drink. At this thought she slowed down even more and indeed began occasionally to stop and dawdle in front of shop windows. The sun had not begun to set, and she figured she could tire him out with this ploy well before dark. He seemed, however, to have divined what she had in mind and to be amused by it. This made his company all the more annoying. He nonetheless was carrying on a fairly lively conversation to which she now and then deigned to reply in monosyllables, as they wandered on along the still crowded avenue.

It was in the midst of some incomprehensible soliloquy on bonds that he all of a sudden interrupted himself to change the topic. "So that pterodactyl is going to keep you locked up in her tower until you get married."

Clara looked at him and blinked. Her eyes, he thought, were just as disconcerting as ever, warm and icy at the same time.

"What pterodactyl?" she asked.

"Oh, Elizabeth, of course. You know she could hand you over your portion of the estate any time, if she felt like it."

Clara continued looking at him, but said nothing.

"Is that news to you?" he persisted.

She blinked in that disturbingly cool way. "I don't see what business it is of yours."

"None. None of mine. Just curious how you were taking it," and glancing down at her, he judged that she had not been taking it well. "So you knew."

They walked on in silence for a while as the light of day began to fade, Clara thinking of her aunt's empty room and Paul wondering how she had found out, since he could not imagine Elizabeth telling her. No, he thought, Elizabeth

Darlinger kept her own counsel and in her imperious way would decide what was for the best, do it, and expect no questions asked. But he could not help puzzling over the attitude of this aloof, mysteriously innocent and angry girl. What did she make of it and why, above all, was she going along with it — why hadn't she said anything? For he was sure she had not mentioned it to her aunt. He dismissed the possibility that she just didn't care or had meekly accepted Mrs. Darlinger's tyrannical will. He had questioned his father enough to know that Clara had no real interest in the career Elizabeth had chosen for her. And as they walked through the hot, dusty twilight, it came to him that Clara was waiting, that perhaps she did not even know it, but she was waiting and biding her time — though for what? — and that in this she might be just as strong and inflexible as her consummately impatient aunt. Clara was, he thought, very much like Mrs. Darlinger, except for this strange, stubborn waiting. He imagined that she was quite capable of holding a silent grudge for years.

He stopped at a street corner to light a cigarette and, exhaling a cloud of smoke, gazed down at his quiet companion who caused the desire to protect and to provoke to alternate so unexpectedly in him. "It's a ghastly family," he finally said and when she looked at him questioningly, he cleared the matter up at once: "Ours."

Clara was somewhat taken aback. "I didn't know that's how you see Elizabeth."

"She raised me," he answered and smiled ruefully. "From the time I was two. They got divorced when I was just a few years younger than you are now. It was delightful."

"The divorce."

"Yes, nothing like it. Every kid should go through at least one."

"Why didn't you go into your father's business?" Clara could not help asking, and, as she did, she saw something ironic and hard and something that seemed full of implication for her come into his blue eyes. "Because I didn't want to," Paul answered, uttering each word quite distinctly.

They looked at each other until Clara, who could not but observe that this remark did not reflect especially nicely on her, shrugged and resumed walking.

"The little liar," Paul thought and hurried to catch up with her. Approaching, he noticed the firey tints in her hair from the weak, crepuscular light, and how slender she was, and that her briefcase seemed a bit too heavy for her. "But you, on the other hand, like the business," he resumed, falling in stride beside her.

"I adore it," she acidly replied.

"I thought so. You look like the entrepreneurial type," he blandly went on. "From the first moment I set eyes on you, I said to myself, that girl belongs in real estate. Here, let me," and he reached over and took, not without some resistance from her, Clara's briefcase. She glared at him. The tussle over the briefcase, which had caused on passerby to stare, had discommoded her somewhat. Her blouse felt slightly out of place and, already uncomfortable from her walk through the ninety degree heat, she was now flushed and perspiring. She looked like a woman about to lose her temper. Paul did not appear at all displeased with having produced this effect on her. "Lovely business, isn't it?" he grinned. "Throwing people out of their homes."

"I don't have anything to do with that part of it," she snapped.

"Oh don't you. What do you think's going on with those tenements in Chelsea?"

"Shut up," was her only reply, as she darted past him into a quick jay-walk across the street. But he, tossing his cigarette into the street and leisurely following her across, caught up with her almost at once. He continued at her side and shortly began whistling. "Yes I could tell right off you'd take to the work, just like Elizabeth," he said after a while. "Or mom — that's what I used to call her. Sort of hard to imagine, isn't it, anyone calling Elizabeth mom. Marilyn, now that was a different story."

Clara looked up. "You knew her."

He nodded, glancing down at her.

"You liked her," Clara went on.

He nodded again and resumed whistling. Clara found this most bothersome. Though eager to question him about her parents, she was determined not to appear too interested in anything this extremely offensive man might say. What made the predicament positively infuriating was her certainty that though aware of her discomfort, he had no intention of obliging her or making things easier by volunteering the information she wanted. By now they had turned onto the cross street that led to Elizabeth's apartment building. The air had not cooled at all, but a breeze had sprung up and rustled the leaves and branches of the trees above them.

"Clara, look!" Paul had caught hold of her elbow and was gazing up at the sky which had turned deep violet.She was, however, in no mood to appreciate natural beauty. She glanced up quickly, and when she caught him looking at her, said, "Fiddlesticks," and marched on. She heard him laughing behind her.

On her way to the elevator, the doorman, Roberto Rodriguez, gave her the message that Elizabeth had gone to Long Island for the weekend and that she should come along, that night or Saturday morning, if she wanted. The moment she stepped into the apartment she began to undress. By the time she reached her room on the second floor of the duplex she was stark naked. She had just changed into shorts and a T-shirt which Elizabeth had bought her as a gag and the back of which sported the sentence "Get ahead or drop dead," when the buzzer rang. It was the doorman, sounding rather perplexed. Paul Fairless had apparently asked permission to come up. "Well for God's sake, he has a key," Clara nearly shouted in a sudden burst of ill temper.

"Maybe he lost it," Roberto said.

"Maybe he lost his marbles," Clara retorted.

"Hmm. Maybe. Maybe not," was Roberto's equivocal reply.

Clara had gone downstairs and poured a glass of lemonade by the time the front doorbell rang. "That was fast," Paul commented upon her change of attire. "I always was partial to hot pants."

"They're not hot pants."

"Indeed."

"You know something?"

"What?"

"You're obnoxious." That said, Clara turned on her heel and headed back into the kitchen for the lemonade.

"Wait a minute — get ahead or drop dead?" He had followed her to the kitchen counter and was scrutinizing her back.

"In your case the latter," Clara went on, while gulping down the entire glass of lemonade.

"Have some more," Paul held the pitcher up for her to drink from.

"What is <u>wrong</u> with you?" Clara exclaimed, snatching the pitcher away and pouring herself another glassful. "No. Don't answer," she went on. "I'll tell you. You're pushy, insulting, arrogant and you have no manners."

"So you're in love with me. How convenient. Is the pterodactyl at home?"

Clara simply looked at him, then turned and headed off to the living room. Out of habit she went toward the blue and white couch, but then bethought herself and decamped to one of the Mies Van der Rohe chairs. A newspaper lay on the coffee table. "Oh terrific," Paul said, flinging his jacket and tie onto the couch and then stretching out in the chair opposite her. "Read to me from the real estate section. You don't know how I've missed it." And his blue eyes settled on her with mirthless irony. But Clara, for the first time since they had met on the street that afternoon, began to laugh. He did not join in, though he smiled, still gazing humorlessly at her.

"Be a sport kiddo, and fix me a drink," he went on, lighting a cigarette with a silver lighter much like Clara's and with the same resounding snap.

"You're being mean to Elizabeth," Clara laughed.

"And you don't know how to have fun."

"I do too," she replied before she could stop herself and immediately regretted it. It sounded ridiculous, more like a confirmation than a denial of what he had just said.

He leaned forward, still gazing at her mirthlessly. "Yes little one, darling, kiddo, my child — fun is working for Elizabeth nine hours a day five days a week, eating lunch alone, and collapsing on the weekends when you're not going out with her rich, middle aged friends. Oh, and I forgot, fun is also reading science books in your spare time, whenever Elizabeth's not reading to you from the newspaper or giving you her screw around yes but marriage no lecture. Of course I realize it must pale in comparison to the rollicking time you had in Florida, growing up with the Tyrannosaurus Rex. Now that must have been one barrel of laughs after another. I wish I had it on video tape. But we try hard here in the New York branch of the family to help everyone enjoy themselves."

"It wasn't so bad in Florida," Clara pensively replied, gazing down at her legs— they still even had her Florida tan. When she looked up she noticed he was watching her sharply.

"Left your true love in Florida, huh? Or was it loves?"

"Maybe" she answered, annoyed at his nosiness, and went back to the kitchen for more lemonade.

"So it was love, singular," he said to himself, "maybe not even that."

She came back with the pitcher and an extra glass. When she offered him some lemonade, he accepted, saying, "that's better. So she's in Sag Harbor for the weekend with the unbearable Moores." And with that he stood up and kissed Clara who was still bent over the lemonade.

"Now you've made me spill it!" she exclaimed.

"Don't worry about what's not important."

"Stop it. I hardly know you."

"Well now you've got a great opportunity —"

"And we're practically related."

"To get better related."

"You're bananas." By this time Clara had backed out into the hall. She tripped over a useless little antique side table. It crashed against the uncomfortable little chair, covered with antique needlework, which decorated that portion of the apartment. The Limoges vase filled with tiger lilies, water and ice cubes — Elizabeth was a great believer in ice cubes as a floral preservative — which had adorned the side table, spilled onto the chair then bounced and shattered on the floor.

"Now look what you made me do," she began. "Listen, I'll go to the movies with you, but that's that."

He looked her in the eyes.

"For now anyway," Clara lamely concluded.

"It's a deal," he said, smiling. "Now pick a movie, any movie, just so long as it's got lots of sex and gore in it."

***

"You've got to do something about it," Elizabeth nearly shrieked, letting go the Venetian blind with a loud snap. She had been standing by the living room window, gazing out at the bright September day. The sunlight streamed into the room as it always did when the weather was good, but that day it could not flatter the angry face of the woman in the silk, chocolate brown, designer-made suit who stood tapping a high heeled foot noiselessly on the oriental rug.

Ward Fairless, seated on the very modern blue and white striped couch, mopped his wide, tired, but still ruddily attractive face with a handkerchief. "Why?" he asked at length, in a deep, exhausted voice.

"Because it's scandalous. They're running around all kissy faced, carrying on like some soap opera, and they're practically related." With that she marched across the room to the walnut cabinet, removed a cigarette from the gold and crystal cigarette case and lit it. "Besides, I tell you that child was a virgin when she arrived here, utterly inexperienced. Not anymore."

"Libby," her ex-husband exclaimed in a tone of genuine surprise. "I never knew you were a prude."

"Prude, smoode," Mrs. Darlinger snorted. "You've got to do something."

"You do something. She's your niece."

"He's your son. And he's almost ten years older than she is. The cradle robber! She's a baby, an absolute baby. And he's using her."

"I doubt it," Ward sighed. "Not that tough little cookie."

"Oh. So now she's a tough little cookie. Don't you talk about Clara like that. That poor girl's in love. Or she thinks she is. But she's too young to be in love. You've got to tell Paul —"

"It's useless. He's acting like as much of an idiot as she it. That's what happens when people fall in love, if I remember correctly."

"Well, it really can't go on like this," Elizabeth continued, smoking vigorously. "I can't bring people over, because God knows whether or not I'm going to find them banging away on the couch. For Christ's sake, he's all over her, even at the dinner table. And it's useless sticking around to try to keep things under control, because he — and it's him, Ward, not her — pays no attention to me. Besides, they'll just go off to his apartment."

"Right you are. I think she's meeting him there on her lunch break."

Elizabeth gasped. "What is he doing?"

"You've got to admit. It shows determination."

"An unhealthy determination. He's obsessed with her. Have you seen the way he watches her? All the time, watching, watching. There's something neurotic about this. I don't like it at all." Elizabeth crushed her cigarette out in the ashtray. "Ward, I'm going to send that girl to a psychiatrist."

"But he's the one with the obsession."

"Well," Elizabeth grandly but somewhat incoherently concluded, "it takes two to tango."

***

"Paul?"

"Clara?"

"I love you."

"You'd better."

"Shut up you creep...Paul?"

"Clara?"

"Elizabeth thinks I should see a psychiatrists."

"Oh. What's wrong with you?"

"She thinks I'm obsessed with you."

"You'd better be."

"I am."

"Good."

"His name is Dr. Shatzenkammer."

"Who's that?"

"The psychiatrist. Wake up you big dope. He's a specialist in sexual disorders."

Paul sat up with a bolt. It was one o'clock on a Saturday afternoon, but with all the shades pulled in his bedroom, it could just as easily have been dusk. He looked down at Clara, lying next to the spot where he had lain on the rumpled bed, and demanded, "What sexual disorders?"

"I don't know what. Elizabeth thinks we're obsessed with each other. She thinks there's something incestuous about it. So does Dr.

Shatzenkammer. She had a consultation with him on the phone. Boy, you should see your hair."

"What's wrong with it?" And then, before she could answer, he said — scowling and tousling his hair even further — "Katzenjammer?"

"Shatzenkammer. She might have a point you know."

"No I don't."

"Well I've never been like this before."

"Like what?"

"Lying in bed all day."

"Neither have I. But," he yawned, "all the best doctors prescribe it."

"Like who?"

"Katzenjammer."

She hit him over the head with a pillow. He grabbed another pillow and hit her back. This went on for a while. It soon gave way, however, to other activities and sometime after that Paul and Clara were snoozing their way into mid-afternoon. They slept in something of a tangle, Clara curled up half under him, her head on his arm, facing his chest. She dreamt that they were swimming in the Gulf of Mexico. He dreamt that he was sleeping with Clara in his arms and that a funny-looking psychiatrist, not unlike Groucho Marx in demeanor, was trying to get into the room. "Some doctor! I thought you knew everything," Elizabeth sneered at Katzenjammer who was fumbling with the lock in the hall. She crossed her arms and tapped her foot in annoyance. "Lady, your family's dental problems may be beyond the reach of science," Katzenjammer retorted, shifting his cigar from one end of his mouth to the other.

"Not dental, mental."

"Mental! Who's mental?"

"You're asking me?"

"You mean you're asking me?" And with that Katzenjammer began pounding on the door with both fists and kicking it with both feet.

"It's hopeless," Elizabeth cried. "Who ever could have dreamed he would act like this? An absolute sex fiend..."

"You're telling me?"

"...And voted Democratic in the last election."

"That won't fly on Wall Street. Market was down six points today. Better get a look at those molars."

"What about that East Side real estate? And the Xerox stock? And our defense investments? He's probably got her pregnant!"

At this Katzenjammer began running around in circles, staring intently ahead of himself like a lunatic and screaming. "He's on first, he's on second and, yes, folks, it looks like...It is! A home run for Fairless!"

A delightful, musical sound interrupted Katzenjammer's insane shrieks.

I

"Paul?"

He opened his eyes but at first was conscious of nothing besides the feel of Clara's shoulder blades and the back of her head against his hands.

"Yes beautiful?" he said after a moment.

"Elizabeth says she thinks it's peculiar for two healthy young people to spend their entire weekend, every weekend, in bed. She says we'll have back problems in our old age."

"Hmm..."

"What do you think?"

"I don't.

"Ever?"

"Not any more. Since I met you my mind kind of went on vacation."

"This happen often?"

"Only once."

"But what do you think about at work?"

"Your legs."

137

"Come on. But when you're closing a deal and things."

"Your arms."

"On the subway?"

"I'm trying to be polite, Clara."

"You know, I think there was a knock at the bedroom door."

By this time Paul was otherwise occupied. He didn't answer.

"It would be very embarrassing, you know," Clara went on.

"Hmm...what?"

"If someone came in and found you doing this."

"It takes two to tango," he reminded her, pulling the sheets up over their heads.

"Good God, it never stops!" came the dulcet tones of Elizabeth Darlinger's voice. "Even at three o'clock in the afternoon!"

Under the covers Paul and Clara looked at each other. She had frozen at the sound of the first footstep. But he continued doing what he had been doing before.There was laughter in his eyes.

There came a loud snap and then another and another, as the shades went flying up to the tops of the windows. Pale yellow light penetrated the busy cocoon on the bed.

"She's gonna throw a fit if you keep it up," Clara whispered.

"You have a way with words, Clara Darlinger, I mean Chimes," Elizabeth went on, yanking back the sheets.

"Leave us alone," Paul yelled, sitting up and covering Clara with a blanket. "We're busy."

"Busy, busy, busy," Elizabeth snapped. "What are you trying to do? Repopulate the earth?"

"As a matter of fact..." he began.

"Don't you go getting any ideas. Paul Fairless. Your behavior has been ghastly. No child of mine is ever — Get your hands away from her. It's disgraceful. Clara stop giggling. Listen to me, young lady. We're going home."

Paul, resting his elbow on his knee and his chin on his hand, leaned forward. A rather hard, deliberate look came into his blue eyes. "No she's not," he replied slowly, and then suddenly, like someone awakened with a start, he said, "Besides, we're getting married."

Clara looked up in surprise and then smiled. She reached over for his hand and kissed it.

"No!" Elizabeth insisted, stomping her foot. "You're both going to get your heads shrunk. I will not have it. I don't care if you marry out of your race or even into your own sex. But the two of you are not, I repeat not, marrying into your own family."

II

After two months of therapy, Paul and Clara had begun to squabble. After six months, they were fighting regularly. After a year they were no longer speaking to each other. By the time Clara had turned twenty, Paul was living in Hong Kong, "doing something or other in somebody or other's venture capital division," as Elizabeth, with characteristic precision, put it. He had given up on the therapy long before Clara, proclaiming to the amazed Dr. Shatzenkammer, "I don't know what women want and you don't either." Unfortunately, neither did Clara, but once she had declared, in the midst of a memorable dispute in front of an outdoor restaurant in Greenwich Village, that she never wanted to speak to or lay eyes on Paul Fairless again, she had at last something really to be depressed about. Prior to that moment, when a look of such insane ferocity came into Paul's eyes that she could not but believe his final, coldly controlled words, "I will never forget the things you've said to me tonight. I will never forget this," she had not had all that much to tell her psychiatrist. Now she had plenty. She discovered, with Dr. Shatzenkammer's help, that she had a great deal of "repressed rage" with regard to Paul, that she had a "deep ambivalence" about him "not unconnected with the early trauma" of losing both her parents, that she had "sought her absent father in him" and had, "like a true passive aggressive encouraged his neurotic sexual fixation" upon her. All of this was at first rather incredible to

Clara, but she was soon coaxed into thinking that her own skepticism was"resistance to the emotional truth," and therefore, by an unusual leap of logic, proof of it. She also discovered that what her dislike of the real estate business concealed was fear of her own aggression, and that in fact she was refusing to accept a natural aptitude for it. So by the time Clara turned twenty-one, she was hard at work in her aunt's firm and lonelier than ever.

The one thing that the psychiatrist could make neither heads nor tails of was Clara's predilection, developed two years after she got her own apartment, for Jewish mysticism. It was ultimately Shatzenkammer's undoing. "Enough of this mumbo jumbo," he had said the very first time Clara had mentioned Gershom Scholem's name. She had happened the week before, to come upon a copy of <u>Main Trends in Jewish Mysticism</u> in a bookstore and by the time she arrived for her therapeutic session, could talk about nothing else. At first the short, bald analyst had tried discreetly to direct Clara's monologues away from supernatural beings and back to her "conflicted feelings" about her mother. Later he had taken to asking leading questions, like, "precisely what is it about this so-called Great White Rabbi that appeals to you?" Then one afternoon Clara had glanced up from the couch after thirty minutes of talking to see Dr. Shatzenkammer, his head in his hands and his horn-rimmed glasses on the desk. "Dr. Shatzenkammer?" she asked with concern and sat up. He glanced up but kept his hands pressed against the lower portion of his face. Above his fingertips, his little brown eyes stared at her with desperation. "Has it ever occurred to you that this, this," for a second it seemed that words had failed him, but he finally regained his composure and managed to get out the word, "interest in Judaism is in fact a denial of your own non-Jewish roots and of the intense Christianity of your grandmother?"

"No." Clara answered, "because what I was just getting to was that I've started reading St. Augustine —"

"I don't want to hear it!" Shatzenkammer cried. "I don't want to hear any more about dybbuks or demons or angels or God. This is an obsessional neurosis —"

"Last time you said it was a neurotic obsession."

"Well it's getting worse. You should be going out with men, not staying home and reading books by, by..." he began sputtering but at last got the word out, "saints!"

"Scholem isn't a saint. He's a scholar."

"I don't care who he is. I've had enough. No more God in this office."

Shortly thereafter Dr. Shatzenkammer went on vacation to Italy. Unfortunately he took a plane destined for Israel and full of Orthodox

Jews and got hijacked. As a result of his two days on the runway of a Middle Eastern capital cooped with nearly a hundred religious zealots, Dr. Shatzenkammer was a changed man by the time the passengers did safely disembark. It was not, alas, a change for the better. When he realized that he had landed not in Rome but in Jerusalem, he apparently had some sort of a fit and had to be hospitalized. He never returned to New York.

"Gadzooks! Who ever would have expected it!" Elizabeth cried one Saturday morning in the living room of Clara's West Side apartment. She had just come from her game of tennis and was dressed accordingly in white shorts, blouse, sneakers and knee socks. Since the <u>Times</u> had already sold out at the nearest newsstand, she had bought a <u>Daily News</u> instead and was now staring wide-eyed at its rather racier headlines, in particular the one that read, N.Y.SHRINK BONKERS IN ISRAEL.

"So old Shatzykatzy's toys got lost in the attic," Elizabeth said, half way into the first paragraph description of how the doctor shrieked and began foaming at the mouth in the airport terminal. An Orthodox rabbi was quoted to the effect that it had started on the Kabul runway, that they had alerted their Muslim captors that there was a lunatic in their midst, that the Muslims had taken one look at him and muttered something about Allah being very angry at this American and suggested that they all pray, which they had, to no avail.

"Hunh?" Clara asked, while gulping down lemonade and not looking up from the article on orgasms in the latest issue of Cosmopolitan.

"Bananas on the brain. Cookies were cracked. Who would have thought it?" Elizabeth went on.

"Went wacko?"

"Yup. Says here he started screaming 'I'm not Jewish, I'm not American, I'm the Great White Rabbit.' Apparently started running around in circles. Rolled his arms in the air. Made noises like an airplane. A fixed stare ahead of himself. Started screaming 'He's on first! He's on second! It looks like, it is, a home run!' Jesus Christ. Talk about half a deck!"

Clara looked up pensively. "I always thought he was a bit neurotic about religion," she said and then returned to what she considered a rather dubious section under the subhead, "Size Has Nothing To Do With It."

"I hope you're ready," Elizabeth said, having finished with the funnies and the crossword puzzle and tossing the newspaper with its sad tale of Shatzenkammer's demise into the trash can.

"I don't want to go," Clara said, and then, looking up, "he really was a sex maniac. It says here that it's actually quite rare for men to want to do it more than a few times a day, at the most."

"You had a very unhealthy effect on Paul. He was already half way round the bend when he met you. Voted Democratic in the last election. You loosened the few remaining screws, as it were. But this business in Hong Kong ought to straighten him out. Get your things."

Clara scowled, which made her face look even rounder than it was. She had let her hair grow to her shoulders and customarily kept it pulled back in a high pony tail, which now bobbed and made her look quite silly when she shook her head.

"Don't you make funny faces at me. You're coming. And get dressed. Don't you ever wear clothes?" Elizabeth cast a critical eye upon the semi nudity of her niece.

"It so happens I wasn't expecting you."

"Why not?" Elizabeth snapped. "Change your underpants. They've got a stain."

"And you're going looking like that?"

"Of course. Like everyone else on the Main Line they have tennis courts. You wouldn't know. You've never deigned to visit them. My gown's in the car. I want you to take that Yves St. Laurent thing I bought you. And leave those Angelica papers at home."

Philip Angelica, thorn in Mrs. Darlinger's side, was a most determined tenant lawyer, currently engaged in obstructing Elizabeth's plans for portions of Lower Manhattan. He had also and therefore become the bane of Clara's life, for whenever she saw her aunt — which was fairly often because Elizabeth, despite early objections to Clara's apartment, had since all but moved in with her — she received a lecture upon the depredations of this attorney whom she had never met, but who had caused so much paperwork that she got a headache at the thought of him. "I can't," Clara replied. "There's something or other that has to be filed in court on Tuesday."

"Then get it to the lawyers Monday night. I will not have that monster ruining my weekend. He's already ruined my life."

"Frankly that may be a moot point," Clara replied, still not moving from the couch. "If we go up in that plane with Rita."

"Nonsense. It's a very short trip from New York to Paoli or Berwyn or wherever it is in Pennsylvania. And Rita's an excellent pilot. Quite an enthusiast."

"I don't like the way she flies. Always at a tilt. If she got the right prescription glasses, I'd feel safer."

Elizabeth just glared and began tapping her foot. When she was angry her pupils contracted, making her eyes two small discs of amber determination.

"Oh, you annoy me!" Clara exclaimed, but rose to her feet and headed into the bedroom to pack. She began tossing some clothes into a small leather suitcase. "I had planned to spend the weekend reading!" she shouted. "And let me tell you, The City of God is a lot more interesting than Sunny and Monica." She marched into the living room with her suitcase.

"You forgot your clothes. And what's wrong with Sunny? She thinks you're the greatest. You're just jealous because she's getting married and you're not."

"She's an idiot and she's marrying an imbecile. I predict mongoloid children."

Elizabeth nodded. "He is a bit dense. Solid wall of cement between the ears, I'd say. But sometimes that's an asset in a husband. How such stupid people can be so rich. What's his name again? Flupper? Slupper?"

"Klupper. And you don't have to have all your batteries working when you come from

Oklahoma and your father owns a slew of oil wells."

"You mean Texas."

"Oklahoma."

"Texas. I'm positive this Slupper's from Texas."

"Klupper! Tom Klupper!" Clara fairly shrieked and dropped her suitcase on the uncarpeted floor.

"Get some clothes on. Slupper, Klupper. It's all the same."

"You said it. Won't mean beans to us if we go up in that plane," Clara retorted, turning on her heel and heading back into the bedroom. "We'll just be so many charcoal-broiled spare ribs, strewn all over the Jersey turnpike." When she returned, she was wearing tight blue jeans, high-heeled sandals, a Hawaiian shirt and sunglasses.

"How unique," Elizabeth said. She turned on the radio and was smoking briskly.

"Except for the shoes you look just like what's his name."

"Klupper."

"No. Sunny's father."

"Horace. But his hair's longer. In the jeans it's rather undistinguished. But in those suits, now that's quite a combination. He looks like a hippie stock broker."

"Always wore it like that. Even thirty years ago. Bad enough being named Horace LaMarque and a nincompoop. That hair's just the icing on the cake. Monica says he bought another motorcycle. People like that, it makes you understand how we could have had a president like Gerald Mayaguez Ford. Talk about a dim bulb. I can just see Horace in the voting booth next year, torn between the Liberty Lobby or whatever those fanatics are called and Ronald Reagan. Quite a quandary. Then he'll look down at Sunny and say 'what do you think?' And when Sunny goes woof woof, he'll close his eyes and pull a lever."

Behind her sunglasses Clara stared. "Sunny? Going woof woof? And in the voting booth? Libby! You've really gone off the deep end."

"What do you mean?" Mrs. Darlinger snapped. "He takes that nauseating creature with him everywhere. Bad enough he had to name it after his daughter."

"Oh. I thought you meant Sunny the girl."

"No. Sunny the dog. Quite a participant in the electoral process, old Sunny boy is. A real kingmaker. Which way will Sunny dog go? None of the pollsters can ever predict. The canine vote — that's something you have to watch out for. Old Sunny boy's a real card in the primary. Didn't like Nixon, not too keen on Reagan either. One thing's for sure — Sunny's a lifelong fan of Harold Stassen. Definitely a left-leaning wolf hound."

155

Clara snapped off the radio, and they went down to Elizabeth's Mercedes. Mrs. Darlinger liked to ride with all the windows open. She also liked to drive very fast. To distract herself from her aunt's terrifying vehicular maneuvers, Clara sorted out the detritus in the glove compartment. There was an ancient pack of Winstons, a comb, a tube of lipstick, some crumpled road maps, the automobile registration, a snapshot of Clara in a bikini at Myrtle Beach, a pack of suppositories, and illegible list of some sort and a photograph of Paul, evidently stark naked, diving off a rock in Tahiti. Clara studied this for quite some time.

"That was taken five years ago," Elizabeth said. "Hurry up buster. What do you think this is — a parking lane? Always a problem getting him to keep his clothes on. Just like you. It must run in the family. Marilyn was that way. So was Frank. She had a load of pictures of him from the war. Here's Frank, naked in Southern

Italy. Here's Frank, swimming naked outside Rome. Here's Frank, with all his clothes off in Germany. Impression you got was he ran naked all over Europe. Ward used to be like that too, said clothes were a nuisance. Sometimes I think the whole family should've been packed off to a nudist colony. Check and make sure I remembered the gum." Elizabeth always armed herself with at least two packs of Juicy Fruit before any flight.

They arrived at the airfield in record time, to find the six-foot Rita Longhill and her five-foot five inches husband quarreling over the lunch she had packed. Ray Longhill was a very determined man who reminded Clara of a terrier and spoke with a distinct Chicago accent. Rita, born on Long Island, had the unmistakably affected pronunciation of a New York snob.

"But darling, not everyone likes egg salad," Rita was saying as they approached. "And you're not, remember, the only one who will be eating."

"The way you've arranged it, I won't be eating at all." Mr. Longhill barked back. "Dear."

"You might have told me, sweetheart, what you wanted."

"After twenty nine years, wonderful, you might have known."

Clara and Elizabeth looked at each other. Clara pulled down her sunglasses and rolled her eyes. Elizabeth put on her "let me handle this" expression.

"What have we here? Ham and Swiss on rye," Mrs. Darlinger began, rifling through the sandwiches. "Ham and Swiss on white bread. Ham and Swiss, hmm...ham and Swiss. And an extra — ham and Swiss." Elizabeth glanced up at Rita who, in her slacks, Merrill Lynch sweatshirt, gold hoop earrings, yellow tinted aviator glasses and yellow silk scarf tied at the side of her neck, did not in the least, Clara thought, inspire aeronautical confidence. Meanwhile Ray had turned a most interesting purplish hue. His dark eyes, behind his black rimmed glasses, seemed molten with suppressed rage.

"Well it's a good thing we all like ham and Swiss," Elizabeth went on, sticking her foot, Clara thought, right in it.

"We don't." Ray said. "I detest ham and Swiss. I've detested it since the army. The only thing I detest more is spam."

"You never said anything, dear," Rita rather inconsequentially replied, "when I made it for the boys. They used to love ham and Swiss."

"And they used to love applesauce, darling. And I've detested it since 1944. But every night with dinner, what do we have? Applesauce."

"Don't exaggerate. Since they went off to college, my love, you know that's not the case."

"Yes, sugar, it most certainly is the case. I've kept track."

"Let's see what we've got to drink," Elizabeth chirped and reached over to the bigger of the two coolers, the one with the Styrofoam top which had, oddly, several holes bored in it. Before either Ray or Rita could say a word, she had removed the lid. Out jumped a beautiful, long-haired, orange and white cat that looked Clara thought, rather like a blurred creamsicle, as it shot off down the runway.

"Hank, you come back here!" Rita shrieked and started down the runway after the cat.

"I've had it!" Ray Longhill growled and climbed into the plane with the other cooler, whose contents — it came to Clara in a flash of intuition — were probably alcoholic.

"Don't just stand there you wretched child," Elizabeth, following Rita, called back at her niece. "Bring the cooler!"

A few minutes later the three women were chasing the cat around a plane at the other end of the runway. A young couple with five-year-old son got out of the plane to assist. So then there were five people chasing the cat and a little boy, running around in circles, rolling his arms in the air and making noises like an airplane.

"What the hell are they doing?" A truck driver said, pulling to a stop on the roadside.

"Beats me," his companion replied and then, looking more closely, "that boy looks bonkers, if you want my opinion."

"Better go have a look"

Shortly there were seven adults chasing the cat on the runway. At length the truck driver and his companion, who seemed to regard this pursuit as a chance to try out a number of innovative football plays, became so absorbed in their own activities that when the driver, charging under the wing past his companion posted as an imaginary fifty-yard line, scooped up the cat — which had paused to regard them with what could only be described as a look of feline amazement — he hardly knew what to do with it. "Over here! Over here!" Rita, Elizabeth and Clara yelled in unison, jumping up and down like a trio of oddly assorted cheerleaders. The driver turned, broke into a trot and amid, cheers, deposited the still astonished beast in the cooler. By the time everyone had congratulated everyone else and the three women had turned back toward their own plane, the two men had resumed their antics, with the five year old enthusiastically racing alongside whichever one he thought was winning.

They found Ray drinking a can of beer in the seat next to the pilot's. "Well Hank, you had the right idea," he said, glancing at the cooler. "Better luck next time."

"Oh botheration!" Rita exclaimed, turning on the engine and fiddling with her glasses. "That optometrist can't do anything right."

"All thumbs," Elizabeth commented, straightening out her knee socks. "They always are."

Clara gazed at Rita with horror and then closed her eyes. She tried to think about <u>The City of God</u> while the little plane bounced down the runway, but this somehow became entangled with Paul diving off a rock in Tahiti. Above the roar of the engine, she heard Elizabeth's gleeful shriek, "Bombs away!" and knew they were airborne. Clara opened her eyes once to look out the cockpit window. As usual Rita was flying at an angle. Elizabeth was chomping happily on gum. Ray was belting down beer in gloomy silence. Clara did not open her eyes again for the rest of the trip. When she didn't think she was going to be sick, she wondered what would happen to her soul when she died, an event which she expected momentarily. Since her discovery of the wisdom of the great Moses of Leon such questions had taken on uncommon urgency. Old Mrs. Darlinger's simple bromide with regard to what the hereafter was like — "You'll find out when you get there" — now seemed to leave something to be desired. The one thing Clara had come to be fairly sure of was that her repressed rage, passive aggression and early traumas would not be of much interest to the Almighty. He doubtless had more important things to worry about than the chimeras she and Shatzenkammer had so fussed over. Happily, these and other such transcendental musings kept Clara's mind off the dips, swoops and tilts of Mrs. Longhill's rather feckless aviation.

They landed with a bump. The first thing Clara saw when her feet touched terra firma was Horace LaMarque's grotesque salt and pepper mane. Behind her sunglasses she allowed her eyes to cross at the folly of human ways. He was eating a carrot.

"Horace!"

"Ray! Rita!" chomp, chomp on the carrot.

"Looks like Bugs Bunny," Elizabeth muttered under her breath and then, "Horace!"

"Libby! Sara!"

"No, it's Clara."

"What? Oh." chomp, chomp. "I get all Sunny's friends mixed up."

"Ray, darling, be careful not to drop Hank. He's bumping around in there."

"You mean be careful not to drop dead of hunger, don't you sweetheart?"

"Have a carrot," chomp, chomp. "Lots of vitamin A."

"He detests carrots. He's detested them since the war. Right, Honeybunny?"

"Old Shatzykatzy would have a field day with his crew."

"What's that Libby dear?"

"Don't call me dear, you dreadful girl. I saw you meditating on the plane. How's Sunny?

Ready to jump out of her skin from excitement, I'll bet."

"Sunny's okay. I don't know about jumping out of her skin though."

"Just an expression."

The salt and pepper mane nodded knowingly.

"And what about that Flupper?"

"Klupper."

"Is he going to find the solution to what's left of the oil crisis?"

"That boy couldn't find his way out of a paper bag," chomp, chomp.

"What I always used to say, when Ray was insisting that John, our oldest boy, could put the village idiot to shame, was, no matter, neither of us exactly worked on the A bomb."

"The world wouldn't be the same if you had, wonderful."

This time Clara's eyes crossed of their own accord.

"How's that boy of your in Bangkok?"

"Hong Kong. Fine. Running around without his clothes on, probably."

"Funny. Sunny said it was Bangkok. She was a geography major. Can't tell up from down, in from out."

"Paul always knew about that," Clara remarked.

Her aunt glanced at her critically.

The ride to the LaMarque's enormous house in Horace's Lincoln Continental though uneventful, was quite busy. Clara sat in the front with Horace and Sunny dog, who seemed most anxious to get at the cooler containing Hank on Ray's lap in the back. Elizabeth put on makeup. The Longhills bickered. Every thirty seconds Sunny dog would lunge at the back seat, the cooler would rattle belligerently and Clara, holding onto the dog's collar, would be jolted out of her seat. Meanwhile Horace, on his second carrot, carried on a spirited conversation with Sunny dog about his new motorcycle.

"But the brakes are tight. What do you think Sunny, should I fix that gasket?"

"Woof, woof.

"Right" chomp, chomp.

"I'll tell you whose gasket needs fixing," Elizabeth muttered.

"What was that Libby? You're getting just like Ray darling. Enunciate. You don't even have his excuse. Which is a defective palate."

"After twenty nine years of starvation lovey dovey, I'm lucky to have one at all."

Woof, woof.

"Rover here seems to agree with you. Quite the conversationalist, aren't you old woof woof?"And with that Elizabeth gave Sunny dog a friendly smack on the chops. This precipitated a series of excited barks and leaps. The car swerved.

"Hold on Sunny. Remember, I'm the driver."

"Thank God for small favors," Elizabeth said and then, as they went up the driveway. "Jeepers! What's that?"

Everyone gawked. A pink baby Rolls Royce was parked under the porte cochiere. There was something unspeakably ugly about it.

"Wedding present," chomp, chomp. "From Klupper."

A look of horror had come into Elizabeth's eyes. "But she's not going to drive that thing."

"Who?"

"Sunny! Your daughter."

"Why not? Klupper says he sees 'em all over Texas."

"Sounds like Klupper's got the DTs."

Sunny came running out of the house in a red bikini and struck a pose in front of her garish new automobile. Her hair, light brown the last time Clara had seen her, was now blond. Sunny started imitating a Texas accent. It did not become her.

"Excited?" Elizabeth asked.

"Why, I'm just going out of my little old mind."

"Little's the word," chomp, chomp.

"Might as well go out of it now," Ray said "Once you're married you won't have any choice."

"Twenty thousand smackeroos and can't tell Hong Kong from Bangkok."

"Now, now. None of us exactly worked on the A bomb."

Woof, woof.

"Speak for yourself, Rover."

At that Sunny dog took off a full speed in the direction of the LaMarque's duck pond.

"Uh-oh" Sunny said.

"So where's prince charming?" Clara asked, picking up her bag and walking to the front door. She and Sunny had hung back a bit from the crowd. At this question Sunny came to a halt and regarded Clara with unaccustomed seriousness. This rare attitude made her look more insipid than usual. Nonetheless, with her greenish eyes she was still very pretty. "We have to talk," she whispered.

"Uh-oh," Clara said.

Clara changed into a black bikini and went down to the pool. But Sunny was not there. Monica lay on a long beach chair, exhausted from the effort of showing her guests to their rooms. Monica tired easily. In her black and gold bathing suit, with her deep tan and thick black hair, however, she looked the picture of health. Monica was Italian and from Pittsburgh. She told people she was French and from Philadelphia. She did not look up from the latest issue of Cosmopolitan in which she was reading the article on orgasms which had so engaged Clara earlier that day.

"So size has nothing to do with it," she said aloud.

"Where's Sunny?"

"Quite an eye-opener, this article. Hunh? I thought she was with you. Rita's out of her mind bringing that cat. I hope it's been declawed."

"Nope," Clara said and dove into the pool. She swam a few laps then ran out onto the lawn, performed a handstand, ran back, dove in and started swimming again.

"A regular little gymnast," Elizabeth commented, crossing the terrace to the pool, cigarettes and lighter in one hand, Horace's <u>Times</u> in the other.

"If it's not the star spangled banner herself," Clara replied. Elizabeth was wearing her red, white and blue skirted bathing suit. Her flip flops made quite a lot of noise. Without even being asked Monica handed her an extra bathing cap, which she put on. Elizabeth then seated herself on the edge of the pool, dangled her legs in the water and began reading an article on real estate. After a while she looked up and watched Clara swimming back and forth.

"You know, you're practically naked in that thing."

"So?" gurgle, gurgle.

"You're lucky Paul's in Hong Kong."

"Depends," gurgle "how you define lucky."

At this Elizabeth plunked into the shallow end, leaned against the wall of the pool and resumed reading. "Lucky, in my book," she said at length, "does not mean having sex ten times a day."

"Says here most men don't want to do it more than once or twice anyway," Monica remarked. "I didn't need to read a magazine article to find that out."

"I don't thing that shrink really helped you," Mrs. Darlinger went on. "I'm not satisfied with the results."

"Ask for your money back."

"You never used to read religious books."

"I used to read science books."

"That's right," Elizabeth snapped. "You're going backwards."

Clara floated on her back and tried to imagine Tahiti. It looked, she thought, very much like Florida, except with rocks. There were long white beaches with nobody on them. She could take all her clothes off and go swimming and not worry about getting arrested. The air was sweet, and exotic birds cawed in the palm trees. For some reason, however, she could not picture the tropical flora beyond the shore without also picturing an offensive, pink baby Rolls Royce in the midst of it. She sighed and climbed out of the pool.

At that moment, out of the corner of her eye, she detected a flash of red in the distance, down by the duck pond and, from afar, heard a scream.

"Oh God!" Monica cried and sat up.

Clara broke into a run toward the pond. Half way down the lawn, she saw Sunny running toward her. A few yards ahead of Sunny raced Sunny dog, with a dead duck in his mouth.

"You filthy, horrible monster!" Sunny cried and threw a stick at the dog. There were tears in her eyes. Clara tried to tackle the animal which dodged her. She chased it around the lawn. The duck's head, dangling from its broken neck, bobbed up and down from Sunny dog's bloody snout. Down by the pond, the ducks quacked and fluttered in alarm. After a while the dog headed off toward the woods, Clara hard on its heels. But Sunny dog was faster and soon disappeared, prey in mouth, into the still and dark of the woods. Clara stood at the end of the lawn and pitched a stone after him. Then she walked despondently back.

She found Sunny, sitting on the grass by the edge of the pond, sobbing.

"I can't marry him," Sunny said.

"Oh."

"He bores me. He bores me to death. It's terrible."

"Oh."

"Please, you tell them."

"Tom?"

"No. Them."

"Oh." Clara lingered for a while by the water's edge. The trees stirred in the late afternoon breeze. Now and then she caught the scent of honeysuckle. Finally she turned and walked back to the pool. Everyone was astir, recounting the depredations of dogs. This was not, apparently, the first time Sunny dog had slaughtered a duck. The had all observed Clara's spectacular chase, and Elizabeth was now portraying in vivid and grisly detail the probable goings on in the woods. Clara walked over to Monica's chair. "Got a minute?" she asked.

By evening a mood of gloom had settled of the LaMarque household. Monica had made over a hundred phone calls. Horace and Ray, well into their cups in the study, were holding forth on the fickleness of women for a second time. It was the subject over which they had commenced drinking and, having enumerated every other possible feminine defect, the one to which, with glum relish, they returned. Elizabeth and Rita were organizing the wedding gifts upstairs. "Everything," Monica had clucked, "everything he gave her will have to be returned." Having spoken with her betrothed on the phone, Sunny had locked herself in her room. By the time the moon sailed into a fully blackened sky, Clara, in her jeans and Hawaiian shirt again and drinking lemonade, was lying on a long recliner by the pool.

She had stepped out there at twilight and watched it grow dark. The fireflies had come and gone. So had the mosquitoes. At the far end of the pond, the ducks slept in the rushes. Now and then on the diving board a round, dark form turned its head. It was Hank, the Longhill's cat, crouched there and transfixed by the movement of silver light on the water below. That light, rippling over the pool, extended in a long path down the sloping lawn and eerily illuminated the distant pond and rushes. Aside from the crickets who were hard at work and an occasional noise from the gigantic house, all was silent. Aside from the moon and the light from two or three bright windows, all was dark. But in that silence and darkness, everything, it seemed, was alive.

She lay under the moon for hours as the chain of being from the most inconsequential microbe to herself to beings who were of an entirely unmaterial essence paraded before her mind's eye. Evil, she had gathered from Augustine, was non being and though she understood the words, they conjured no image. This perplexed her for some time. She could not imagine something that did not have a soul; she could not picture evil or non being. Nor could she picture absolute being. Instead, every sort of creature and spirit crowded her mind. Nothing else but these pagan pantheistic spirits, she concluded, really existed. And in her imagination, she conversed with them all.

Angels and snails, bacilli and centaurs, anemones and naiads busied the humid, sylvan air with their whisperings. Behind her, trees rustled softly about the melancholy peace of staying forever in one place. Everything had something to say, all of it clear and lovely, none of it merry. The ice cubes clinked in the glass of lemonade and from afar came the chimes of bells. It was ten o'clock. "There will be no wedding tomorrow," Clara heard in the teeming and magical night air. "There will be no husband and there will be no wife." The words made her unaccountably morose. After all, she had never approved of this particular marriage.

Out on the shadowed lawn, something moved. It was Sunny dog, who had cowered in the woods all evening, now bounding through the summer moonlight. He frisked over to Clara, ignoring the hiss from the diving board. "Wicked, wicked, wicked," she said, nonetheless giving the animal a pat. With that Sunny dog plunged into the pool, splashing and barking and then trotted off to the garden to dig up Monica's flowers. Hours passed. One by one, the lights went out in the house.

At midnight, as Clara lay in a flood of moonlight, she heard a step on the terrace. Sunny came over and sat in a chair beside her. "Let's go to a party," she said. Clara blinked. Sunny thought her friend's eyes looked very cold when she did that. She asked if Clara thought she was awful.

"I just feel sorry for Tom," Clara replied.

"I want to go out. Some friends of mine are having a party in Philly."

Clara wrinkled her nose. Sunny reached over to the lawn, pulled up a handful of grass and threw it at her.

"Your friends!" Clara huffed. "Last party we went to I got stuck with that Ivy League jerk. Talked my ear off. About himself, natch. I didn't even get to dance."

"I didn't know you really liked to."

Shortly they were speeding along the expressway in Sunny's sports car, smoking cigarettes, with disco blaring over the radio. Sunny had begun to lecture Clara about not having a boyfriend.

"But I don't like anyone."

"You liked Paul."

"I hate Paul."

"You're too picky. You judge people too fast. Guys can't help it if they're morons. That's part of the deal."

"Like Tom?"

"Not fair," Sunny pouted and turned up the radio. She had a way of all but dancing to the radio as she drove. It made life on the road very exciting. The two of them danced in their seats all the way into town, parked near the University of Pennsylvania campus, right below the second floor apartment of Sunny's friends, whence music thundered out onto the street, then danced their way upstairs and into the party. The rooms were jammed with college and graduate students. Clara, who had always liked dancing, had not had such an opportunity in years. An energetic Penn quarterback with whom she exchanged scarcely ten words after he introduced himself, asked her to dance. Hours later they were still dancing, and the apartment was still packed with people.

"I had no idea you were such a good dancer," Sunny gasped, collapsing on the couch.

But Clara, ecstatic, did not stop. At sunrise, she was till dancing.

***

By degrees Clara had become more and more essential to her aunt's firm. She had taken over much of the business previously executed by Ward Fairless and had quickly become vice president of Darlinger-Fairless. As a result, she had to travel from time to time—aside from its several offices in and around Boston and New York, the firm had branch offices in five other cities across the country. Though generally well liked, Clara was regarded in these other offices as something of a terror, as demanding as Elizabeth had been before her, or in the words of one competitor, "the toughest foreman in the business." She had more than one occasion to travel to Florida, where she often stayed with Stanley Katz and his girlfriend. Stanley had persuaded her to become his partner in a racetrack which, contrary to Elizabeth's predictions, had done quite well. "You've done it, bless you. You've made me eat my words," Mrs. Darlinger proclaimed upon seeing how lucrative this sort of investment could be. Meanwhile Ward Fairless watched in amazement. He had long had a heart condition and was glad to reduce his responsibilities. He was not, however, wholly delighted for Clara's sake, nor with certain changes which he thought he detected occurring in her.

She had become exceedingly efficient and rather imperious, by the summer of Shatzenkammer's decline and fall. Though she socialized a great deal, she seemed, to Ward Fairless, even more profoundly unsociable than the shy orphan he had met four years before. Prior to her spring romance with religion, she had seemed at times even cynical. Now she alternated between cynicism and what he considered just plain strangeness. And yet she had such irrepressible energy and appetite for work that he had come to think of her, in his own pet phrase, as someone always and forever "energetically alone."

He told her so one summer evening after everyone had left the office. It was well past nine when he walked out toward the reception desk. On his way he passed Clara's office. The door was open.The desk lamp was on. She sat in a little circle of light by the window, a sheaf of papers in her hand. When she looked up she said, by way of explanation, "Angelica." He nodded, crossing the threshold, and then sat down on the leather couch in semi-darkness. She told him that he need not wait, that she would be there several hours more. He replied that he was worried about her safety in that district, so busy during daylight, so deserted after dark. "I can take care of myself," she said with a hardness that, once imitated from her aunt, was now completely her own. He sat in silence for a while and then commented that this landmark co-op conversion case against Angelica was gaining some notoriety. She replied that New Yorkers and the New York press were insane about real estate, that in the rest of the country it was regarded differently and that she didn't care a fig about notoriety anyway. He looked up in surprise. "Most people do," he said.

"And do you do what you do according to what most people think?"

He had thought that one over for a moment and then said, "You don't."

She glanced up from the papers and blinked in that way of hers. "I did once, four years ago, according to what Elizabeth thought. It was an irrevocable mistake. I won't do it again."

She returned to her papers. In the yellow light he noticed that her hair was getting redder as she got older. Once chestnut, it was now auburn, and for some reason this wonderful color made him say, "We're alone enough as it is. But you'll be very alone."

She put the papers down and turned and faced him. "And what, precisely, do you advise me to do to avert this catastrophe?" There was anger in her voice.

"Change," was his reply.

"What if it's my nature?"

"You made a mistake, but you're proceeding right on the path that leads from that mistake."

"I can't stop."

"Then hope something stops you."

She seemed taken aback at this, but then, after a moment, shrugged and returned to her work. In her pretty hazel eyes, he had seen startling, alien lights when she spoke to him. Those lights worried him; they seemed ferocious. He had told her to change but, he mused sadly, she was already changing, learning to walk the road that had been built for her, the road that of her own accord she would never have chosen but which she had been too young or too weak or perhaps something else that he had never divined, to refuse. And as he sat on the shadowed couch gazing past her, out the window at the fierce nocturnal splendor of the city, he thought it very unfortunate that what she could not know was that the road altered the traveler and that it had never been otherwise. Closing his eyes for a moment, he envisioned it, the way that led into her future, that had been his past and considered that it had not at all been bad for him but that he, unlike this girl, unlike his own son, was not the sort to ask for something else. Money and freedom, he mused, that was success in life. But somehow for Clara, it was not. He had no idea why but was as sure of this as he had been, one summer afternoon in the country years ago, that when his son said no he meant it. At that time he had behaved like

Elizabeth and had shared her indignation. The divorce, he had argued, gazing into those young blue eyes suddenly so wild and critical and cold, had no bearing on the situation. But Paul had just tossed his tennis racquet onto the lawn and looked at him and said no and never been quite the same. In that moment he sensed that he had been judged and so had Elizabeth and that, oddly, it had changed neither of them. The person it had changed was his son, or rather their son, for sometimes, even afterward, it seemed that Elizabeth had appropriated him entirely. She of course had raged against him, against Ward, against everything in sight except herself. Even old Mrs. Darlinger had been cursed and consulted. "Get him a job on Wall Street," had been the old woman's only advice. And they had, but he had refused that too and gone and found one himself. Mr. Fairless sighed and opened his eyes and gazed with incomprehension at Clara. He did not understand these children. Nor, he believed, did they understand themselves.

He did not rise from the couch. The thought of the long drive through the night out to his home on Long Island, of the occasional lights flashing by on the highway, tired him. But he thought about it anyway and especially about the big, darkened house at the end of his journey. He saw himself going through it, room by room, turning on the lights and wondering which would be the one he would collapse in from his final heart attack. Certainly not the first floor study, he found himself rather irrelevantly thinking. He had never much cared for that room with its memories of quarrels with Elizabeth. Why they had always gone in there to argue, he could never say, but at that moment saw, as vividly as Clara before him, Elizabeth's manicured hand shutting the door to keep Paul from hearing. No it would not be there, he said to himself, and in his mind resumed walking from room to room of the spacious, deserted house where every light blazed at night, searching for a suitable tomb.

His reverie was soon interrupted by Clara asking if he was allright. He replied that he was just "being vacant," like Elizabeth. She smiled, and when she did he thought it no surprise that his son had gone berserk over her. Despite the cool, acquired business air, Clara still had a marvelous smile. He wondered gloomily if she would lose that too. He had noticed that smile her first day in New York, though it was Paul who had made him think about it with his arid remark, "too toothy." That tune had certainly changed, Mr. Fairless said to himself and then began musing over what his wayward son — for Elizabeth's pronouncement that he was wayward stayed with him always — would think of her now. Paul had never had much use for the parties of celebrities, socialites and business moguls that his Junior League stepmother and Rotarian father had regularly attended. He would invariably meander through the crowd, then return to his parents and say "what do these people do all day?"He had gone as infrequently as possible. Clara had the same attitude, yet whenever she was not busy working, she went. And she went with grim relish.She had met the debutante of the year six times and upon each encounter had to be reintroduced — because Clara was not in the social register, "deaf and dumb" as she referred to the debutante — would not say hello without an introduction. This was the sort of detail Clara never missed and in which she seemed to take bitter delight. What she liked even better was to confound some idle youth, dazzled by her fearsome reputation in real estate, with remarks on fifteenth century Jewish mysticism. She could be relied upon by gossip columnists for the mordant quote of the evening and even for an occasional shocker. It was not at all, Ward thought, healthy.

In light of the latest turn the business had taken under her stewardship, it seemed even less healthy. It had always been, predominately, a commercial real estate firm. In the past six months, however, there had been a distinct increase in the number of residential properties bought redeveloped and sold. Ward had always had what he considered sound business reasons for "staying out of residential," especially in New York with its bellicose tenants and rigorous laws. The degree of ruthlessness simply was not worth it. But the market, as Clara was wont to point out, had changed.The laws, she liked to remark, would change with it. Indeed she and a number of other developers already had a pretty clear idea of the sort of legislation they desired. Ward could not disagree that there was a fortune to be made. But he was tired, his heart was bad, he had no appetite for it. Above all, he had no heart for battles with the likes of Philip Angelica, for court appearances or for the bad publicity, of which there had already been quite a lot.

In all of its residential transactions, Darlinger-Fairless was represented by the oldest, most prestigious and powerful law firm of the landlord bar, named, with rather unfortunate evocation, for the three brothers who ran it, Batter, Batter and Batter. They were a most efficient and well connected group of attorneys, on such warm terms with the housing court judiciary that Batter senior was known to drive the chief judge of civil court to work every morning and to gamble with him in Las Vegas. Batter, Batter and Batter routinely picked up the judicial tab at a local watering hole and had by long tradition at Christmas time cordially distributed white envelopes containing cash gifts to all judges and most clerks of the housing court. Needless to say, Batter, Batter, as it was commonly called, rarely lost a case. It was hard to tell whether this success was due to the attorneys' fraternal interest in all judicial goings on or because of the unhappy example of the few judges who now and then ruled against them. Those judges did not advance. They did not go up to State Supreme Court nor to the Appellate Division, nor did they become powerful judicial administrators. They were generally transferred out of the housing court, which was regarded as a dump, and into family court, which was regarded as a hellhole. They were shunned by their judicial brethren who ate at the table, drank the wine and from time to time took the Caribbean vacations of Batter, Batter. All of the three senior partners, who now and then had served stints in city government, were excellent fund raisers for the politicians they favored. A surprising number of Batter Batter's clients, including executives of Darlinger Fairless, were court-appointed receivers for bankrupt buildings, always a jolly and lucrative affair.

Ward Fairless had worked closely with Batter senior for over thirty years and had a keen appreciation of his attorney's acumen. For five years old Mr. Batter had urged him to expand the residential interests of Darlinger-Fairless. For five years this advice had been greeted rather coolly. Then along came Clara. She did not, Ward saw, fully appreciate the more perilous implications of Batter, Batter's courthouse activities. She did, however, grasp the wisdom of the sagacious old lawyer's advice at once. Ward yielded because he had to admit that from a business perspective she was right. But he did not like it. And with each notice of eviction and each summons to appear in court he liked it less.

The current co-oping case, in which Clara was so hotly embroiled, was out of Ward's hands entirely. He would not have gone for it himself. The legal expense had already been staggering, the publicity ghastly. Twice a group of tenants had picketed the housing court. They would probably do so again. The usual allegations of judge shopping and case fixing were circulating vigorously even, according to one rumor monger, through the airy chambers of the district attorney's office. All of this put Ward in a rather sour state of mind with regard to the case. Clara's evident lack of caution bothered him even more. It could become, he thought, lack of scruple. And that could be bad for business — especially at a time when the ever watchful Angelica was lurking on the fringes of so many of Darlinger-Fairless's affairs. That attorney, Ward often said, had a nose for even the slightest impropriety. Though Elizabeth habitually dismissed such observations with the withering disdain summed up in the phrase "a self-righteous stuffed shirt," by which she so often designated her adversary, the sense of a far-seeing and minatory presence always haunted Ward in his dealings with this man who seemed at times more of a bloodhound than an attorney. Ward was ever aware of the fact that for a number of years Angelica had been a prosecutor who liked nothing better than to put some luckless white-collar entrepreneur behind bars for fraud. Angelica was, in Mr. Fairless' eyes, a most loathsome and dangerous creature. Ward thought of him as a member of the police, working in areas where no policeman was needed or belonged. "A self-righteous, opportunistic stuffed shirt," Elizabeth would scoff, if Ward became too anxious on the subject. But she never allayed his fears. Over the years he had come more and more to agree with Batter senior when the old man nodded his distinguished white head and remarked that that law firm was a madhouse and Angelica was deranged.

In the current West Side co-oping case, Ward had no doubt that Angelica intended to sue Darlinger-Fairless at the first opportunity. And he had no doubt that they would be sued for a lot of money. The whole business made him vaguely ill when he thought about it.Batter senior, who had managed to get the case before a charmingly lunatic judge given to lecturing tenants in his courtroom on the criminality of non-payment of rent, the evils of communism, the dire state of the municipal government and anything else that chanced to pop into his fertile brain, was only guardedly optimistic about the likelihood of success. Judge Pepper had a healthy sense of freedom in regard to the application of the law and indeed rarely felt himself confined by it. But he was quirky. In a superstitious mood he would go by the book.

Fortunately such moods were easily detected. They occurred on days when Judge Pepper refrained from shouting at tenants and instead indulged in muttering to himself. There had, happily, been very little muttering so far. Indeed in recent months Judge Pepper had been in a most excitedly extroverted state. Two weeks before, he had punched another judge in the mouth. On Darlinger-Fairless's most recent court date Judge Pepper had arrived in the courtroom two hours late as usual but had immediately gone about making his dynamic presence felt. At the judge's entrance everyone in the crowded courtroom had risen to their feet and said "good morning your honor," though by then of course it was nearly noon. "What's good about it?" Judge Pepper had snapped and threw a tantrum from which it was deduced, though with difficulty, that he was displeased with the manner in which he had been addressed. "Good morning you honor," had not, apparently, been said in unison. Everyone in the courtroom, therefore, had to remain standing and repeat their salutation to the judge over and over until he was satisfied that they had got it "all together." This lasted forty five minutes, by which time Judge Pepper had noticed that he had an appetite, and so adjourned for lunch.

Even more fortunately, old Mr. Batter had observed, Judge Pepper had a most violent dislike of Philip Angelica whom he correctly suspected of having testified against him at an investigation into his judicial conduct. Most judges — and Angelica had testified against a number — would and did react by treating Angelica with great caution, or at least tampering with their taped court record when they forgot to. Judge Pepper had no such qualms since he kept his tape recorder off all the time anyway and only allowed a stenographer to set foot in his courtroom on the rarest occasions. He was thus free to disport himself as he pleased, which usually meant hurling insults at Angelica all afternoon. When he tired of this, he engaged in other activities, such as summoning Angelica to the bench, then screaming for him to step away, then summoning him again and so on. This particular ploy amused Judge Pepper no end; but as a result, the case proceeded rather slowly.

It did not, however, amuse Ward Fairless, who believed that such antics would only harden Angelica's resolve "to get" Darlinger-Fairless and to get Judge Pepper thrown off the bench. But he consoled himself with the certainty that at least Judge Pepper would rule consistently against the tenants. Clara, who had not yet had the experience of seeing Judge Pepper in action, was by no means as sanguine as Ward. She said he sounded like a flake and that flakes could not be trusted. Yet she seemed hardly at all troubled by the prospect of the inevitable appeal. She wanted, she said, to clear the matter up as soon as possible, hopefully without having to testify in court. Batter senior did not want her to testify either, for he was afraid that despite his careful coaching, she might, under pressure, tell the truth. In that case, they might not be able to evict the tenants forthwith. And the girl, as Elizabeth said, was "a lousy liar." As he gazed at Clara in the lonely circle of light, however, Ward Fairless wondered how Elizabeth knew that, for he himself had never yet known Clara to lie.

Before it was done, Ward foresaw that this case would require more than one lie. Mr.Angelica, of course, knew that too and, being the menace he was, was sure, Ward thought, either to make them engrave every lie in stone, swear to it under oath or both. For when he sensed what he decided was injustice, Angelica generally displayed a rabid determination to "bring everything into the light," as he put it. The only thing capable of obscuring that light, but liable to obscure it like a big black cloud was Judge Pepper. If the judge contented himself with routine misbehavior, all would be well. Frequent yelling was no problem. Nor were most of Judge Pepper's other most common pranks. He liked, for instance, to make funny faces at the people in the courtroom. And he did not like to sit still, but preferred to roam around between the bench and the audience, haranguing the attorneys and plaintiffs, scowling and waving his hands. He was also given, in fits of pique, to ordering the attorneys to conference in his chambers. When the attorneys arrived he generally asked them what they were doing there. On occasion he had been known to take everyone in the courtroom on the Judge Pepper lecture tour of the courthouse. All of this was tedious, but certainly within the limits of the expected. It was the unexpected that preyed on Mr. Fairless's mind. Whenever he thought about the co-op case —which in recent weeks happened more and more often — the vague, alarming and most unpleasant premonition of making history with Judge Pepper in some awful, unspeakable way haunted him like an incubus. He knew it was not rational, but Judge Pepper had begun, in Elizabeth's phrase, to give him the creeps.

Batter senior had told him not to worry, that Judge Pepper, though psychotic, was benign. After all, he ruled in favor of Batter, Batter every time the firm came before him. Judge Pepper, evidently, was fully capable of grasping who his friends were. After all, Batter senior had got him on the bench in the first place. But Ward remained uneasy and became uneasier still whenever he thought of Clara being in charge of the entire matter. She had labored on it, had spent many costly hours in old Mr. Batter's company. Messengers constantly went to and fro between the uptown offices of Darlinger-Fairless and those of Batter, Batter in the financial district. Although in the past Clara had shown a tendency to overwork, this transaction confirmed her, in Ward Fairless's mind, a workaholic. She routinely stayed in the office until eleven at night and had lately begun to snap at whoever urged her to leave sooner. And when she left, she did not go home to rest but went instead to one of the parties on the endless social circuit she secretly disdained. There were circles under her eyes. She smoked a pack and a half of cigarettes a day. As oblivious to food as ever, she now rarely ate a regular meal. She did not look especially harried, indeed she was better dressed and groomed than ever, but her peculiar intensity was evident in subtle ways, such as the vaguely mad glints in her eyes when Ward had told her how alone she would be. Those glints, he had observed, appeared whenever she suspected someone of trying to stop her, thwart her or get in her way. But she never lost her temper, which, considering the pressure she put on herself, was quite surprising. Instead, she had become more stubborn than ever. Indeed the remarkable extent of Clara's stubbornness had only recently revealed itself to Ward. From the very first she had had a mild air of the intractable. Four years ago he and Elizabeth had found it endearing. Over time he had come to think her ornery, or, alternately, a young woman of marvelous patience. By the time of their court case, he believed her the most stubborn person he had ever known.

What mitigated this relentless stubbornness was the intelligence, if she perceived herself in the wrong and someone else in the right, to abandon her position and take up the other, which she invariably did with the exact same degree of tenacity. There were, however, times when she failed to see that she was wrong. Such times were most unpleasant, since it was impossible either to reason or argue with her. On these occasions, which were fortunately rare, Ward could only wait and hope she would come to her senses. She usually did; it usually happened all in a flash; and it usually happened only after a certain amount of damage had been done.

He rose to go and left Clara as he had found her, alone in the quiet, deserted office in the middle of the night, scribbling notes, leafing through papers, occasionally turning to punch something into the office computer. And all the way down the elevator, then to the parking lot, through the darkened streets and at last on the lonely highway, the image of her stayed with him, and although there was no physical similarity aside from the color of her eyes, he thought how much, how very much, she had come to resemble Elizabeth Darlinger.

***

One fine June morning when the sun beamed brightly in the cloudless sky — the kind of extraordinary morning that makes everyone think how foolish it is to be carrying briefcases to work when they could be lolling about in the park — a taxi, crowded with passengers, came to a stop in front of one of the many imposing municipal buildings down by the courts. Out stepped a number of men in suits and a young woman in a tan skirt, tan jacket and pinstriped shirt. Everyone stood for a moment on the sidewalk, dazed by the beauty of the summer morning, and commented on the weather. Everyone said "Thank God it's Friday," and everyone happily imagined themselves twenty four hours hence, lounging in semi-nakedness like pagans on the beach.

Across the street in a little park where derelicts snored on the benches and birds chirped merrily in the trees, a man who had decided to disrobe was being questioned by the police. From the direction of city hall, sirens could be heard, neither approaching nor retreating, which doubtless had something to do with a colossal traffic jam in the vicinity of Park Place. Two teenagers, carrying radios the size of suitcases, passed by on a cross street, the jovial obscenities of the lyrics audible for blocks in either direction. A plane buzzed through the radiant sky and, completing the symphony, a subway rattled under the street. Everyone in the little crowd on the sidewalk thought of the sun and the water, seafood and cocktails. The young woman completed her own mental image of paradise with a pitcher of lemonade. After a moment, they turned and walked inside the courthouse.

"A mere technicality," Batter senior was saying about something in regard to the title to the West Side property as the group strolled down the hall.

"Then why fudge on it?" Clara asked, lighting a cigarette.

The distinguished white head nodded as if to say "I see your point, but there are a few things you haven't taken into consideration." Indeed after a second he said exactly that. They continued, apart from their assistants, the authoritative old counselor and the woman young enough to be his granddaughter, strolling and chatting, pausing now and then by a window and then walking on through the light and shade of the deserted corridors of justice.

One of Batter senior's assistants beckoned to them from a door down the hall. "I don't believe it," he said. "The judge is on time."

Batter senior looked up in alarm. "Is he muttering?"

"I don't think you could call it that."

When they entered the courtroom, a tall, elderly man with short, dark hair, thick glasses and his judicial robe slightly askew, was standing very upright and screaming at a group of lawyers from the bench. "You want to make a record? You'll get a record." He repeated this over and over, and each time Judge Pepper finished his question and answer, he gave a little jump of fury. A number of the tenants were sitting in the courtroom. In the second row Clara observed an angry looking, gray-haired man, discreetly taking notes on a long, skinny pad of paper.

"You honor, I think this proceeding —" one of the attorneys began.

"Shut up." Judge Pepper snapped. "What are you saying?"

"I would like to make a record."

"Shut up." Judge Pepper began fidgeting with some papers. "Mr. Angelica, you want to make a record?"

"Yes your honor."

"Shut up. You're giving me a headache." With that Judge Pepper hopped down from the bench, strode over to the audience and, waving his hands, began lecturing upon the meaning of his own career. He said that he had been a defense lawyer and a prosecutor, that he knew all about crime and punishment. His son in law, he added for emphasis, had been mugged only two weeks before. And as he rambled on about crime, deterrence and incapacitation, some of the attorneys began looking at each other. Judge Pepper demanded to know why they were making funny faces.

"Uh, judge, this is not a criminal proceeding—"

"I know very well what this is."

"— it's a civil —"

213

"Shut up." Judge Pepper resumed his noisy monologue, now and then asking one of the stunned tenants a question, to which they generally replied in monosyllables. The angry looking, gray-haired man stopped scribbling and studied the judge closely. By now his honor of the civil court of New York had proceeded to a rather tangled explication of the purpose of a trial. He said that it was to determine guilt or innocence and that there was a good question in his mind as to whether or not these tenants might be liable for criminal prosecution. Property, he noted, was the basis of American democracy, and thereupon launched into a paean on the splendors of his country, in its rolling rhythms not at all unlike the Battle Hymn of the Republic. The dark eyes of the angry looking man met those of Philip Angelica. In that glance something ominous, it seemed to Clara, was communicated. But she paid little attention to it. Her mind was otherwise occupied.

It was not until Judge Pepper reached "dulce et decora est, pro patria mori," that the attorneys began rolling their eyes. "At the top of his form today," one of them whispered. "You ain't kiddin there's no one upstairs," another muttered. "Somebody left the door open and all the furniture went bye bye." Clara said nothing. She was still preoccupied. The gray-haired man in the audience was writing as fast as he could.

Judge Pepper carried on for twenty minutes. Then after a bang-up conclusion, "I urge you all to go out and vote, vote, vote," he turned and grandly marched back to the bench.

"What is it Mr. Angelica?" he asked, seating himself with a flourish and removing his glasses.

The attorney again requested a record, and this time the judge directed that the stenographer be brought into the room. Things got quickly under way. The judge ruled consistently in favor of Batter, Batter, pausing now and then to make a speech, waving his glasses in the air as he did so. More often than not, he directed the stenographer to stop typing.At one point Angelica rose, but before he had uttered a word, Judge Pepper beat him to the punch with a defiant "Motion denied."

"I didn't even make the motion."

"Shut up."

Clara watched the proceeding but took none of it in. She was dimly aware that she was being called to the stand. To Batter senior and the other attorneys there seemed nothing particularly out of the ordinary. Clara Chimes appeared as reserved, dry and professional as ever — the incongruously young, pretty, and auburn-haired real estate mogul, about to do what was exactly in her interest, namely, tell a white lie about a missing date in order to empty a building of a group of contentious tenants and make, as usual, millions of dollars. Nor did the tenants' attorneys perceive anything unusual. Philip Angelica knew very well what questions he would ask and what lies to expect in response. It was not, after all, the crux of the case. That would come later. But to Clara it seemed that she was in a trance. And as she contemplated the cause of this state, she knew she ought to be alarmed. But she had no time for alarm. As she answered the preliminary questions she knew she should be thinking of all those nights in the office, of the thousands of dollars she had paid Batter, Batter and of the four long years working for Darlinger-Fairless. Instead she was thinking of the room in Elizabeth's duplex, white and modern and empty. And in her mind she stood in the doorway, wondering at it and at herself for wondering.

To Judge Pepper, scrutinizing the palms of his hands, nothing was amiss. To the people in

217

the audience everything was proceeding rather dully and depressingly. Batter senior and his associates were day dreaming about their upcoming weekend. But despite the perfunctory replies to his inquiries, a light had come into Angelica's eyes. He did not as yet know how or why, but he sensed suddenly that he might be able to make mincemeat of Batter, Batter's case. He walked over to his associate, picked up a paper, returned to Clara and asked the first of what he thought would be a series of questions about dates.

"Was that before June first?"

Clara paused. And as she did, two things happened. A voice sounded like an alarm bell in her mind — "You little idiot. This is the enemy" — and into the blue eyes regarding her, critically and cynically expecting a lie, there came a frightening light.

"No, it was June 13," she said before she could stop herself and immediately regretted it.

The light in those eyes had gone from a flash to a blaze and Batter senior was on his feet requesting an adjournment.

"I'm hungry too," Judge Pepper remarked.

"Judge, I move that —"

"Shut up."

But this time Angelica did not. He began to demand something in legalese that Clara could make no sense of, though she knew that whatever it was, it could not be good for Darlinger-Fairless. Angelica was ordered to shut up again. "And you know what I can do to you if you don't," Judge Pepper bellowed. The lawyer said that he wanted to ask the witness about a certain other date. And Clara, to the astonishment of everyone, said that it too had been June 13. Angelica just stared at her. The angry looking man in the audience was on his feet now scribbling openly. A murmur had arisen from the table of Batter, Batter. And at that instant, Judge Pepper flew into a rage and held Philip Angelica in contempt of court.

The repercussions of Clara's two little slips of the tongue were manifold and inexorable. Darlinger-Fairless dropped its case. The tenants of the West Side property were allowed to remain peacefully in their homes. Further plans for expansion into the residential market were, for the moment, dropped by Clara's firm. Judge Pepper, quickly overruled in his attempt to put the attorney in jail, made many headlines. Indeed his conduct sparked a series of articles — in which Clara and her firm did not exactly appear in a favorable light — by the gray-haired reporter whom Clara had observed taking notes. The series gave the commission that was investigating Judge Pepper an incentive to do so more briskly. Under this extraordinary strain, Judge Pepper testified to a number of things that a number of people wished he hadn't. This led ultimately to another investigation of a much more serious nature, brought by different sorts of people with rather more extensive powers. By the time Judge Pepper stepped quietly down from the bench and was paying regular visits to one of Dr. Shatzenkammer's less excitable colleagues, a number of prosecutors had become most interested in the activities of Batter, Batter and Batter. Indeed they became so interested that several other judges decided to retire; as did Batter senior himself — to a sunny, foreign country of beautiful women and stringent laws prohibiting extradition.

These events, of course, all took a while to unfold. In the meantime, immediately after her day in court, Clara's life resumed fairly much as it had before, except that she was noticeably gloomy. Although she knew that the cause of her low spirits was the same as that which had prompted her courtroom debacle, she did not understand it, and so sank into an even worse funk. She worked as hard as ever, but went to fewer parties and devoted more and more of her spare time to the arcana of religious history. From that she soon moved on to arcana in general. Elizabeth became concerned. But Clara, who at first had not dared to mention what was on her mind, soon decided, in defiance, to keep it to herself.

Since her aborted wedding, Sunny had taken to visiting Clara in New York and staying in her apartment. Elizabeth assigned her the task of finding out "what's eating that kid." Sunny, alas, was not up to the job. She found Clara too clever and too intractable. During a spate of rainy weekends in late June and early July, when nobody was going to the beach, Sunny had plenty of opportunities to observe her friend but found her as inscrutable as ever. Clara spent a great deal of time in bed, reading, sleeping, eating, smoking cigarettes and conducting business over the phone.

Indeed, on the weekends, that bed became the center of the apartment. At almost any hour Clara could be found there, in her bathrobe, curled up in some strange position, eating chocolate cookies, absorbed in Eunapius's <u>Lives of the Sophists</u>, and surrounded by a heap of books, newspapers and fashion magazines. Now and then the phone would ring, she would rap out a few commands, and return to her book. Clara always sounded annoyed on the phone. Perhaps that was because, as she often said, she could never escape it. At Elizabeth's insistence one had even been installed in the bathroom. Sometimes Clara listened to the radio in bed and in the evenings watched TV. When Sunny came in in the morning, they would gossip for a while, then Clara, who had developed a passion for reading aloud, would read from Eunapius.

"Well did they know the meanings of the omens then revealed," Clara read to Sunny late one hot, damp, Saturday morning as the rain came down in torrents outside the window. "Now Chrysanthius was overwhelmed and awe struck by what he saw, and biting his tongue he said: 'Not only must I stay here, beloved Maximus, I must also hide myself from all men.' But Maximus asserted the force of his will and replied: 'Nay, Chrysanthius, I think that you have forgotten that we have been educated to believe that it is the duty of genuine Hellenes, especially if they are learned men, not to yield absolutely to the first obstacles they meet; but rather to wrestle with the heavenly powers till you make them incline to their servant.'"

"Your aunt says you'll go out of your mind reading all this heathen nonsense," Sunny remarked, while applying a coral-colored polish to her nails.

Clara peered over the top of her book. "Where'd you get that?"

"Elizabeth Arden. They have the greatest colors. I'm giving you a gift certificate there for your birthday. An Elizabeth Arden pedicure."

Clara looked down at her toes and wiggled them.

"You're going to be twenty two," Sunny went on.

"So?"

"You shouldn't be such a loner."

"Neither should you. So there. And don't tell me to go out more. I go out all the time. I just don't like anybody." And with that Clara tossed a pillow at Sunny. "Has Libby hypnotized you to torment me?"

In dodging the pillow Sunny lost what little covering she had, namely a towel, since she had just stepped out of the shower. "She thinks you have some kind of secret," Sunny went on, wrapping herself up in the towel again.

Clara snorted and began munching on a chocolate cookie.

"How you can eat all that junk and never gain weight," Sunny complained, but then, a little more brightly added, "you're probably horribly malnourished. Ravioli out of the can, cheeseburgers, Coca Cola, chocolate cookies, potato chips, hot green peppers. You'll get rickets. Your hair will fall out. Your skin will turn green. You've already got those telltale glints in your eyes."

The phone rang. "Hello," munch, munch. "Well then don't close it, wait for them to come down. What?"

"Squawk, squawk, you sound like a bird," Sunny editorialized.

"I don't care about the goddamn city contract. No abatement, no contract. I'm not in business to help the government get rich. What?"

"Squawk, squawk."

"I could leave that money in the bank and get a better return. If the city's nearly bankrupt that's the city's problem. You tell him." Clara slammed down the receiver. "Democrats!" She sputtered and rose and went into the bathroom. The phone rang again. From the bathroom, Sunny heard Clara's musical shriek, "No abatement, not contract!" There was silence, followed by the sound of water filling the bathtub and then, "They want jobs, they'll get jobs. But I'm not paying a fortune in taxes, to give a mob-run union a bunch of jobs." Sunny heard Clara splashing around in the tub. Suddenly the splashing stopped. "I read that article. I don't care what that newspaper says. That reporter's a liar. What?" There was silence and then a scream. "Angelica? What the hell has he got to do with this? This is commercial real estate. What? Represents the union? No, no, no, no, no. I will not meet with him. No abatement, no contract!" With that there came a loud crash, as Clara hung up the receiver and threw the telephone against the wall.

Sunny moved over to the window and gazed down through the rain at Central Park. Except for the top of an occasional umbrella, there was no sign of anyone out and about in the wet tangle of green that stretched before her below. In the buildings across the park she made out the darkened window of Mrs. Darlinger's abode. Elizabeth was in Maine for the week, entertaining the Longhills. When Clara emerged from her bath looking fresh and indolent, Sunny reminded her to water her aunt's plants. Clara frowned and tried to talk her friend into doing it, but with no luck. So, complaining and fretting, she put on her jeans, clogs, Darlinger-Fairless T-shirt, shiny red poncho and tromped out into the rain.Half way across the water-logged park, her feet and legs drenched from the downpour and still absorbed in the morose financial ponderings prompted by that morning's telephone call, Clara was distracted by a soft, pretty sound. She paused in the middle of a damp, deserted path, on the edge of an immense puddle that extended to a park bench. She heard it again, very faint and sorrowful. But after looking around, she could not detect its source and so proceeded a few steps. It came again. She turned, and there, on the far side of the puddle, muddy and miserable, sat a skinny, black and white kitten.

"I can't get to you, stupid," she said, contemplating the murky pool before her. A soaked and ragged drunk, lying on a nearby bench, looked up curiously, thus rumpling his bedspread of sodden newspapers. The kitten mewed again.

"Oh, I can't bear it," Clara exclaimed and began splashing through the water. Reaching the kitten, she saw that it was filthy, but nonetheless picked it up and carried it back to the path, where she sat it down. The drunk began clapping and yelling "hurray!" She continued walking and musing disconsolately, until she heard the sound again. The kitten was following her. She stopped and looked down at it. "You're too dirty," she told it. "I'll probably get a disease." At this the pathetic creature merely began crying again. "Stop, stop!" Clara beseeched it and scooped it up and jogged with it all the way to Elizabeth's apartment building.

The doorman, Roberto Rodriguez, greeted her with a look of surprise.

"Want a cat?" Clara asked.

"I don't think so," he said, regarding the wretched animal with curiosity and distaste. "He needs a bath."

"Maybe Elizabeth will want him."

"Maybe. Maybe not," the ever equivocal Roberto replied.

For once, all the lights in Elizabeth's duplex were off. Clara carried the kitten through the unusually somber apartment to the kitchen and fed it a bowl of milk. As it drank, she cleaned it with damp paper towels. It was all skin and bones and, in no time, finished the milk. Hunting through the refrigerator, Clara found some pate foi gras. It devoured that in a matter of seconds. "You are a rainy little pig," she said, passing it some leftover caviar.At last, in one of the cabinets, she found a can of salmon. For the first time in her life, Clara made salmon salad with mayonnaise and celery and fed it to the cat. When the animal finished that and had begun cleaning itself, Clara noticed a postcard on the kitchen table. It was from Paul in Hong Kong, in his uniquely curt style. "Dear Libby, everything's fine, making lots of money, how's Clara? Love Paul." It had evidently arrived some weeks before, and for some reason the fact that it had and that Mrs. Darlinger had not shown it to her, annoyed Clara. She dropped it back on the table, went into the pantry, watered the plants and then wandered up to the second floor. Her old room was exactly as she had left it years before, except without flowers. The next room, which had been Paul's, had the same timeless aura, as though it had been deliberately kept exactly as it was when the departed child lived there. In his closets she found every imaginable variety of athletic gear including a rifle. Several novels by Joseph Conrad lay on the desk, in one drawer of which she found a pornographic magazine, an ancient issue of <u>Sports Illustrated</u> and a high school term paper on <u>Macbeth</u>. Outside the rain came down faster than ever, a wind had sprung up, and the sound of it made her suddenly very tired. She lay down on the bed, began to doze and was joined by the kitten who curled up at her feet. She woke up a little while later, hot and uncomfortable, took off her clothes and went back to sleep. Hours passed.

She was awakened from a mournful and frantic dream by the telephone. It was Sunny, wondering what had become of her and reminding her that she was expected at a jet-set affair at a posh club right off Park Avenue that evening.

"I'm not going," Sunny said. "I won't know anybody there."

"Neither will I probably."

"But you have professional reasons for going. I don't know. I think I'll take in a movie."

"You okay?"

"No. I'm depressed."

"So am I," Clara said. "But then, I've been depressed for years." She went back into Paul's room and slept and slept and slept.

***

When she awoke it was dark, and the kitten was frisky. She therefore put it in a box and took a cab home through the rain. By the time the kitten was chasing its tail in her apartment, she had named it Rainy, partly because of how she had found it and partly for

Sunny, who she thought, without much hope, might want to take it back to the Main Line. Sunny had gone to the movies, leaving a take-out container of half-eaten Chinese food in the refrigerator. Clara showered to wake up and then, as she finished the moo-shoo pork, changed into a sleeveless black dress and high heels. After what Elizabeth called the ritual application of war paint, Clara grabbed her raincoat and umbrella and went out once again in the rain. She hailed a cab with a talkative Middle Eastern driver, who, by the time he deposited her on Park Avenue, had proposed marriage. When refused, he merely shrugged and asked if she had any sisters. In a moment of wickedness, she gave him Elizabeth's phone number and told him to call it next week. Either he was deliriously grateful or a very bad driver — in any event, as he sped away he grazed the side of a limousine, which precipitated a rather noisy street altercation in the rain.

Clara's name was on the guest list at the club. Even had it not been, the doormen would have let her in out of deference to her notoriety. She had, after all, lately been featured in a number of very unpleasant articles on real estate. She went up to the second floor past the bar to an entirely mirrored room decorated with white balloons and filled with politicians, TV pundits, real estate tycoons, mobsters, gossip columnists, actresses, press agents, athletes, models, idle millionaires and other such delightful celebrities. She was immediately greeted by young Schmeckenkopf, her twenty-eight-year-old competitor in commercial real estate. The first pulse of a headache throbbed between her eyes. But she banished it with the thought that even she had not received as much horrendous publicity as Schmeckenkopf. She said her hellos and made a quick escape to the bar, where she was immediately accosted by an old friend of Elizabeth, a reactionary, mob-connected and reputedly homosexual lawyer. He had also been confidant of old grandfather Chimes. Therefore he had what he called "a paternal interest" in Clara. He was perhaps the most charming and repulsive person she had ever known.

They started chatting, and she went to work on her first brandy. She had not got very far when, all at once and with a shock, she realized that she had come face to face with IT, the cause of her unshakable funk. It was amused. It had at once taken in her close relationship with the fey and notorious attorney. It was curious. It was about thirty three years old, black haired, blue eyed, the most handsome man she thought she had ever seen and, most unfortunately, named Philip Angelica.

"Yes, I've had the pleasure," it said to the notorious attorney when introduced to Clara.

"That was quite a courtroom performance Miss Chimes."

Clara smiled sweetly and lit a cigarette. Her underworld intimate moved off at the first opportunity. He seemed not to like the company of the former prosecutor.

"Why'd you do it?" Philip Angelica went on.

"Do what?"

He smiled. "Tell the truth."

"Oh, yes, the truth. A rare commodity, that. Very scarce in these quarters."

He regarded her curiously. "I see."

"Well it's not as if I'm on the stand."

"The one place no one ever wants to be," he smiled, "because then they just might, just might have to tell the truth. You broke the rules.It was very curious."

This line of conversation somewhat displeased Clara. "You found out <u>what</u>, now you want to know <u>why</u> too? That's asking a lot, considering your remarks about me to that reporter. I think I'm entitled to a question."

He nodded.

"What brings you here, of all places?"

"I'm studying the tribal customs of my enemies," and he smiled again.

"Well in that case, let's go over and talk to Hilda Honker, the stupidest critic in town." She led him over, introduced him and the three of them chatted for a while.

"Ah" Clara breathed, once they had stepped away," and there's the dullest celebrity who ever lived. Let's go say hello to him."

"And there's the most vacant actor who ever walked the earth!" she said a little later and directed Philip Angelica in that direction.

"How about some of the sleaziest paparazzi? Let's go get our picture taken."

"And there's the rudest debutante who ever came out. She should be good for a snub."

"What have we here? Schmeckenkopf, the most tedious rent gouger in the business."

In half an hour they were back at the bar and Philip Angelica had met nearly a dozen of the most illustrious citizens of New York. "You come to these things often?" he asked, regarding her coolly and rather critically.

"I'm a regular."

"I see." And then, after a moment, he looked at her as he had that day in the courtroom. "You knew that if you said anything beyond June first, you'd ruin the deal —"

"Back to that," Clara interrupted. "I see you don't like it here."

"I don't. You don't. Let's go somewhere else."

Clara had never thought of herself as someone given to living dangerously, but in the weeks that followed she had to admit that that was what she was doing. No one knew that she was seeing Philip Angelica, although Ward, she thought, had surmised that something unusual was going on. She knew she seemed more harried than ever and that she was working on entirely false energy. So did Ward Fairless, and he had several times suggested she take a vacation.But Clara had reached the point where she could not imagine what she would do on a vacation. Her current routine had become something of a prison from which she could envision no escape. Instead of leaving the office at eleven p.m.to socialize with the dreadful acquaintances of her adopted milieu, she went at that hour to consort with the enemy. Since her work repelled Philip, they could not discuss that. But since he was the most intellectual person she had ever met, they had plenty else to talk about. It seemed to Clara that he had read every book ever written and remembered them all with complete accuracy. Not only that, he spoke about them with a self-confidence and excitement which, she knew, Elizabeth or indeed anyone in her family would have considered very bad taste. He was somewhat startled at her patchwork self-education and, ashamed of her ignorance, she quickly moved from arcana to the more mainstream books that he and everyone in his acquaintance seemed to have read long ago. She went on a vigorous self-improvement spree, borrowing regularly from his extensive library. By midsummer, she was thoroughly immersed in <u>Capital</u>.

It was one of the ironies of her situation, and one which Philip Angelica had quickly observed to her, that she, who had been raised in the very heart of mammon, as he liked laughingly to put it, had been unable and unfree to do the one very simple thing she liked, namely, to continue her education. For him, on the other hand, coming from a family with little money, there had never been any question on the subject. He had gone to City College because it was free, because he wanted to be educated and because that was how he could secure a decent life in the middle class. He found Clara's summaries of her aunt's views on the subject offensive and incomprehensible. Indeed from time to time he asked why she did not just quite Darlinger-Fairless and go do what she wanted. After all, from the Chimes side of the family, she now had the money.

Clara had no convincing reply to this question. In fact her answers were so hollow that she could not but observe that she really had no idea why she was doing what she was doing. There was, all too evidently, no necessity in it. Darlinger-Fairless did not need her. And there was no reason why she should work in the firm rather than do anything else in the world, except that, somehow, she had come to need the firm. When asked why she needed it, she could only reply, "because I'm good at it." To this Philip Angelica always retorted that she would be good at anything she chose to do. But Clara did not really believe it.

For her, there was something unprecedentedly painful about these discussions. They led to depressions, long, aimless, solitary walks through the city and occasional tears. They led to the phrase, persistently in her mind, and that seemed to speak out at her from everything she saw: "You're wasting your life." But at other times she became outraged with this man who seemed to be sitting in judgment upon her life. She would decide that he was wantonly torturing her and not answer his phone calls for a day or two. He seemed quickly to catch on to the meaning of these sudden silences, but that, in turn, seemed only to bolster his certainty that he was right. That year, at the beginning of August, it started to rain, and so the unlikely pair spent hours on the weekends in Philip Angelica's apartment, hours that, for Clara, were not often happy. The rain came down; all

the buildings looked gray and sad. And Clara
wondered what was going wrong with her.

One dark Saturday afternoon, when Philip
had departed for his office downtown, Clara
stayed behind in his study, reading Capital and
now and then gazing out at the downpour.
From the window she could see the murky East
River and the cars making slow headway along
the slick, hilly streets of the east thirties. The
canopies of apartment buildings shook and
rippled under the rain. Few people were out
and about, and the air that drifted through the
half-open window was clammy. There was
something forlorn about the empty chairs on
the roofs of the buildings below. The forms of
water towers and chimneys stood out darkly
here and there in the distance. The city looked
shut-up and forbidding.

As she sat by the window, listening to the
thunder and gazing emptily at the summer
rain, the telephone rang. The call was from a

friend and client of Philip, a state assemblyman
who, rightly assuming her to be Philip's
girlfriend and being in an angry and somewhat
indiscreet frame of mind, left the massage that
one Marty Stein, noted slumlord, had just
phoned to persuade him to abandon his
demands with regard to an East Side
development. Mr. Stein's approach had been
most crude. He had promised to get the
legislator elected to any higher state office he
chose. The now furious assemblyman Berlin
had taped the conversation. Clara said she
would deliver the message as soon as Philip
returned.

Immediately upon hanging up the
telephone, Clara got a headache. She, Marty
Stein and a multi-national conglomerate based
in Paraguay were partners in the multi-million-
dollar development. And Mr. Stein had just
tried to bribe a government official — an official
with whom no one in his right mind would ever

attempt such a thing. She reached over and began to dial Stein's number, but then hung up. It occurred to her that alerting her partner, at this stage, might somehow endanger the assemblyman. After all, she had already heard the rumor that one person opposed to the development had received a bomb threat. Both of her partners had professed amazement at this tale, yet when she had checked the conglomerate's list of partners in other ventures, she had discovered a number of disturbing things.

With an American company based in Chicago, International Waste, her Paraguayan partner had a monopoly on garbage collection in six major Latin American cities. Clara had good reason to suspect that International Waste was a mob-run company. And she thought it possible that if she suspected it, in time other people, with a much keener interest in such matters would come to suspect it too.

Furthermore, she had discovered that the Latin American company had tried to conceal its rather questionable origins. Once wholly owned by the Paraguayan military dictatorship, it was now private, though still in partnership with several construction companies owned by various Latin American juntas. There was one company of which she was particularly leery, fearing that it was a silent investor in the Manhattan real estate deal.

It had, unfortunately, been easy to brush these worries aside. The Paraguayan group had more money than anyone had ever seen so lavishly disbursed, and no one, especially no one in city government, had asked where that money came from. Only a few community activists, upset at the magnitude of the gargantuan development, had raised that question. No one, above all the press, had bothered to try to answer it. The newspapers had contented themselves with puff pieces, while the politicians had hailed the development as "good for the city." It was also, Clara knew, good for them. After all, Dr. Vittelini, the Paraguayan firm's representative in New York, had already contributed generously to the campaign chests of everyone in city government from mayor to dog-catcher. Clara did not like this Dr. Vittelini one bit. She did not like it when he paid residents of the community to testify in favor of the project before the city planning commission, no matter how much he insisted that they were "consultants." Despite his PhD in genetics, Dr. Vittelini had abandoned science for real estate, something Clara had disapproved of from the first. Furthermore, she had no idea what the very cultivated doctor had done in Italy during the Second World War, prior to his emigration to Paraguay. But she had an intuition it had not been very nice.

Nonetheless, every elected and appointed city official thought him wonderful. The real estate community was in love with him. So were the banks. Marty Stein sang Dr. Vittelini's praises everywhere, from the American Jewish Congress to his local synagogue. This was in part due to the fact that upon his arrival in Manhattan, Dr. Vittelini had bought everyone in sight. He had hired several people straight out of key positions in city government. His press agent was the former spokesman for the most important state housing agency. His army of lawyers, who had all performed lengthy stints in government, were known as the people to go to if one wanted to do business with the city. He had befriended one of the city's most powerful publishers.The city had had to commission studies on the environmental impact of the development, and Dr. Vittelini had graciously paid for the studies. At one point when there looked to be considerable community resistance to the project, Dr. Vittelini had arranged for a counter-demonstration in favor of his multi-million-dollar dream. He had rented the buses and hired the citizens to go down to city hall and demonstrate their enthusiasm for the project, right under the already enthusiastic mayor's nose. In short, he had become, overnight, quite a man to contend with in New York. Philip Angelica had never once mentioned to Clara her association with this group.

But now, Philip's close associate, assemblyman Berlin, had a piece of political dynamite in his hands. And the more Clara contemplated the ramifications of this tape-recorded attempted bribe, the more convinced she became that either the minority share of Darlinger-Fairless or the minority share of Marty Stein had to go. It was not much of a quandary. She soon telephoned her attorney at home, telling him to begin negotiating to sell Darlinger-Fairless's share of the project to the Paraguayan company forthwith. She wanted the sale official by Monday afternoon. She also told him to be very reasonable about the terms.

The advice proved unnecessary. Dr. Vittelini had never much cared for what he considered the overly cautious way in which Clara's firm did business. Since he had only come to Darlinger-Fairless for its political and financial connections, of which he had already made maximal use, he was delighted that Clara wanted out, and by late afternoon a price had been agreed on, and the lawyers were drawing up the papers. Everything would be taken care of upon the resumption of banking hours Monday morning. By the time the sky had turned from gray to brown and a distant church bell was tolling six o'clock, Clara saw that she had done almost everything she could to insulate Darlinger-Fairless from whatever disaster was about to occur. Only one step remained. She waited rather tensely for Philip to return.

He came in looking tired but, as soon as he saw Clara, asked what was wrong. She told him to call assemblyman Berlin. He looked at her curiously and then, while taking off his tie, dialed the number. Following the perfunctory hellos, he sat down and began to listen. After a moment, he raised his eyes, looked at Clara and continued listening, now and then saying "I see," all the while watching Clara. At length he promised to call his friend right back and hung up the phone.

They sat and looked at each other for a while. Finally he asked if she had known Stein was going to do what he had done. Clara shook her head.

"But it doesn't surprise you."

"No," she answered. "Nothing about this deal surprises me anymore."

He inquired why she had not phoned him immediately at work. She fibbed that she had not been sure he was in his office.

"Maybe we'd better talk about this deal," he resumed.

"I'd like to have Darlinger-Fairless kept out of it."

"Out of what?"

"If you and Berlin go to the press with this."

"No, we won't be going to the press. We'll be going to the U. S. Attorney."

Clara groaned and gazed out at the rain. Then she asked how her company could be kept out of it, and he replied that if they had not participated in any of their partner's chicanery, he would try to see to it that they were. Clara nodded and assured him that they had not; this produced a smile, and then Philip came over and sat beside her and pointed out that her assurance was not quite enough.

Clara regarded him coldly. "You mean someone will have to look into our affairs." Since he didn't reply, she soon went on that that was fine but she would have to clear it with one or two people first. He nodded, brought her the phone and then went into the next room.

Ward was not exactly overjoyed by the situation. He blamed himself, since the deal had originally been his idea. He said that he, like Clara, had had his suspicions about these people, but had ignored them because of the possible profits. He thoroughly approved of her move to sell their share and concurred on the need for absolute discretion.What he did not understand was how Clara had been so lucky as to find out what was afoot. She explained that it was quite by accident and reiterated that they could be kept out of it if they could show, right at the beginning that they had been entirely above board.

"No problem with that," Ward replied. He planned to speak to his attorney and accountant about letting whichever investigators were involved look over their papers. "By the way," he concluded, "I was trying to reach you last night and this morning."

"Oh," Clara replied, "I've been out with friends."

When Philip returned, he made a joke about how she had bought time "to cook the books."

"That is not funny," Clara retorted. "We're a clean company, whatever you may say about our partners."

"What may I say? Tell me. I'd like to know."

She looked up and smiled. "Tell you what — once we're out of this, I'll tell you exactly where to look."

"And what will I find?"

Clara smiled again. "Enough to keep you and your prosecutor friends busy for quite a while."

By Monday, Darlinger-Fairless was no longer associated with Stein or Dr. Vittelini's firm. By Tuesday, Clara had planted an item to this effect in an article on local business. In a very short time, they had been given "a clean bill of health by the Feebs," in Elizabeth's words. Both Elizabeth and Ward considered it to have been a close call. Both considered Clara's luck and ingenuity just a bit too miraculous.

"That kid's up to something," Elizabeth remarked to Sunny one damp August weekend. They were standing in Mrs. Darlinger's kitchen, munching on caviar out of the jar.

"She said she found out by accident."

"Accident my ass. Nobody finds out about a federal investigation by accident. Next thing you'll be telling me is God protects the working girl."

"Well somebody protected her. And you. Maybe it's that Angelica. Didn't Ward say he was involved in this?"

Elizabeth's eyes lit up. "That's it," she shrieked and gagged on the caviar.

"What?" Sunny shrieked back.

"In bed," Elizabeth coughed.

"Hunh? Libby, you're not making much sense."

"Shut up you birdbrained child! She's in bed with him."

Sunny nodded and made a face as if to say, "it's possible," but before she could utter the words, Elizabeth had grabbed her shiny, black and very fashionable raincoat and was out the door.

"Get me a cab!" Mrs. Darlinger commanded Roberto Rodriguez, who marched in military fashion out under the canopy and began blowing his whistle. She stood below the lintel, tapping her foot. At length Roberto came back, dejected.

"It's a rainy Friday afternoon. Rush hour," he said.

"Well, don't they usually let a lot of people off around here?"

"Sometimes yes, sometimes no."

"Give me that," Elizabeth glared.

"Is something wrong?"he asked, handing over the whistle and gazing at her curiously.

"You're darn tootin' there is," she snapped, marched out into the street and began vigorously blowing the whistle.

"I bet it's that cat she picked up," he muttered to himself, as three cabs converged upon Elizabeth. "It looked diseased." Unfortunately his veterinary musings so distracted him that it was not until Mrs. Darlinger had driven off that he realized he had lost his whistle.

"Took it with her," commented the elevator man, who had observed these goings on from the hall. "Think she'll bring it back?"

"Maybe, maybe not."

"Strange woman."

"Whole family's cracked if you ask me."

Ward was surprised to see Elizabeth at company headquarters, but she swept by without giving an explanation and then swept grandly into Clara's office, slamming the door shut behind her. Clara needed only to look up from her word processor to know that her aunt knew.

"You know."

"I know." Elizabeth replied, standing next to the desk, her arms akimbo, gazing down at Clara. "Can't you ever keep out of trouble?"

"So happens it saved you a lot of trouble."

Elizabeth nodded. "It's not that I mind your doing reconnaissance work behind enemy lines.

But it happens to be dangerous. What if you talk in your sleep?"

"I don't."

"You do too, Clara Darlinger, I mean Chimes, or whatever your name is. Whole conversations. Loud and clear. Just like Marilyn, Paul, and every other blabber-mouth in this family. I'm the only one who's ever been able to keep her mouth shut."

"Ha!"

"What ha? Just because I've had bad dreams lately. What do you expect with some maniac Syrian cab driver calling me ten times a day? The police think I'm making it up. Under normal circumstances I don't utter a peep. But you! Quite a little chatterbox."

"I'll wear a muzzle."

Elizabeth flung herself down on the couch and glared. "And what about Sunny?" she demanded after a moment.

"Hunh?"

"She comes up every weekend. She thinks you're the greatest. And you leave her alone. No manners."

"What am I? Her mother?"

"I don't like it. It can't lead to anything good."

Clara gazed at her abstractedly, "you may be right."

"Of course, my child. I'm always right."

Though far from convinced that her aunt was always right, Clara had nonetheless come partly to believe that nothing very good could come of her alliance with Philip. Not knowing why she thought this, she associated her unexpected despair with the painful self-criticism he provoked in her. And when at last she realized that she could not imagine being with him forever, at least under the present circumstances, she began to wonder what she was doing being with him at all. Though these thoughts vanished when they were together, they nagged her when she was alone. Yet even in those moments when she began to think, "Oh, well. That's that. I'll never see him again," she began to be afraid, not so much of losing him, but of losing her one link to what she considered integrity. He was, it seemed, the only person in her acquaintance with real values and certainly the only one who lived by them. And the thought of what might become of her if she cut herself off from this other perspective, this distinctly honorable point of view on the world she lived in, terrified her. Philip provided balance. Although his very existence was a condemnation of almost everyone in her acquaintance, it was a condemnation which she had long shared — but it had been a subterranean condemnation, and one she had not heeded. Now it was out in the open and not at all shattering. On the contrary, she turned to it in need, to remind her what was real and false, and to remind her not who she was, but who she could be. He was necessary. But somehow, she thought, he would not be permanent.

Clara spent that night alone, and the next day; indeed she passed the entire weekend in bed, eating cookies and finishing <u>Capital</u>. She read long passages to Sunny, who had the most irritating habit of either falling asleep or asking utterly irrelevant questions about the author's personal life. Since these invariably led to questions about Clara's personal life, Clara had become rather adroit at heading them off. Sunny did not like forfeiting her vicarious fun or being outmaneuvered. Whenever it happened, she would pick up the kitten and talk baby talk to it, thus interrupting Clara's recitations. It was not a harmonious arrangement.

"What do I care about Mirabeau or M. Molinari or le roi de Prusse?" Sunny shrieked after one particularly acrimonious altercation.

"I never heard of these people. I've never met them."

"It would be quite something if you had," Clara retorted, "since they're dead."

"Dead! Everyone you like is dead. I'm sick of dead people. I'm sick of imaginary people. Read to me about real people." Sunny's green eyes flashed with indignation. "Dead people," she repeated in disgust. "Nothing but dead people. Do dead people go to parties? Do dead people go on dates? Do they buy interesting clothes? What have you or I got to do with dead people? Nothing. We have no business with them. We have nothing to say to them. We can't do anything for them and they can't do anything for us."

"Some of them happen to be very smart," Clara loftily replied.

"If they're so smart, how come they're dead?"

II

"I've got to admit, Sunny," Clara acidly went on, folding her arms across her chest, "you've got me there."

"Then cut it out. This is the me generation, remember? I'll bet that Philip Angelica doesn't waste his time thinking about dead people."

"No. He thinks about how to put live ones in jail."

"Libby says it's a miracle any man that handsome could be such a stuffed shirt."

"Libby's got low standards where miracles are concerned. Aren't you two going to the health club?"

Sunny shrugged. "She hasn't called yet. I wonder what she's up to."

"I don't even want to guess," Clara replied, taking off her clothes, then marching into the bathroom. By the time Elizabeth arrived in her jogging outfit, which consisted of a yellow sweatshirt, white sweat pants and what Clara had long considered very peculiar looking

265

shoes, Clara was lying limply in the tub, staring glazedly at the ceiling.

"So the Queen of Sheba takes a bath," Elizabeth commented, barging into the bathroom.

"Running in the rain," Clara remarked. "You look like a drowned rat."

"Talk about the pot and the kettle," Sunny called from the bedroom.

At this Clara slumped down in the water to nose-level and began blowing bubbles.

"If only the stuffed shirt could see you now," Elizabeth remarked. "You're going out with him tonight, I presume."

"Maybe," bubble, bubble. "Maybe not."

"Only your hairdresser knows for sure. Except you haven't been to the hairdresser in about two months. Your personal hygiene leaves a lot to be desired.But I suppose he likes it like that."

"Who he?"

"The stuffed shirt. Or is there more than one?"

"Thousands."

"Must be hard to tell 'em all apart."

"Very hard."

"Let me help you. One of them, a particularly pompous stuffed shirt, a.k.a. Angelica, has just been retained by a group of small manufacturers who rent several floors of a midtown building we're planning to lease to a communications conglomerate as their New York headquarters. Does that jog your memory?"

Clara narrowed her eyes, but before she could say anything, Elizabeth went on, "I don't mean to tell you how to run your personal life — heaven forfend I should ever presume — but surely even a love-struck creature like yourself is capable of seeing how useful it would be to know exactly what these revolting tenants are up to."

"Useful?" Clara pronounced the word very slowly.

"Something wrong with your hearing? Yes. I said useful. Useful to you, me, Ward, the family, Darlinger-Fairless. Useful. U-s-e-f-u-l. You want me to get a dictionary?"

Clara just glared at her aunt who haughtily drew herself up. "You must have known the time would come for you to make a choice."

Clara continued to glare.

"Stop that," Elizabeth commanded. "It's probably bad for your eyes. Already got reading glasses. Besides, it makes you look ugly."

"What choice?"

"Why, us or him, little one. Us or him." And with that Elizabeth, so absorbed in the grandeur of her announcement that she had forgotten her gym date with Sunny, turned, marched out of the bathroom and out of the apartment.

Her exit was immediately followed by Sunny's entrance. Miss LaMarque was clearly excited by all this drama. "Just like a soap opera," she burbled. As she sat on the toilet top, brushing her long blond hair, she bemoaned the iniquities of parents.

"She's not my mother, she's my aunt," Clara said sourly.

"Same thing in a situation like this. She's getting in your way."

"Just like Romeo and Juliette," Clara said, even more sourly.

"It really is," Sunny went on enthusiastically. "That was my favorite book in high school and college, aside from Love Story. The language kind of got me down, though. All those 'tises and 'twases. You're not going to kill yourself?"

"Shut up."

"Come on Clara, why don't you?"

"What?"

269

"Kill yourself. It would make life so much more interesting."

"Baloney."

"Well you've got to do something."

"Don't worry. I'm going to."

Sunny looked at her eagerly. All at once Clara brightened. She had just had an idea. "I'm going away for a week, to visit my friend Stanley Katz."

Sunny was disappointed. "That's it? You're going away to Florida? Not even to a monastery or a sanitarium — what a drag."

"No you ditz. Las Vegas."

A week on Stanley's ranch in Nevada helped immensely to clear Clara's mind. Lying on the porch, gazing out at the flat, scrubby landscape day after day, Clara became more and more convinced that she and Philip were not made for each other. Stanley and his girlfriend had a very simple view of such matters, but oddly, one which, Clara noted, they themselves did not heed.

"Do you want to be with him all the time?" Stanley would ask.

"You mean marry him?"

"Yeah."

"No."

"Then you better break up."

This seemed very sound advice, especially in light of Philip's growing disapproval of her real-estate work. Ever since the first revelations in the Stein/Paraguay disaster, he had begun urging her to reconsider her occupation. Although certain that he only voiced such views because he knew that she in part shared them, she had begun to consider him meddlesome. She was dimly aware that it was easier to be angry with him than to consider the substance of his remarks, which, after all, might have made her angry with herself, but this awareness did nothing to change the course of her emotions. And then, she would tell herself, what if, after a hard look at what she was doing, she discovered she really did like it? That would, she thought, once and for all, separate them, because at bottom it was not merely a matter of Philip sharing her doubts. His opposition went much further, was, in fact, total. He would not stay with her for long, she believed, if he though that really and truly she was never going to abandon her ill-chosen career.

The case of Marty Stein had given her some pause though. Under pressure several citizens had already admitted to receiving cash gifts for their testimony in favor of the development before the city planning commission. The had provided the names of some thirty other citizens hired in the same manner.There was already the suggestion that several city officials had accepted what the Paraguayan conglomerate might call fees, but what Philip's friends would undoubtedly call bribes. She had stayed abreast of the situation not because she chose to but because Philip insisted on keeping her informed. With the uncovering of each new scandal, it was as if he was saying, "Look, these are the people you deal with; this is the way your world <u>really</u> is." And though she knew it was stubborn of her, she could not help but resent the implied criticism. There was something too knowing about it, too self-righteous — as if she herself might, alone, be incapable of shock at what was revealed.

There had already been more than one dispute on the subject. Clara had several times accused him of "not believing in" her, and he had never had a satisfactory reply. Now, to make matters worse, there was Elizabeth, demanding that she behave in a manner that would inescapably justify his worst doubts. It was bad enough that Elizabeth wanted her to use him. What was insufferable was that this demand came at a time when she could not merely shrug it off and forget it, but when she had to consider all of its possible meanings, because it fell baldly and rather hideously into the cruel light to which Philip Angelica had somehow subjected all of her affairs. Not that she minded judging her aunt. She had done so many times — but privately and of her own accord. Now, it was as if she was being forced to. And this sense of coercion made it seem that her privacy had been invaded.

The only way to preserve that sense of privacy and to prevent an irreparable falling out with Philip was, she had decided, never to discuss with him this matter of the midtown manufacturers. Indeed, if in general they could stay away from the subject of her work, they might have a chance, she thought, of getting along. She recalled with some nostalgia the first few weeks of their acquaintance when he had shied away from any mention of real estate. Then it was she who had been surprised at this discretion. Now it was she who would have to insist on it. That was the one hopeful conviction she came upon, during her stay in Nevada. She returned to New York more resigned about the differences between herself and Philip, yet more optimistic that within certain limits, "things would work out." Unfortunately that optimism vanished on her second night back.

He was the one who brought it up — the matter Elizabeth had urged her to investigate. They were midway through dinner in a Chelsea restaurant when he mentioned that they might be on opposite sides of a legal battle. The steak in Clara's mouth suddenly tasted very dry. She took a swallow of wine and tried to change the topic. This proved futile since Philip, who had not yet made up his mind about taking the manufacturers' case wanted to use the situation as an example of the difficulties besetting them. Clara replied that she knew very well about her difficulties with him, and that they did not need further amplification. He replied that on the contrary they did. She contradicted this remark; he contradicted her. So it went, as the steak grew cold. At length he began marveling at her obstinacy. This was followed by Clara slamming down her fork and informing him that there were, contrary to his apparent conviction, a few things in the world he knew nothing about and that might be better left unsaid. Philip answered that if she had something to say she had better say it forthwith, since he was getting ready to leave. Clara observed that her meal might go down much better if he did. But by then he had apparently changed his mind, because he was demanding to know what, exactly, she wanted to keep unsaid. That, she coldly explained, was precisely the point — not to say it. Unfortunately Philip thereupon began insisting rather firmly that she say whatever she had to say. This went on for quite some time and, now and then, loudly. The couple at the next table began to stare.

At last Clara got up and walked out of the restaurant. Philip paid and followed her out. And there on the sidewalk on Eighteenth street in the balmy, late summer evening air, they began somewhat noisily, and in a manner one often has the misfortune to encounter on the sidewalks of New York, to examine their disagreements in great detail. After some time, amid accusations and counter-accusations, and oblivious to the cautious passersby who crossed to the other side of the street, Clara inadvertently and in the heat, as it were, of passion, revealed that Mrs. Darlinger had already indicated some interest in the question of the manufacturers, and had indeed attempted to recruit Clara as a sleuth. This revelation did not have a soothing effect upon

Philip. It seemed in fact to do something most unpleasant to his physiognomy: in short, he flew into a rage. Clara at once became calm and, after a rather icy comment upon his infantile behavior, hailed a cab and went home.

The instant she walked into the apartment, the phone rang. It was Philip, and she promptly hung up. A few minutes later, when she had changed into her bathrobe, the doorbell rang. At his point she began really to lose her temper. By the time he arrived in the apartment, she was too angry to observe that her visitor was in a similarly livid state. The two of them, in fact, were too angry to notice much of anything. But Clara's next door neighbor noticed, and called the police.

Officers Ryan and Brown were most agreeable. Ryan took Clara's side and Brown took Philip's. Rather like two interpreters at the UN, they proceeded to mediate.

"But he doesn't like getting books thrown at him," Brown explained. "Especially when, what's that? Oh. When they're <u>his</u> books."

"Well then he shouldn't call her a, what was that?" Ryan asked Clara.

"A lying, underhanded bitch," Philip elucidated.

"Arrogant pig," Clara replied.

"Now just a minute," Brown remonstrated. "There's been enough name calling for one night."

But since the choleric pair did not seem convinced of this assessment, it took another fifteen minutes or so for Ryan to impress upon them how unpleasant and inconvenient it would be to resolve their differences at the police station. Philip was the first to see the logic of this position. And as he began to calm down, the tone of the mediation between Ryan and Brown took on the sharp eagerness of labor and management at the bargaining table, when both sides scent a compromise.

Finally Philip put his offer on the table. He agreed to leave, but would not, he said, ever come back nor would he ever speak to Clara or set eyes upon her again, until she made certain necessary adjustments in her career.

"Such as?" Ryan asked with noticeable curiosity.

Brown looked puzzled, but conveyed the terms: "No more evictions, no more co-ops, no more developments."

The two officers looked at each other in some confusion. Then Ryan looked at the disheveled young woman and said, "Well?"

She glared at Philip, then glared at Brown, then nodded as they walked to the door. "Tell him," she said to Officer Ryan," he can take a long walk off a short pier."

***

After that eventful evening, it was quite plain to Clara that she and Philip were, as she put it to Sunny, "through." Sunny marveled at how quickly Clara got over it. She never mentioned him. She seemed rarely to think about him. Indeed that was pretty much the case. Clara was too busy thinking about something else.For although he was now only occasionally in her thoughts, he had, she knew, irrevocably changed her. And this was both perplexing and disheartening at the same time.

Clara thought about this change a great deal. It preoccupied her. It made no sense. By all logic it was something that should have occurred while she still cared about him, not once she had given up. But there it was, evident and inescapable: Clara no longer wanted to work in real estate.

She did not discuss this discovery with anyone except her cat, who had, on this subject as on everything else, the most inscrutable opinions. Yet she did not act on it either. She went to work every day as before, and, just as before, stayed at the office until very late. However, she no longer went out in the evenings. Instead she went home and read; or, in fits of melancholy, watched TV. At one point in early September she became downright despondent and, for a brief period, took to drinking herself to sleep every night. By then she had an active aversion to the office and anything associated with it, but still, unaccountably, she could not bring herself to quit. "After all, what will I do if I quit?" she asked her cat, over and over again. "What will I do then?"

Ward meanwhile had become alarmed. It seemed that Clara's mind was not on the business. And since, for all purposes, she was running the business, this was very bad. Not that she didn't work hard — he had no complaints about that. But he could not help observing that her intuition, usually so keen, seemed to have dulled lately. Her quick discernment for a good deal seemed to have vanished. She was no longer aggressively on the lookout for ways to expand and enrich Darlinger-Fairless. She seemed to be treading water, and in real estate, as he loved to say, if you weren't going forward, you were going backward or, in Elizabeth's rather pithier phrase, it was "eat or be eaten." As Ward watched Clara, he had the unmistakable sense that Darlinger-Fairless was not doing the eating.

He said as much to Elizabeth, who told him not to worry, "the kid's depressed, she just broke up with her boyfriend, thank God." But it bothered him all the same, and every morning when he saw Clara, it bothered him more. In the context of her previous, workaholic excesses, Clara's latest absent-mindedness struck him as the violent mood swing of a perhaps imbalanced personality. He began to wonder if this inattention was to be expected every time she broke up with a boyfriend. This notion was so disturbing that he concluded it might not be bad idea for her to get married. Then at least they could take her husband into the company.

Early on Friday morning he tried to broach the subject of whether or not she wanted another vacation. He brought it up by explaining that he would be glad to take care of one of their most recent and, he hoped, final residential ventures. It was a nasty business. Darlinger-Fairless was drawing up a contract to rehabilitate a number of buildings on East Thirteenth street, if the current landlord, a Mr. Peabody, first emptied them of tenants. Mr. Peabody was not known for his gentle methods, which generally did not stop with turning off the heat, electricity and hot water. He had apparently moved some friends of his into the building, and they were making life unpleasant for the other tenants most of whom, Ward guessed though he preferred not to think about this, were probably impoverished. In their current condition the buildings were little better than slums. Most of the tenants, represented by a public defender named Bartly, had been easily cowed. Only a few remained and they, Ward guessed, though again he did not like to think about it, were probably the most desperate cases, the people with nowhere else to go.

So he urged Clara to take the day off, even the following week if she liked, and suggested that henceforth he deal with the Peabody contract. Clara looked up at him from what evidently had been a glum daydream and said, "what?"

"The Peabody buildings," he replied. "I'll be glad to handle it."

"Oh yes," she answered quietly. "Now what stage is that at?"

"If I'm not mistaken," Ward went on, gazing down at her with his tired blue eyes, "the city marshals will be evicting the last tenants this afternoon."

Clara blinked at him. "But it's Friday."

"So?"

"Where will they go on a Friday?"

"And where will they go on a Monday or a Tuesday or a Wednesday?" he impatiently replied. "That's not our concern."

"Oh," she said and then, even more quietly. "I just meant that it would seem a little more difficult on a Friday. It seems rather hard."

Furrows of concern appeared on Ward's wide, ruddy forehead. "What do you, or I for that matter, know about such things? I should think it would be difficult any day of the week, if you'd planned your life so badly that you got into the position of being evicted." He paused and gazed out the window at the towers of midtown Manhattan. The sky was dark and threatened rain. "Hard? Yes, I guess it is hard. But that's not our concern. The poor shall always be with us," he intoned. "Every Christian knows that."

Clara looked up at him. "I'm not Christian."

This was certainly unexpected; more than anything the tone in which it was said. Ward's first reaction was to take it as a joke, but Clara was not smiling. She was looking at him coldly, and then she turned and looked away, out the window. "On a Friday afternoon in September in the rain," she said.

"What?"

"That's when we're putting them out on the street. As I recall there's a Mr. Lopez in the building, whose wife just died, leaving him with four infant daughters. Batter says he looks very young."

"That's none of our concern."

There was silence for a moment, and then Ward said he guessed he had better handle the matter.

"No. I can take care of it," Clara replied. "But I think you're right about a short vacation. I'll take the rest of the day off."

Ward retired to his office with some relief and thought no more about their conversation until he saw Clara, an hour or so later, in her raincoat, carrying her umbrella, going down the hall on her way to the elevator. And as he watched her and recalled portions of their talk, he had a sudden premonition that he would never see her in that office again. "Oh Libby," he thought, "it's never the way you think." And with that, he returned to his work.

By the time Clara reached the street, it had begun to drizzle. She put up her umbrella and went to a nearby delicatessen for lunch. Long after she had finished eating, she sat in the booth, sipping her coffee and watching the rain.

She finally left and went aimlessly shopping. She wandered in and out of the department stores and shops that her aunt so loved to frequent, all the while thinking of Mr. Peabody's buildings. She knew where they were. And although she herself had never seen them, she could well imagine what they were like, having met Mr. Peabody. He was a short, wiry, white haired man, whose demeanor suggested that he was accustomed to the reverence of those around him. He thought himself exceedingly noble and was given to fits of temper when he imagined himself slighted. He spoke about his tenants as if they infested his buildings like termites.

It was late afternoon and pouring rain, when Clara went down the stairs of the Lexington Avenue subway. She got off the train at Union Square, put her umbrella and walked east, toward Mr. Peabody's buildings. When she came to the correct block, they were not hard to spot — two run-down tenements that looked like lumps of green rock in the rain. The street was nearly deserted. Small brown rivers of rainwater coursed along the curb. Here and there an orange peel, a bottle top, a piece of decomposing newspaper bobbed on the water. Two stray dogs rifled through an overturned trash can. Huge potholes in the middle of the street had already become small ponds, and whenever a car passed by, its windshield wipers going futilely, the water from the potholes splashed even to the window of the bodega behind her. The shopkeeper, visible in the yellow light behind the windowpane, gazed out at the inclement weather and now and then shook his head. Across the street, in front of one of Mr. Peabody's buildings, was what appeared to be an immense heap of wreckage. Peering out from under her umbrella, Clara discerned a bedstead, several box springs, mattresses, chairs, two bureaus, and a crib.

There were heaps of clothes on one of the mattresses. The white shade of a stand-up lamp swayed in the rain.

At length a woman ran out of the building with a piece of plastic and threw it over the clothes. She ran back in and when she opened the door, Clara heard shouting inside. Clara turned and saw the shopkeeper in the bodega shaking his head. But for quite some time after that, no one came out of the building. The furniture on the sidewalk looked very peculiar — the bed and bureaus seemed abject, resigned to their unseemly fate, while the empty, soaking chairs seemed shocked and seemed, in that unfamiliar context, to be asking how they came there and where they would go next. The swaying lamp shade reminded Clara of the duck in Sunny dog's mouth, its head dangling from its broken neck.

The door opened to reveal the marshal carrying a kitchen table. An old woman was scolding him in Spanish in the hall. For a moment her sparse white hair shone in the dim interior light. In her faded blue dress that hung well below her knees, she could not have been much more than four feet tall. The door swung shut, the image vanished. By the time the marshal went back into the building, the woman had gone. The street returned to its previous calm. The top of the kitchen table gleamed in the rain.

After a few minutes the shopkeeper darted out with a large plastic bag. He raced across the street, and as the rain smeared his little spectacles, wrapped the bag over the lamp. Then he ran back into the shop and stood behind the door, panting, wiping his glasses on his shirt, and watching the building. When a group of nearly ragged children passing along the sidewalk, began to poke curiously at the furniture, he opened the door, screamed at them, and they scampered away in the rain.

In the next ten minutes, the scene became much busier. The marshal, accompanied by a policeman, hurried in and out of the building. With each foray, the pile of furniture grew bigger. As it did, people began coming out of the building. Some wrapped their possessions in plastic bags, some began carrying things away. One frail old man hurried out and, to Clara's amazement, picked up a huge, moth-eaten armchair and carted it off down the street. He disappeared around the corner and did not return.

Despite her raincoat and umbrella, Clara was now quite wet. The rain had soaked through her shoes, gotten into her hair, on her hands and, as it splashed up from the sidewalk, onto her legs. To make matters worse, a wind had started up, and although it was slight, it was almost cold, and seemed to come from all directions at once. She backed up under a fire escape, but that provided little shelter. The shopkeeper beckoned for her to come inside, but for some reason she felt she had to stay out on the sidewalk. She did not know what that reason was, nor did she care to examine it. She was too absorbed in the goings on across the street even to wonder why she was there or what this visit could possibly accomplish. Though vaguely aware that she was in part responsible for that furniture being on the street and for the frantic attempts of its owners to shield it from the rain, that responsibility seemed distant, and from time to time she imagined she heard Mr. Fairless's words, "That's none of our concern."

Yet at the same time these thoughts seemed inconsequential, seemed to belong to another mind, another person. For her, at that moment, the immediate concern was what she saw and trying to make sense of it. This should have been simple, but it confounded her. She thought she must be in a daze to find what was before her so incomprehensible and to find it provoking only one rather moronic thought — "why is this happening?"

In those ten minutes, fifteen people must have come out of the building, grabbed their belongings and disappeared. Some made return trips, some, like the boy with three dogs on three leashes, just stood for a while in the rain looking startled before they went away. It was not until a young man carrying two little girls appeared on the threshold that Clara matched one of the names she had heard to a face. Of course it was Mr. Lopez. He stepped out in the rain, looked around anxiously and went back inside.His daughters were not crying; they looked terrified. It was at that point that Clara began groping in her pocketbook for some change.

She hurried off to the corner and, hardly thinking about what she was doing, pulled out her little book of telephone numbers and dialed

Mr. Peabody's attorney. He was surprised to hear from her and displeased to learn that Darlinger-Fairless was backing out of the deal. It created difficulties, he said. Since they had begun to empty one of their buildings, now they would not even get their rent. She told him that in that case, he had better get someone down to Thirteenth street, with an order for the marshal to desist. She hung up and then phoned Batter, Batter to inform them of Darlinger-Fairless's decision. "Too bad," one of the bright, young associates said. "Just when it looked like Peabody had 'em licked."

Clara wandered up the street to the scene of the eviction. By now the policeman, a big, dour fellow, was standing in the bodega, talking to the shopkeeper. Clara entered and overheard him saying that earlier he had phoned a clerk who worked in housing court for the attorneys who had obtained the order to evict, in the hopes of getting it postponed until Monday. He had, he said, urged the clerk to do anything in his power, licit or illicit, to stop the eviction, but to no avail.

"You might have better luck now," Clara remarked. When the policeman looked at her in surprise, she merely said that she worked for someone associated with the landlord, someone she had just spoken to on the phone, and that the landlord might indeed be in a mood to postpone the eviction.

"If you say so," the policeman answered, and hurried outside in the direction of the pay telephone.

Clara went back out into the rain. The last thing she saw, as she put up her umbrella, was Mr. Lopez, carrying one child and pushing a baby carriage that contained three others. He negotiated it carefully down the front steps and then stopped on the sidewalk to straighten the hood of the carriage. In seconds his shirt and pants were soaked through. But he did not seem to notice. He went about his arrangements methodically and, when he was done, wheeled the carriage away in an easterly direction. The last Clara saw of him, he was turning south on the avenue, pushing his carriage cautiously through the rain. The storekeeper opened the door and gazed out after Mr. Lopez.

"He better not go to the men's shelter," he remarked.

"Why not?" Clara asked.

"He's on welfare. If he goes there, they'll take the babies away from him. Happens a lot. What do they call it? Oh, it's when they deem you an unfit parent."

***

Clara walked uptown through the rain. Once or twice she lit a cigarette, and then a little cloud of smoke would travel with her under the umbrella. By now it was early evening, the rain came down in thick, slanting sheets, and the streets of east midtown were deserted. She was just as glad for that — she was in no mood to contend with a crowd. In fact she was in no mood to contend with anything, since she could scarcely think. Instead, an incongruous array of images passed through her mind — Mr. Lopez with his children in a carriage disappearing around a corner in the rain, old Mrs. Darlinger in her white nightgown sitting back for the last time in her hospital bed, the policeman looking at her with surprise and walking out of the bodega, Paul Fairless turning away from her one beautiful summer evening in front of a Greenwich Village restaurant.One after another in her mind people she knew and even scarcely knew turned their backs, shut doors, closed their eyes and died, or vanished forever around a street corner. Everyone seemed to be going away. Everything seemed to be ending. And whenever for a moment the images ceased, all she could see or imagine seeing was the rain, coming down like cold tears, everywhere.

Pausing before the smoked glass of a restaurant, she realized all at once that she was hungry. She bought a newspaper at the tobacco shop next door, went into the restaurant and ordered dinner. The waiter regarded her sopping high heels critically, but when he saw that she would be dining alone, his attitude changed to one of sympathy. Clara found this a little annoying and so hastened to appear absorbed in her newspaper.As always, she turned to the gossip columns first, since she knew most of the people written about. Indeed there was an item on a party Elizabeth had thrown for some political bigwig at a fashionable restaurant. As Clara read her aunt's menu, she calculated that it must have cost a small fortune. For some reason this realization, which ordinarily might have amused her, suddenly put her out. She turned the page and her eye was immediately lured to the twenty-eight point print of the headline, JUDGE SLAMMED BY GOV'S PANEL, STEPS DOWN. There followed a rather bracing column of type on the recent activities of Judge Pepper with quotes from sundry courthouse denizens, foremost among them one of the commissioners who had deemed the judge delinquent. These were by far the punchiest: "He ran a kangaroo court"; "He may say it's a speech defect, but we have testimony he spat on a litigant"; "Oh he had plenty to say about his colleagues. But I can't comment on that now"; And "Judges scream and yell all the time, but it's my understanding that generally they do not sing 'God Bless America' in open court." The commissioner's comments perked Clara up considerably. Indeed the waiter thought it a bit strange that the young woman eating her desert alone at the corner table was giggling.

He said as much to the cashier. When he handed Clara her check, he asked, with elaborate casualness, just what was so funny.

"Here," she said, handing him the paper and pointing to the item on Judge Pepper. "Read this." By the time she had paid and left, the waiter's eyes, as he read the article, had grown round with disbelief.

"Well?" the cashier asked.'

"Some judge, Popper, Pepper — spitting on people, singing 'God Bless America' in court. A real cuckoo bird."

"How he got on the bench, that's what I'd like to know."

"You and everybody else, apparently."

Inexplicably cheered by the odd tale of Judge Pepper and more explicably by the fact that the rain had turned to fog, Clara continued making her way uptown on foot. Now and then she stopped to study the displays in shop windows under the eerie fluorescent light.

Small, multicolored neon signs glimmered through the fog, and the occasional passers-by appeared and disappeared so swiftly that it was easy to doubt they had ever been there.The lonely, loud sound of her high heels on the pavement reminded her of her destination. Much later, as she drew near, she began to go slowly, to doubt and reconsider what she was about to do. But these hesitations passed surprisingly quickly. At another time they would not have; they would, in fact, have overcome her and made her turn back. That day, however, had changed everything. Above all and most illogically it was Mr. Lopez who had changed everything. And in its very incongruity it even began to seem fitting that one whom she had never met, who had for weeks been merely a name, usually uttered with imprecations by the people she did know and who, in the end, had crossed her path for scarcely five minutes, as fleeting, she thought, as a ghost, that <u>this</u> one should have succeeded where others much more important to her and whom she knew well had failed — it was remarkable, but fitting. Mr. Lopez, she thought, didn't know her from Adam. He would never know the effect he had had; just as she would never know what became of him. It was fitting that he had turned her away from something awful and unspeakable, without even trying, by accident. It was fitting that even if he had known the change he caused, he would not have cared, because it was useless to care — the place Clara stepped out of would not be empty long, not even five minutes. There would always be someone to step in, as long as there was money to be made. And that, Clara thought, as she walked down the final side street, was forever.

Roberto Rodriguez greeted her with a question about her cat.

"Eats like a pig," she answered.

"Hmm. He looked sick to me. But then sometimes I'm right and sometimes I'm wrong."

No one was home at Mrs. Darlinger's duplex, so Clara settled down on the very modern, blue and white couch and waited. She picked up the newspaper which was open to an article on real estate and began to read. She did not take off her raincoat.

An hour later Elizabeth arrived, in very high spirits from a cocktail party and on her way, once she had changed her clothes, to a rather formal soiree.

"Jimminy Cricket!What have you been doing — swimming in the Hudson River?" she exclaimed, shutting the front door behind her. "Quick. Change! You'll catch pneumonia. To say nothing of ruining my priceless Darlinger antiques."

Clara looked down at the couch. "If this is an antique, I'm a monkey's uncle."

"No, you're a poor old woman's niece. And as usual you're giving me heart failure. I don't need two of you in the hospital."

"Since when are there two of me?"

"I'm referring to your step-cousin, or whatever he is."

"Paul?"

Elizabeth nodded.

"He's in the hospital? In Hong Kong?"

She nodded again. "I mean no. In and out. Didn't even tell us till this afternoon. Imagine, calling Ward on the phone with news like that. His poor father nearly dropped dead. The thought of him in some Chinese hospital! Probably got whatever he got running around without any clothes on."

"He's cured?"

"Depends how you define cured," Elizabeth snorted. "Acupuncture!"

"Well if it cured him —"

"It's a lot of humbug if you want my opinion. That boy should see a psychiatrist. I always thought there were a few marbles missing. Shock therapy, something medically approved. That's what he needs. Not a bunch of witch doctors sticking needles in his joints. Talk about a banana." And with that Elizabeth stalked off to the kitchen. "Have a drink," she called and then, sticking her head out into the hall "see that article on Judge Pepper — spitting on people. He didn't ever spit on you, did he?"

"Not that I recall."

"A lunatic like that, you never know, it could be catching."

"Lunacy?"

"You bet. Could be a microbe, a virus, like meningitis. Friend of Rita's just died of meningitis. Got it and two days later, whamo, kicked the bucket. Rita's scared half out of her wits she might have picked it up. Tell you the truth, I'm not exactly comfortable about it myself. Kind of makes me cautious about shaking Rita's hand and things like that. For God's sake, will you get out of those clothes?"

Clara rose and walked into the kitchen. Elizabeth, who had mixed two martinis, handed her one. "That's better," she said. "If you're going to be dripping, you might as well drip on the kitchen floor!"Elizabeth took a swallow of her drink and then surveyed her own black silk and black sequined dress. "Formal enough?" she asked.

"I don't see how it could be any more formal. What's wrong with Paul?"

"He's up a tree. That's what's wrong with him now, that's what's always been wrong with him. Acupuncture! Next thing you know he'll be moving to the country and making clay pots. What do they call it?"

"Ceramics. Why did he have acupuncture?"

"I told you. He's working on half an engine. He's out of his gourd. How in heaven am I supposed to know why he had acupuncture? You think I can penetrate the mysteries of that twisted brain any better than anyone else? The boy sings loony tunes."

"But what," Clara asked in a very low voice, audibly controlling her impatience, "was wrong with his body?"

"Nothing a few days at the funny farm wouldn't cure. Some tropical disease."

"A tropical disease!" Clara shrieked.

"Don't get so excited. I told you he was better. It has a long Latin name. Ward couldn't get it down, what with the waves."

"Waves?"

"You know, the ocean, the sound of the waves on the telephone cable. Anyway I'd never heard of it before. Paul said it made him dizzy but this voodoo business took care of that. Won't be any after effects."

"How do you know, when you can't even remember the name of the disease?" Clara was trying not to lose her temper.

Elizabeth finished her martini and proceeded to mix another. "That was the first thing Ward asked about. He always does. After all, his brother got that awful disease, whatever it's called, and they thought he was cured and the next thing they knew, his legs were falling off. Had to be amputated, both of 'em. First the right and then the left.Gruesome business. He eventually died."

Clara's eyes had become very round. "You mean Paul has a disease that could mean he'll have to have his legs amputated?"

"Now don't go mixing things up, dummy. Paul's got what Paul's got, and Ward's brother had whatever he had. They're two separate things. Unless, of course, there's something that runs in the family. Hmm...I hadn't thought of that."

Clara's eyes crossed.

"Don't you go wiggling your eyes at me, young lady. One of these days you'll cross them like that and they'll get stuck. That happened to a friend of Horace LaMarque. His eyes got stuck, right in there next to the nose. Looked hideous, to say nothing of the fact he couldn't see straight. And in his line of work — he was an architect — not seeing straight presents some problems. Though you wouldn't know it the way buildings look these days, swooping around at all sorts of crazy angles. He had an operation."

"Who?"

"Horace's friend, the architect, the guy they wanted me to marry. I took one look at him after that operation, boy, no way. A gibbering idiot. I mean, that was it — a complete vegetable. The surgeon screwed up, went after the wrong nerve or something. They sued him for a mint."

"Who?"

"The architect's kids by his first marriage. They sure made a pretty penny out of it. Sued him, sued the hospital, sued everyone in sight. Case was tied up in the courts for years. Horace had to testify that he hadn't been like that before the operation. Not a very hard job, you would think. After all, the guy was a mindless moron. A zombie. There was no way he could have been like that before the old sawbones got to him. I mean how could a vegetable run an architecture firm? How could friends of mine try to fix me up with a basket case? Self-evident that something went wrong on the operating table, right? Wrong. By the time Horace got off the stand, he'd set the architect's case back six months, what with his ditherings about how Joe used to say this and Joe used to say that. Impression you got was Joe was a babbling numskull."

"Joe — the architect?"

Elizabeth nodded. "Boy, his kids were mad as hell, at Horace, I mean. Can't say I blame them. Out of the millions they made, old Horace must have lost them ten grand. No matter how rich you are, that's nothing to sneeze at. You ought to write Paul a letter. It might cheer him up."

"I doubt it."

"Don't be a pill. He's over you just like you're over him. And a good thing too. Last thing we need in this nuthouse is incest. A brood of inbred, three-eyed brats, that's what it comes to. Just like in Maine."

"I've never seen any three-eyed anythings in Maine, for all your carryings on about how all they do is sleep with their brothers and sisters. Besides Paul and I aren't related. Just tell me, is he going to be okay? I mean, he's not going to be a cripple or anything."

"Physically no. Mentally, the prognosis is grim. Especially if he's chasing after Oriental women."

"He's what?" Clara demanded.

"I said <u>if</u>, <u>if</u>. The last thing we need in this family is miscegenation. You, my dear, are as close as we get to that experiment. And I'm not at all sure I'm happy with the results."

"So he's not chasing after women."

"I don't know that he's not."

"Doesn't sound very sick to me," Clara remarked and then rather bitterly added, "too bad he won't be crippled."

"My thought exactly. The minute I heard he was in the hospital I thought, good, that'll take care of the wild oats problem. Next thing you know, he's out and around. And I was dreaming he might come back home and work in the firm."

"Speaking of which," Clara said and took a large swallow of her martini, "I'm not."

"Not what?"

"Working in the firm."

For a moment Elizabeth did not speak. Her hazel eyes looked Clara over from head to toe. At length she said, "since when?"

"Since now, this minute. And it's final."

Elizabeth opened her mouth to argue, but then saw the look in Clara's eyes and shut it. "You'll kill him," she finally said.

"Ward?"

"Yes. His heart. He can't handle it alone and you know it. If you quit, it's as good as killing him."

"Then he should quit and let you run the firm."

"That will kill him even faster."

"Then it looks like he's destined to die, like the rest of us."

They glared at each other for a moment until Elizabeth said, "I hope you don't expect me to support you."

"No, I'll get a job."

"A job! You have a job. You're not suited for anything else."

"We'll see about that."

"It's a tough world out there, kiddo."

"We'll see about that."

After Clara had left, Elizabeth stood for a long time in the kitchen. At last she turned and smashed her martini glass in the sink.

III

Early one spring afternoon in the mid-1980s, a young woman was walking slowly and rather aimlessly in the vicinity of Rutherford Square. It was an uncertain day, at times gray and full of clouds and then, suddenly, just as full of sun. The woman, wearing an elegant tweed skirt, a cream-colored silk blouse and low-heeled, leather shoes, ambled along, gazing curiously at the old brownstones on either side of the quiet, tree-lined street. In that peaceful, old section of town, she was the only person on the sidewalk, and she seemed to feel her solitude, for as she went, her tired and somewhat disappointed expression grew melancholy. At length she stopped, so as not to disturb a squirrel that had run out into the middle of the sidewalk. For a moment they looked at each other, until the squirrel, suddenly timorous, darted back to the locust tree whence it had come and scampered up the trunk. The woman watched it ascend and then cross by means of a branch to another nearby locust tree. To see it better, she walked toward the tree at the corner, gazing heavenward. The squirrel seemed to know exactly where it was going and even paused every now and then, as if to make sure the woman was watching it. There was something so deliberate, so nearly intelligent about these feral glances that she stopped in the middle of the pavement and studied the animal closely. By now it had raced out onto a limb that extended from the tree to the tiled roof of the ancient, ivy-covered house on the corner. The branches intertwined with those of another tree from the other side of the house, and in seconds the squirrel had disappeared in that direction. Even after it had gone, the woman remained, still gazing upward, her attention now absorbed in the peaks, turrets and protruding attic windows of the magnificent old house. Its roof was dappled by the sun, filtering through the branches of the trees. Pigeons cooed under the eaves. Otherwise, the elegant yet not ostentatiously rich neighborhood, leafy though densely urban, in all its vernal splendor, was suddenly and, it seemed to the young woman, almost supernaturally silent. And as she lowered her gaze to the plate glass of the first floor window, a look of puzzlement mingled with the melancholy of her hazel eyes as they settled on the antediluvian curls and twirls of a quaint window sign. For all at once the sun had vanished behind a mass of gray clouds. As it did a warm, benign and indeed soothing wind had struck up and blew gently in her face, wetting it with a fine, silver mist. Through that strange and unexpected cloud, she saw, but in a blur, the door beside the window swing open. And there, standing on the threshold was a remarkable, tall, lean and truly ancient man. Above his well tailored gray suit and beneath his mane of white hair was the one of the most unusual and commanding faces she had ever seen. His features were dark, aquiline, and despite his venerable age and the thousands of lines in his leathery skin, he was handsome. One hand held a cigar. Evidently he was a habitual smoker, for the edge of his luxurious white moustache had turned brown from tobacco stains. In the other hand he held a marvelous cane, eccentrically carved with a lion's head knob and clearly an antique. At his side, on the threshold, sat a regal and spotlessly white hound. But all of these details were mere accessories, secondary to the miracle of his dark, limitless eyes that had sparkled at her through the blue, curling cigar smoke and the sudden mist, drawing her own gaze to him and away from the sign that read:

Tannini's Bookshop

Foreign Classics

They stood thus for nearly thirty seconds, staring at each other. In that glance it seemed that she was not only studied, she was taken in. Those limpid, ageless eyes looked into her and beyond her, seemed to recognize and claim her as part of some other world from which she had strayed so long ago she hardly knew when, a world whose existence she had until then forgotten; those eyes seemed capable of seeing incontrovertibly and once and for all who she was. She looked at him as he gazed at her, and she did not know what to say.

"So you're lost," he said rather than asked and did not seem to expect a reply.

"Not really," she said after a moment. "But I'm rarely in this part of town."

He nodded and the myriad lines in his face all moved wonderfully and at once and for some reason made her think of the shifting patterns of sun and foam on the surface of the ocean.

"It's a nice place to walk," she went on. "To kill time."

"If only we could," he answered, with no trace of humor, as his dark eyes concentrated upon her with renewed seriousness and an unmistakable look of regret.

"That would be something," she found herself saying, "to kill it, once and for all. Too bad, it kills us first." And with that, the surprise of that unique moment began to fade, or rather, she grew accustomed to its extraordinariness and her melancholy returned.

"Such thoughts, on this beautiful afternoon of sun and rain — being lost, as I recall, has its

322

dangers." And thereupon the old bookseller took a step back into the interior of his shop.

"Do you mind if I come in?" she asked, peering at the rows and rows of books behind him.

"I think," he answered, still studying her with those startling eyes, seeming still to scrutinize her very soul and to wonder at it, "I think you'd better."

This remark did not surprise her in the least, nor did any part of their unusual conversation — for it seemed to her that she had long been expected.

Inside his shop the bookseller ensconced himself high up, behind the raised cashier's desk and gazed down at his visitor over stacks of books. His hound took up a post at the entrance to the residential wing of the house.

"I'm looking for something," the woman began, "completely escapist."

"You won't find it here," came the deep, yet unreproving reply.

"No?" she turned and gestured at the rows of books. "Not in all that literature?"

"Not in any of it. It won't take you away from reality; it will bring you closer to it. You see, these are <u>good</u> books."

She signed but resumed chatting. Shortly he asked her name.

"Clara Chimes," she said at once. "And you must be Mr. Tannini."

"You read the sign."

She nodded and, when they continued talking, soon found herself explaining that she had a great deal of time on her hands because she had just been fired from her clerical job at a book publishing house. He knew the particular house and had nothing good to say about it, but asked why she had been fired.

"For labor organizing."

"You hardly look like my idea of a trade unionist," Mr. Tannini smiled. "But then the ones I knew — that was long ago, and in another country, and they weren't fired, they were killed."

Their conversation continued throughout the afternoon. In the course of it, two things happened. Clara realized that she was speaking with a man whose values and outlook had been formed in another era and that, as a result, he regarded the present time as something of a dark age. He had much to say about the decline of literacy and about the rise, throughout the world, of torture. This, to him, appeared to be the absolute and fearsome portent of the decline into modern barbarism. It had nearly disappeared from the West, he remarked, after the Enlightenment. But now it had returned in such Western countries as those in Latin Amreica. He was extremely gloomy on this subject and had evidently thought about it a great deal. This decline into ignorance and brutality and modern mindlessness was, he said, as advanced in Europe as in America and he, originally from Italy, who had lived all over Europe, the Mediterranean and Russia had never, he said, had so much reason for pessimism as in the present time.

Secondarily, Clara was encouraged to talk about herself. By the time she reached the events of the preceding summer and her abandonment of real estate, Mr. Tannini had become very curious. She explained that at first she had not known what to do with herself. She had passed the early autumn disconsolate and disoriented. She had signed up for some first year philosophy courses at a local university, and though these had kept her occupied through the short, hot days of the Indian summer, they had not dispelled the uncertainty, the vague unease besetting her. It seemed that she did not fit in anywhere, not in school and not in the series of part-time jobs that she had held throughout that year. She had also, she explained, resumed a number of language courses from high school and taken introductory Hebrew.

The old man's eyes sparkled at this. They sparkled as she had never seen eyes sparkle before.

She explained that she had wanted to read the medieval Hebrew mystic poets, but added that she had soon realized that it would take years to attain that level of competence.

"Not necessarily," was Mr. Tannini's reply. And thereupon he commenced a pedagogical lecture, exhorting her to read in these various languages every day. It did not matter what she read, he explained, just so long as she read. For some reason, Clara believed him and said so, but did not, she said, believe in her own ability.

He looked concerned at this, but presently replied: "Then I will help you."

It was not an offer, it was a statement of fact, of how things would be. And the moment he said it, she was immensely relieved. He explained that she could have a job in the bookstore, that there was little work but that he did need help. Above all, it was quiet there. She could read, and he could help her, and this could go on as long as she liked. She asked if she could begin immediately, that afternoon.

"I think you'd better," was his reply. And she did.

To Elizabeth Darlinger, it was at first just another in the succession of Clara's meaningless jobs. Though she and her niece had soon reconciled over Clara's departure from Darlinger-Fairless, she never felt constrained to withhold her opinion of Clara's activities or indeed of Clara's character. As with her stepson, her opinion of her niece had abruptly changed. "A wayward fritterbug," she had proclaimed to Ward Fairless that year. "Who would've thought it? She seemed so stable — but there she is, frittering her life away on books and stupid part-time jobs." She even wrote her stepson to this effect. "You'll be happy to know," she announced in one letter to Paul, "that Clara's turned out to be just as pigheaded a little monster as you. Quite the enfant terrible. No sooner does she turn up her nose at the family business, then she comes to me and demands her portion of the wicked old witch's estate. I, of course, said 'not on your life. After the way you've behaved, I wouldn't trust you with a subway token.' Besides, it's not as if she's in any real difficulty. Though the money from the mob side of her family is tied up in stocks and whatnot, she could always sell. Which is just what I'm afraid of. That Mr. Chimes certainly knew how to invest. It would be just like Clara to go and undo the work of two generations. Fortunately I think I've managed to pound that into her head. So now she's working for some Italian, who's a hundred if he's a day, in his musty old book shop. I haven't seen it, but it sounds absolutely ghastly. The Longhills say to leave her alone, because she'll come out of it. Rita says it's not so bad, look at their oldest son, who's in that horrid EST thing and has got so he talks in a way where she can't understand a word he says. Monica holds the same view. After all, what's going on with Sunny is absolutely, unspeakably UNBELIEVABLE. If you ever decide to come home, I'll tell you about it. It would take two years to write, but naturally the WHOLE THING is Clara's fault. That stubborn fritterbug. It must run in the family. Well, write me more than three words one of these days. And for God's sake keep your clothes on. Toodles. Love and kisses, Mom."

Clara had, to tell the truth, not paid very much attention to the momentous events swirling around Sunny. After all, Sunny had never been happier, so Clara, aside from occasional complaints that she did not see her much anymore, left the matter alone. But then, one bright spring Saturday morning, as she lay in bed reading the <u>Theatetus</u> and drinking lemonade, the whole affair was brought forcibly to her attention. Three screaming and hysterical middle-aged people had burst into her apartment. At first Clara had no idea what was going on, but involuntarily and from long habit crossed her eyes at the sight of the pink Bermuda shorts and salt and pepper mane of Horace LaMarque.

"You've got to stop it!" Monica, in matching pink Bermuda shorts, was shrieking.

"Uncross those eyes, you little fritterbug. Before they get stuck there just like what's his name who became a zombie." Thus Elizabeth.

"Not a zombie, a vegetable. He couldn't even walk," Horace clarified, munching on an apple. "No less play tennis."

"Who said anything about tennis! All you think about is tennis, while our daughter, my daughter, little Sunny has run off —"

"She did, huh?" Clara had sat up with interest. "So they're shacking up?"

"Worse!" Monica moaned.

"Worse?"

"Eloped," munch, munch on the apple.

"Yeah? Where to?"

"Hawaii, where else? Where does anybody elope to?" Monica fumed.

"Oh boy, oh boy," Clara hopped out of bed, "got their number?"

"At the Honolulu Hilton, where else? You can look it up.'

"Oh boy, oh boy!" Clara dashed into the bathroom and started getting dressed.

"I don't know what you're so excited about," Elizabeth said. "They're half way across the world and you're running around like a chicken with its head cut off."

"You've got to talk her into getting it annulled," Monica went on.

"Annulled?!" Clara stuck her head out of the bathroom.

"Kid's got a hearing problem," munch, munch, "on top of that funny business with the eyes."

"Are you kidding?" Clara went on. "I'm going to get them a wedding present."

"But Clara, don't you see?" Monica cried. "She can't be married to him."

"Why not?"

In a gesture of despair, Monica ran her fingers through her thick, black hair. "Because he's a mobster!" she wailed.

"Stanley? Hunh. I guess he is."

"Now you cut that out Clara Darlinger, Chimes, whatever your name is. You know very well that's what he is. Race tracks, casinos and God knows what else; investigated by the FBI. I don't want to think about it. And I don't have to think about it. You have to think about it. You introduced them."

"Well, what could I do?" Clara asked. "It was love at first sight."

"Yeah?" Horace seemed interested. "Just like that."

"Just like that. Whamo."

"Sunny fell in love at first sight?"

"Yup. Head over heels."

"Never could tell up from down. But that's the first time that ever happened. Exactly," munch, munch, "what does this boy do for a living."

"He's a racketeer!" Monica shrieked. "How many times do I have to tell you." And with that she collapsed in one of Clara's director's chairs.

"Hmm. Well, what does his father do?"

"Ditto," Elizabeth replied. "Even went to jail."

Horace looked concerned. "Well, has he ever been arrested?"

"Stanley? Stanley Katz? Except for drunk driving," Clara explained, "he's never been in trouble with the law."

"Just a little matter of a grand jury here and there," Elizabeth put in, "an occasional federal investigation, you know, trifles like that."

"Well," munch, munch, "If he likes Sunny—"

"Boy does he like Sunny," Clara said. "I've never seen him like anything so much. Frankly, I think they were made for each other. They like all the same things."

"Such as?" Monica challenged.

"Yeah," Horace put in. "Name one thing Sunny likes besides Coca Cola."

"Stanley likes that too."

"Name another thing."

"Lying on the beach."

"And another."

Clara looked perplexed. "That's it. Like I said, they're made for each other."

Horace looked at his wife. "Sara may have a point."

"Clara."

"Sorry. I get all Sunny's friends mixed up."

"And she doesn't have a point," Monica contradicted. "I don't see what in the world our little Sunny could have in common with a, a criminal!" And with that she glared at her husband defiantly.

"Hmm. Well, you're father wasn't exactly straight as an arrow. Pittsburgh underworld."

"One lousy bet on a horse and I'm the daughter of a Mafia don," Monica complained. "He'll never shut up about it."

"Got any idea how much he makes a year?" Horace inquired.

"Hard to say," Clara answered. "Touchy tax situation, if you know what I mean. But I'd guess a couple of hundred thousand."

"Monica," munch, munch, "I always said, 'live and let live.' Besides he's a good-looking kid. Honest face. Look on the bright side. None of that wedding nonsense, putting up with your family all over the house. No pink baby Rolls Royces. By the way, that Mercedes he drives — how long's he had it?"

"A year," Clara answered.

"Better take it in while he's still got the warranty. Something's wrong under the hood. Vote for Reagan?"

"Nope. Carter."

"Uh-oh," munch, munch, "a Democrat. We'll have to take care of that."

"Well, I don't know that he's a Democrat."

"All mobsters are Democrats. Democratic party's run by the mob."

At this both Clara and Elizabeth looked up in surprise. Even Monica seemed startled.

"But no matter," Horace went on. "We'll have a talk. When I'm done with Stuart, he won't make a mistake like that again."

"You mean Stanley."

"Stuart, Stanley, Tom, Dick, Harry, I don't care who Sunny picked. Point is he's my son in law, he'll vote Republican. I don't care if he's named Alistair."

That, unfortunately for Clara's peace of mind, was not the end of the Sunny/Stanley complaints. No sooner had they eloped than, it seemed to Clara, they were back on the East Coast to pick up Sunny's things and arrange for her move to the Nevada ranch. Elizabeth and the Longhills sojourned down to the Main Line by plane "to get a look at the love birds." It was an eventful trip. Elizabeth returned with tales of an emergency landing in New Jersey, a monumental quarrel between Ray and Rita over whether they would rent a car from Hertz or Avis (Rita: "But we've always rented cars from Avis, darling, not once can I remember renting from anyone else." Ray: "That, Honeybunny, is because there's something wrong with your memory. I hate Avis. I've always hated Avis. Ever since they rented me a lemon in 1953 and I got stuck in the desert outside San Antonio. I make a point of renting from Hertz. They're number one." Rita:"But sugarbaby you know I always like the underdog. That's why I've used Avis. They're number two. Besides, if you rent a Hertz, I'm not going." And so on.), of more foul play down by the duck pond on the part of the incorrigible Sunny dog, of an endless and stupefying lecture delivered by Horace LaMarque to his son in law on the history of the Republican party, and of Sunny and Stanley necking or worse at every opportunity in every corner of the house. "They're absolute nincompoops," Elizabeth proclaimed. "Just try, I defy you to try to hold a conversation with them for more than ten seconds. A pair of airheads. Their children won't even <u>have</u> IQs. It's beyond stupidity. It's complete vacuity. Positively amazing that boy can make a living. No wonder he had to turn to crime."

By this time Clara had been working for Mr. Tannini for over a month and was well immersed in Hebrew and Italian literature. She arrived in the bookstore every day at nine, but there was so little work to be done that by ten she was seated at a table with a dictionary and her books, reading and drinking lemonade. Mr. Tannini had taken to keeping an enormous supply of it in his refrigerator. Meanwhile Mr. Tannini came and went. Sometimes he too spent the day reading. Often he helped Clara with a difficult passage, and just as often they became entangled in hermeneutic controversies over the substance of what she was reading. These debates were immensely enjoyable for both parties. Since Clara was by nature stubborn and disputatious, while Mr. Tannini delighted in argument for its own sake, their discussions went on for hours. The were frequently interrupted by the visits of Mr. Tannini's friends, who were, in Clara's opinion, a most motley crew. His acquaintance was broad and various. The people who dropped by his shop to chat seemed to come from every part of the social spectrum. And they all had great respect for the old man. But neither they, nor Clara, nor, it seemed, anyone, was ever invited into Mr. Tannini's house. Clara decided that this was most mysterious and for a while engaged in elaborate imaginings about her employer's abode. In the end, "the old wizard," as she had taken to referring to him, explained that his house was so cluttered with memorabilia that he would be embarrassed for anyone to see it.

"So the old wizard's off to Italy," Elizabeth commented one bright weekend morning. She had dropped by to read an article on a change in the rent stabilization law to Clara and had been unpleasantly surprised to find Clara just as ready to read to her from, of all things <u>De Consolatione Philosophiae</u>. "Who is this Boethius?" Elizabeth snapped after a few minutes.

"A great man," Clara explained, "a Roman statesman and philosopher who was thrown in prison by Theodoric the Ostrogoth —"

"Hmmph."

"— and finally put to death in 524 A. D."

"Serves him right for being such a bore."

"That had nothing to do with it. He was executed for treason."

"Another argument for capital punishment."

"Nonsense." Clara retorted and then intoned "Nubila mens est/ Vinctaque frenis; Haec ubi regnant."

"Hunh? Who dat?"

"'For where these terrors reign in the mind, they it do bind in cloudy errors.' Isn't that terrific? And to think, they killed him, the Philistines."

"Let's not bring the Middle East into it. Besides, what do you expect —writing in that jargon. What is it, Latin? Is this what Mr. Tanninski's filling your brain with?"

"Tannini."

"Tanninski, Tannini. All those ethnic names sound alike. Where'd he go — the Riviera?"

"No, Bologna."

"Bologna, baloney. What kind of a place is that to spend a vacation?"

"It's got the oldest university in the West."

"And he may be the oldest man in the West. Spitting image of Father Time, if you ask me, but a little over-aged to be going to college. What happened to the AC? It must be a thousand degrees in this dump."

"Electricity's all screwed up. Landlord's trying to evict us, wants to co-op the building."

"What's his name?"

"Hers. Shatzenkammer."

"Any relation to?"

"You bet," Clara replied. "His wife, Wilhelmina. We call her Willy for short. She's also a shrink. Bought the building a few months ago. I'm the leader of the tenant's association."

Elizabeth's jaw dropped open. Then she snapped it shut with the word, "Fiddlesticks!"

"We'll have her tied up in court for years. Get this: 'Neither do we in vain put our hope in God or pray to Him: for if we do this well and as we ought, we shall not lose our labor or be without effect...There is, if you will not dissemble, a great necessity of doing well

344

imposed upon you, since you live in the sight of your Judge, who beholdeth all things.'"

"Sounds like the junk they used to read us in church. If Marilyn could hear you now, she'd roll over in her grave. Speaking of which, Ward's got at least one foot in his. They're not letting him out of the hospital for another week. You might visit him, you know. Bad enough Paul's been gone five years and all he can do is send telegrams, saying things like 'Acupuncture.' You'd think he'd get sick of running all over the world without his clothes on. Then again you'd think you'd get sick of lying in bed reading hieroglyphics with no clothes on.The both of you are wayward. Only explanation is bad genes. Every time I think of him up in that plane I know we got a nutcase on our hands. Likes to fly upside down."

"What plane?"

"Paul's plane. The one he bought so he can spend all his time flying upside down."

345

"I didn't know he could fly."

"He can't, from the sound of it. Rita says it's a miracle he hasn't killed himself. Especially with that broken arm. I didn't tell you, he broke his arm in Singapore, on an escalator."

"What escalator?"

"In the Singapore airport. Says the escalator attacked him. According to his partner, it was the other way around."

"Paul attacked an escalator? In the Singapore airport?"

"Singapore, Hong Kong, what's the difference? He could have been in Antarctica for all he knew. A four-day bender, walking on limousines and everything, according to his partner. Just our luck. Now we got a drunk in the family."

"A bender here, a bender there. Doesn't mean he's an alcoholic."

"How about a bender everywhere. When you get so you're walking over the hoods of limousines rather than going around them, I say you're ready for AA." With that Elizabeth snorted and seized the opportunity to read aloud to her niece. When she had read to her satisfaction, she commanded Clara to get up and dressed. Mrs. Darlinger wanted to go shopping. And since it was the one activity they could share without disagreement, Clara complied. Not that they bickered all the time, but since Clara had left the family firm, Elizabeth had become more critical than usual. Her attitude suggested that there was much to find fault with in her niece, that Clara somehow and in many situations fell short of the mark. She had even taken to describing Clara to her friends in the same terms she applied to Paul — as someone hovering perpetually on the brink of insanity. It was as if Elizabeth's trust, once shattered, opened the way for any sort of disaster. Indeed she seemed to live in the continual expectation that the worst, as far as her niece was concerned, was yet to come.This had long been her view of her stepson, and so accustomed had she become to predicting catastrophe for him that it was with vague astonishment that, every now and then, she realized that nothing truly dreadful had happened. But with Clara the doubt was nearer, and therefore Elizabeth regarded her more keenly, wondering what form her demise would take. Perhaps, like the Longhill's eldest son, it would be EST, and from time to time, she quizzed her niece to detect any fatal leanings toward therapy or guru cults. So far she had found none, but this had only fueled her conviction that something so awful she had not thought of it was about to occur. For a brief time, at the beginning of Clara's employment in Mr. Tannini's shop, she had seemed so energetic, so cheerful, that Elizabeth thought she might be taking cocaine. Mrs. Darlinger took to poking her head in her niece's refrigerator whenever she visited, but saw no trace of drugs. She took to making leading remarks, to the effect that so-and-so's daughter had "turned into a hopeless coke-head," but Clara would invariably reply, "what do you expect with a bunch of nitwits like her parents?"

For a while, Elizabeth had entertained the nightmare that her niece was going to become a labor organizer. Happily, this storm passed. Thereafter, she had thought that Clara might have some boyfriend even worse than Philip Angelica or Paul Fairless. When repeated probes revealed nothing of the sort, the horrifying idea occurred to Mrs. Darlinger that her niece might be a lesbian. If so, she wondered, with whom was Clara engaging in her depraved practices? Her suspicions immediately settled upon Sunny LaMarque. But, after tormenting herself for a day or so with this notion, she had decided "to take the bull by the horns," and watch the two girls closely. She had ample opportunity, but nothing seemed amiss. Then Sunny had eloped with Stanley Katz, leaving Elizabeth to conclude that Sunny and Clara were probably not having an affair. In the absence of any such calamity, Elizabeth finally came to believe that Clara, like Paul, was on the edge of a nervous breakdown. She had contented herself with this idea until that very morning, when Clara mentioned the tenants' association. "The calm before the storm," Mrs. Darlinger thought of Clara's previous and apparent well being. "I knew something was cooking." And since Elizabeth conceived of tenant leaders as a generally scruffy and ill dressed lot, her idea of a cure, though she knew it would be a long one and take weeks, perhaps months, was to keep Clara busy with such things as her appearance and apparel.

Their first stop was Saks, where Elizabeth announced her intention to buy Clara an evening dress.

"But I don't need one," came the predictable reply.

"Phooey. You can never be too skinny, too rich, and you can never own too many clothes," Elizabeth rejoined.

"But I have more clothes than I know what to do with."

"Then why are you wearing that hideous rag?" Elizabeth replied, indicating Clara's T-shirt dress.

"I like it. Besides I don't need fancy clothes, because I don't go to those deadly parties anymore."

"Which, my child, is another thing I've been meaning to talk to you about," Elizabeth retorted, while marching off in the direction of the designer dresses. They passed the afternoon in one store after another and then retreated to

351

Elizabeth's duplex, to reexamine their loot.
Clara was trying on her new red bathing suit
for a second time when the phone rang.

"For you," Elizabeth gurgled.She was
drinking gin and tonic.

It was a friend of Mr. Tannini's, a semi-
alcoholic poet named Grimes who said he was
on his way to upstate New York and could
therefore no longer take care of the old
bookseller's dog. Clara arranged to meet with
him that evening, get the keys and then go feed
and walk the dog.

"You can stay there if you like," Grimes said.
"It's more convenient since you work there
every day anyway."

"At Mr. Tannini's?"

"Sure. That's what I've been doing. Made
sort of a mess I'm afraid, but it's a nice place all
the same."

At six o'clock Clara was on her way
downtown, with a small overnight bag of

accessories, to take up residence in "the haunted house," as Elizabeth called it. From the street, however, it did not look haunted at all. Grimes had every light on, and the place seemed bright and lively. Clara rang the bell, and the gray-haired poet, smelling distinctly of bourbon, opened the door, saluted her, handed her the keys, and then marched off, albeit unsteadily, into the night.

The four story house seemed much bigger inside than it looked from the street. More than once, after she had fed and walked the dog, Clara got lost in its maze of corridors and stairways. It was, as Mr. Tannini had said, indeed cluttered. But there was something warm, friendly and above all tasteful about this clutter. Huge mahogany bookcases with glass panes lined one hallway, with books on the shelves that Clara had never heard of, in languages she had never know existed. Mr. Tannini evidently had an interest in old prints and cartography — everywhere, in the shadowed halls, in the dim, high-ceilinged rooms, were archaic maps and framed lithographs, mainly reproductions of what looked to be some originals by Daumier. But best of all was a large, oddly shaped room on the third floor, evidently a study, to which there were five entrances, including a spiral staircase in a corner. It was here that Grimes had clearly spent most of his time, and Clara at once understood why. There was something hidden, secret, yet so inviting about this spot with its high windows, leather couches and gray carpet with the maroon floral pattern. The room had many nooks and crannies: here and there were armchairs with antique lamps and side tables. In one corner stood an old, roll-top desk, flanked on either side by plaster busts of Plato and Aristotle. In another, beside an oak table covered with books, papers and two typewriters, was an enormous globe. Maps, paintings and etchings hung on the wall, most striking among them a reproduction of the Daumier oil "Passers by." To Clara it seemed that this picture conveyed all the ominous splendor of people separate and going their own ways scarcely aware of their fleeting partnership in one haphazard moment. It seemed to be the living image, the only possible image and an enigmatic one, a warning, of chance itself. She studied it for quite some time, then turned to the center of the room, where there rose up an immense fireplace. A fire was roaring in it, the heat offset by cool breezes which entered through the high, open windows on the garden side of the room. As Clara approached the large leather couch that faced the fire, one of the many ancient clocks in the room began to chime seven times. Soon the others followed, and for a brief interval the air filled with the sound of clinks and bells, glass, silver, crystal and brass; it was impossible to tell them apart in that mingled tintinnabulation of innumerable chimes.

That night she happened to fall asleep on the huge leather couch, dreaming all the while of the house in which she slept, its halls and corridors radiating from her room like the spokes of a wheel. And now and then in her dreams she traversed those halls which were high and bright and endless and led everywhere in the world. One startling vista unfolded after another, some of preternatural beauty. But not in one of them did she find a single, other human being. And yet, unaccountably, she knew she was not alone.

The morning light filtered into the room, revealing the young woman in her green T-shirt dress, asleep on the leather couch. She slept face down, her tangled auburn hair glinting in the sun and one arm outstretched over a side table, the hand at rest on a black telephone. Across the room, guarding the main entrance, sat the white hound, wide awake.When the clocks began chiming eight times, she stirred and soon sat up, blinking in the light. The profound repose of her sleep and that of the room around her made it difficult at first to wake. But as she stretched and then staggered off in search of a bathroom, the dreams of the preceding night began vividly to recur. And it seemed to Clara, as she splashed water on her face from a sink, that she had been traveling all night, that her dreams had been one journey after another, and that she had never dreamt like that before.

She passed the entire week in this state of strange repose, only leaving the house to walk the dog or buy groceries, telephoning no one, talking to no one except an occasional customer in the bookstore. Every night she returned to that marvelous room, buried, it seemed to her, in the very core of the house, and slept on the couch, dreaming and dreaming, of long journeys through foreign terrain, of travels that never tired her, though she always made them on foot.

Every morning she rose to find the dog awake at the entrance way, as if it had been guarding the house while she slept. Indeed by the end of the week, she had begun to wonder whether she was sleep-walking, and at the cause of these remarkable dreams, and at the nature of the connection, for she was sure it existed, with Mr. Tannini's house. But she had no clue and in the end simply came to believe that the place was magical. It had, undeniably, wrought a change in her state of mind. It had made her peaceful — though how or why, she had not the slightest idea.

Into this splendid solitude and without disrupting it, strode Mr. Tannini one fine May afternoon. His travels seemed to have refreshed him, to have made him look younger. In a glance, he took in Clara's altered mood.

"You've been staying in the house," he smiled with characteristic prescience, as he puffed on his cigar and seemed to point at something beyond a bookshelf with his lion's head cane.

"I hope you don't mind," Clara replied.

"I hope <u>you</u> don't mind," he answered, gesturing as if to tip his brown felt hat, "the clutter. Some people find it a mess."

She explained that on the contrary it had been delightful, especially the very cluttered room on the third floor, to which he replied by informing her that she was welcome to stay in that room as long as she liked. "So the 'Passers by' appealed to you" he remarked and then answered her vigorous nod, "so stay with it. The room is yours." And she did, for the entire month of May.

Suspecting the worst, Elizabeth disapproved of this arrangement. "Damn peculiar," she said to Rita Longhill.

"Well, darling, if you think that's peculiar, what about running around worshiping some quack with a phony German name, five years after everyone else has given up on it. That's what EST is."

"Thing I don't understand is why the kid doesn't come down here and swim in the pool." Thus Horace LaMarque, eating handfuls of granola out of a plastic bag. The were seated around the LaMarque's pool, sunbathing. "Not healthy, if you ask me."

"Well she didn't," Monica snapped. "And at least Clara had to good sense not to run off and marry a Mafioso."

"Not Mafioso," munch, munch. "Katz is a Jewish name. Cosa Nostra's all Italians. You ought to know that. You saw <u>The Godfather</u>."

"Jewish, Italian. Point is I don't like her hanging around the two thousand year old man," Elizabeth went on. "Kid's turning into a real nut job. Just like what's his face, flying upside down with no clothes on."

"Making good money though," munch, munch.

"Who?" Monica asked. "What's his face?"

"No, Stuart."

"Stanley."

"Sorry. I get all Sunny's boyfriends mixed up. Anyway makes a mint. Flies a helicopter around his ranch, says he's going to teach Sunny. I warned him. Another plane in the sky, she'll hit it. A mountain nearby, she'll fly right into it. Never could drive anything, can't sit still. Kid's got ants in her pants."

"She's dancing," Monica explained. "When she's driving, she dances in her seat. She told me."

"Clara does it too. A regular ballerina," Elizabeth snorted. "I just hope what's his name sits still when he's flying upside down,

361

screaming 'bombs away.' Usually bombed out of his mind, according to his partner."

"A little nip now and then never hurt anyone, dear," Ray remarked, finishing his Bloody Mary.

"We're not talking about a little nip," Elizabeth gurgled. She was drinking scotch and soda. "We're talking about caseloads. Got a light?" Ray obliged her with a match.

"Libby," munch, munch, munch, "you ever read the surgeon general's report?"

"Of course she hasn't," Monica snapped, lighting a cigarette. "For the same reason I haven't. It's thousands of pages long, morbid, and boring."

"Maybe dull, but so are most things in life. Look at me. I quit smoking, started eating raw foods. Never felt better. Even my hair's growing faster, not going bald like most people — no offense Ray."

""If I took offense at remarks like that, I'd have been divorced years ago."

"Now sweetydear, you know that's not true."

"On the contrary, honeybunch, you know that it is."

"Ahem," Elizabeth cut in, hoping to head off a dispute.

"Something in your throat?" Horace asked. "Better read that report, Libby." At this Elizabeth began coughing in earnest.

"Here, have some granola."

"Would you stop it, Horace, with your nauseating health foods?" Monica demanded. "Do something. She's choking to death. Do that thing you're always practicing on me."

Horace perked up. "My Heimlich maneuver?"

Rita sat up with sudden interest. "I've always wondered how that was done. I've spent literally hours wondering how it works."

"I always suspected, darling, that yours was one of the great minds of our generation. Now I'm sure of it."

"Too late folks," Elizabeth said, gesturing for Horace to get away from her, "I'm going to live."

"Rats," Horace snapped his fingers. "Let me show how it's done anyway."

"Not on your life. You break a rib or something, then I'll have to sue you, just like that friend of Ward's who was in a car accident. Thrown right out of the window, lying there on the highway, all covered with blood, and some doctor tried to help him. Couldn't have paid me to touch him, bloody mess like that. Oh, what is his name? He sued that doctor and made a fortune. Clara said it was criminal."

"The suit?" Ray asked. "Or the doctor trying to help?"

"The suit."

"Kid's got some strange ideas," munch, munch, munch, "couldn't sue in a spot like that,

364

the whole insurance business would collapse, to say nothing of the American economic system."

Monica regarded her husband with one of her habitual looks of surprise.

"That wouldn't bother Clara," Elizabeth huffed. "She's turned into the most un-American little fritterbug you ever saw. Last month it was labor unions, this month its tenant organizing. Next thing you know she'll be singing the International."

"Uh-oh," Horace's eyes had narrowed, "sounds like a Democrat to me. All those Democrats are half-way to Moscow."

"I beg your pardon," Ray interrupted. "It so happens my tennis partner has voted Democratic in every election since the war."

"That may be," Horace's eyes flashed. "But the question is — is he a registered Democrat?"

"Hmm. Tell you the truth, I really don't know."

"I'll bet you anything Clara is," Mrs. Darlinger put in. "I don't know what's come over her. Used to be completely apolitical. Didn't know Eisenhower from Roosevelt, McGovern from Reagan. All of a sudden wowie zowie — a pinko, intellectual snob. What's his name went through a phase like this too. Voted Democratic at least once I know of."

"You mean Paul?" Monica asked politely and then, "Sometimes our conversations seem to become so, I don't know, so vague."

Elizabeth nodded. "Paul. And we <u>know</u> he's crazy as a bedbug. I hope he doesn't come home while she's in this phase. They always brought out the worst in each other."

"Well, darling, it certainly doesn't sound like it can come to any good." Rita grandly concluded before walking over to the diving board. It was quite a concession. Until that moment, Rita had always fiercely maintained that no matter what Clara did, it just could not compare, in its potential for disaster, with the errors of her oldest son.

"No," Elizabeth muttered glumly, as Rita began bouncing on the board. "It can't come to anything good." At that Rita plunged into the water, with a tremendous splash.

Unperturbed by her aunt's dire predictions, Clara passed a serene and dreamy month at Mr. Tannini's. Toward June, however, she became restive and so relocated to her West Side apartment. That summer, working for Mr. Tannini, passed very quickly. Clara read a number of Italian classics in the original, among them the <u>Divine Comedy</u> and <u>Orlando Furioso</u>, and tormented her aunt with lengthy readings. "She's become an insufferable little egghead," Mrs. Darlinger told her friends. Clara suspected as much, because whenever she saw the LaMarques, Horace would say. "How's that Ariosto? Hear it's one of the best restaurants in town." He seemed to think this a hilarious joke.

Toward summer's end Clara, at first tentatively, but later resolutely, resumed her scientific studies. More than once, Mr. Tannini was surprised to find her reading a college physics textbook. She began inquiring about books on the history and philosophy of science. He was very helpful, but more than once she caught him watching her sadly. Indeed on the very day that she finished the textbook, as she snapped it shut with an exclamation of satisfaction, "Well! That's that!" she glanced up and saw him across the room, gazing at her with a mournful expression in his limpid eyes. She asked what was the matter.

"I'll be sad to see you go," he said, "now that you've found your way."

This reply seemed no more cryptic than most of his comments, but it stayed with her. In the ensuing weeks, Clara found herself mulling it over and wondering at its significance. Then one morning it became clear.

She arrived at the bookstore to find Mr. Tannini on the threshold, exactly as she had seen him on the day of their first meeting. She knew he was there before she saw him, because from the corner she had noticed the blue and curling plume of cigar smoke unrolling over the sidewalk and then spiraling up into the boughs of the locust tree like a secret, evanescent script.

"Something lucky," he said without even a hello, "has come up." He went on to explain that a friend of his, an astrophysicist, who worked at his laboratory at his university on Long Island needed an assistant and had agreed to take Clara on, on a trial basis, starting in the autumn. "Oh boy!" Clara exclaimed and then before she could even thank him, Mr. Tannini smiled and said:"I thought you'd say that."

Weeks before that crisp, sunny day in October when she went to work for him, Clara was introduced to Slava Aster, the strangest looking man she thought she had ever seen. He was very tall, lanky and covered with freckles. From his short, reddish blond hair and extremely pale green eyes, one would never have guessed that he was over fifty. The combination of an East European accent, a slight lisp and his habit of speaking quite softly, made it difficult at first to understand a word the astrophysicist said. But Clara soon got the knack of communicating with Slava Aster. It was his morose face, however, that took the most getting used to. All of his features, from his upward slanting eyes to his downturned mouth, seemed to be at odds with each other, as if the long, rather pointy nose did not like the company of the high cheekbones, as if the slightly receding chin were offended by everything above it, as if his freckles had

III

sprouted up in revolt against his pale, nearly translucent albino skin. He seemed conscious that people found his appearance unusual and, being diffident, this made him exceedingly shy. So Clara —who liked him despite the fact that she found him "a little birdy," as she described his particular form of absent-mindedness — took pains to put him at ease. She soon learned that the key to friendship with Slava Aster was to talk as little as possible. The astrophysicist was uneasy with idle conversation, and he adored silence.

They became great friends, passing many evenings in the laboratory. In the course of a week together, Clara and Slava Aster would exchange maybe a hundred words. To Clara's complete surprise, on the one occasion when they met, Mrs. Darlinger and the astrophysicist liked each other immensely. "He may look like a Martian," Elizabeth said. "But a man who knows how to keep his mouth shut doesn't come

371

a dime a dozen." Slava Aster, in turn, in one of his rare fits of loquacity and indeed in the only comment Clara ever heard him make about another person, observed that "your aunt is an exceptional woman. Though she may seem a little eccentric, she certainly knows a great deal about everybody. She is an excellent judge of character, perhaps the best I have ever met." Clara could not even find words to reply to this. She simply gaped.

A year passed, and then nearly another. By the time Clara was approaching her twenty-fifth birthday, it seemed now and then that there had never been any other life aside from working for Slava Aster. Every day she made the long commute to Long Island. Every day passed in near silence in the company of the astrophysicist, either in his office or laboratory. Often she did not return home until late in the evening, because when the weather was good, Slava Aster would finagle time at the mini-observatory, to gaze at the stars. She had gone up with him many times to watch the heavens at night and never tired of it; and frequently, after an evening of looking at the stars, she would drive her Chevette onto the shoulder of the highway, while going home, park, and step out to look at the night sky again and at the stars, with which she was now so familiar.

Elizabeth found her niece's routine depressing and pestered her to "go out more; after all, anything would be more than nothing," to come to the country and to meet the various sons of her various friends. But Clara had little time for the social life her aunt envisioned. Sometimes she missed it and thought herself very alone. Then she would contemplate the existence of Slava Aster who, as far as she could tell, had no friends and no family, and when she did, her own life seemed a veritable hubbub of social activity.

Suddenly, in the spring, it very nearly was. Her landlady, wife of the little lamented Dr. Shatzenkammer, had become most determined to get rid of her tenants once and for all. Though no longer head of the tenants' association, Clara was an active member, and therefore had to attend numerous late night and weekend meetings. Neighbors began dropping by at all hours. The phone rang incessantly. By the time they went on a rent strike, Clara was sick of the whole business.

But it was with great anger that she returned home one night to discover that she and a number of other residents had been locked out of their apartments. One tenant, who had got the key for the new locks from the very reluctant and surly super, had opened the door only to find his furniture missing, "in storage," as the building's managing agent said. At first merely furious, Clara soon became terrified at the thought of what might have happened to her cat. By the time she got into her apartment and saw the furniture gone, she was in a panic. She ran from room to room, then out onto the fire escape, calling for Rainy. But there was no sign of him. She went up to the top floor and worked her way down to the basement, knocking on every door, checking in all the doorways — no one had seen the black and white cat with the green eyes. At midnight she phoned Elizabeth.

"Well, looks like you better stay here," Mrs. Darlinger said.

But by then Clara was in tears over the cat, so Elizabeth got in a cab and came to get her.

"Check the basement?" Elizabeth demanded.

"Yes," sob, sob. "He's not there, not anywhere."

"What about the roof?"

"He couldn't get up on the roof."

"Oh yeah?" In minutes Elizabeth was drawn into the search, pestering neighbors and poking through old furniture in the cellar, screaming, "Come on you goddamn cat. It's past my bedtime."

At two a.m. they gave up and went down to the street.

"That's him," Clara clamored at the sound of a meow.

"A thousand alley cats in New York City and you think that's him?"

But by then Clara was on her hands and knees, peering under a car parked in front of her building. "It is him," she said, looking up at Elizabeth.

"Well for God's sake tell him to come out and let's go home."

"He won't come out. He's just sitting there, under the middle of the car, looking at me."

Elizabeth let out a snort of exasperation and joined her niece on the asphalt. "You come out of there, you revolting beast," she commanded the cat, who merely pranced gracefully away from her. Clara, on her stomach now, inched over and tried to grab it. But the cat merely walked, rather haughtily, over by another wheel.

"So that's the way it is," Elizabeth said and lunged at the cat, fruitlessly. This went on for some time.

"Hey, uh, lady. Mind if I move my car?" a male voice came from above them.

"No!" Clara shrieked. "My cat's under it."

"How about I just start the engine? That should scare him out."

The two women posted themselves at opposite ends of the car. The man started the engine. The cat raced out under his open door. He accidentally stepped on its tail. The cat shrieked and Clara caught it.

"Good kitty," the man said and attempted to reach up and pet the animal. There came a loud hiss followed by a ferocious spit as the the cat swatted at him.

"Delightful animal. Everyone should have one," Elizabeth remarked, before thanking him and taking her niece home.

***

Clara had not intended to stay at her aunt's more than a week but, one balmy June evening she returned to the duplex to find her aunt sitting alone in the living room, drinking gin and tonic, and looking pale.

"What's up doc?"

When Elizabeth did not answer, but instead just turned and stared at her, Clara knew something was wrong. "Tell me when I'm sitting down," she went on, and seated herself opposite her aunt.

Mrs. Darlinger made an attempt at a sour expression and then said, "went back to the doctor today."

Clara said nothing. After a moment Elizabeth continued, "I'll be damned if they're going to try and keep me cooped up in a hospital bed, even if it is lung cancer."

Clara closed her eyes and, while they were closed, asked, "do they know for sure."

"No doubt about it, kiddo. And very advanced. Says I should have been in for a check up a year ago. Stupid. If they'd found out then, I'd be dead by now, what with their poisons and radiation."

It took a week of non-stop bullying for Clara to convince her aunt to go into the hospital. But Elizabeth did not take well to being an invalid. There was a constant stream of visitors into her private room, where, seated on her bed, clothed in white from head to toe (Elizabeth had, for some reason known only to her, taken to wrapping her hair in a white towel, turban-style), Mrs. Darlinger held court all day long, much to the consternation of her physician and nurses. Visited by Ward and Clara every evening and weekend, she became hypercritical of her niece's attire.

"Black leather pants?!" she exclaimed one evening. "What's next? The cellophane shirt?"

"They happen to be in fashion."

"For who? Aborigines? Are you watering those plants?"

Clara nodded.

"I bet my whole apartment's going to pot. Is what's her name coming in to clean? She's supposed to come twice a week, you know. Sometimes I wonder what I'm paying her for."

"The apartment looks fine Libby," Ward put in.

"What do you know? You're oblivious to your surroundings. Always were."

"He knows and I know that you're having more radiation tomorrow, so you'd better get to sleep at a decent hour tonight."

"Decent!" Elizabeth huffed. "There's nothing decent about this place. Have you <u>seen</u> the food? Canned potatoes! I never even knew such horrors existed. And they won't let me drink. No booze whatsoever. Dr. Schmertz, Schmaltz, whatever he's called, said I'm a borderline alcoholic. The nerve."

Later, on their way down the corridor, Ward and Clara passed Dr. Smeltz. Ward asked about the prognosis and learned nothing he did not know already: that it was very bad, the oat-celled cancer had spread throughout both lungs, into the chest cavity and possibly elsewhere, but that with the cobalt, she might have more than six weeks to live. As they left the grim-faced doctor, Clara noted that Ward looked suddenly very tired and very old. And when they stepped onto the sidewalk, she heard him saying, not to her, not to anyone in particular, "She's all I have." With that, he stepped into a cab and disappeared into the night.

Clara's life had never been lonelier. The duplex seemed vast, sterile and empty. The long drives to and from Long Island were painfully solitary. Often she found herself wishing that Slava Aster liked to talk just a little bit more. The lovely, balmy June evenings only made her feel worse. Several times she caught herself wishing it was raining or cold, so she would not have to see people enjoying themselves in the warm, nocturnal air. But each day was clearer and more beautiful than the last. At night the stars came out by the millions, and they could be seen even in the city. Her visits to Elizabeth's sick bed lasted longer and longer. Ward, it seemed, was all but living in the hospital. His gray hair, Clara noticed, had begun to turn white in places, while his blue eyes, ever old, now looked ancient. And as Elizabeth began to be in pain, his wide, ruddy face became ashen. Often Clara found him gazing blankly out the window into the luxurious sunlight while his ex-wife slept. He had become quiet except that, at Elizabeth's request, he had taken to reading to her from the newspaper.After another week, Elizabeth began demanding laetrile. When refused, she got it in her head to sue the hospital. It took days to talk her out of it and, even then, she sulked. She had not a kind word for either Ward or Clara.

But then, one bright afternoon, Clara walked in carrying a small paper bag. Both Elizabeth and Ward sat up curiously as Clara withdrew a little packet of cigarette papers and began rolling a joint.

"What's that?" Elizabeth demanded.

"No, no, no," Ward said when informed. "It's against hospital regulations. Besides, it involves smoking."

"Balderdash!" Elizabeth exclaimed. "I'm sick of this hospital. I'm sick of their regulations. I'm sick of the doctors. Sick of the nurses. Sick of the technicians and paramedics. Far as I'm concerned, whole disgusting thing could sink into the East River tomorrow and it wouldn't be too soon. Come over here Clara, show me how you smoke that thing." In no time Elizabeth was puffing away quite professionally.

"I don't get it, what's the big deal?" she said after a few minutes, eying the marijuana critically. "Stinks like all get out, but it has no effect whatsoever. Ward, better open the window, smells like a Turkish bazaar in here."

When he sat down again, his ex-wife offered him a joint. "Chicken? I'm telling you, it's nothing. Like sticking your head over a barbecue pit." For a few days, however, Elizabeth smoked her marijuana religiously, now and then exclaiming, "Me, a pothead. Who'd ever believe it? Just wait till I tell Rita."

Rita was intrigued. "Libby, darling, you can't be serious. I mean it's got to have <u>some</u>

effect. Why else would our boys be smoking it all the time?"

"Sweetie dear, sometimes you ask the most puzzling questions." Ray put in.

"Don't ask me," Elizabeth went on. "All it does is make you sleepy."

It made Rita, however, giggly. That afternoon her husband led her out of the hospital in disgust. After another few days, however, Elizabeth tired of "being a drug addict," as she put it. She exchanged her "habit" for a new and, Clara thought, her most insufferable pastime yet: reading aloud from the Old Testament. At first, she harried her family with selections from Job. Then it was Isaiah, next Jeremiah. But what she really seemed to relish was Ecclesiastes.

"The words of the preacher, the son of David, king in Jerusalem," she intoned, sitting up in her bed, her head wrapped in its high white turban. "Vanity of vanities, saith the preacher, vanity of vanities; all is vanity. What profit hath a man of all his labor which he taketh under the sun? One generation passeth away, and another generation cometh. But the earth abideth forever."

"Libby please," Ward beseeched her. "It's morbid. Let me read to you from the Times."

The Times!" she snorted, and then, rather biblically, "What need have I of the Times? It's eternity I'm interested in. The Times! The very name suggests transience. You heard me: it passeth away!" And then very loudly, "The thing that hath been, it is that which shall be; and that which is done is that which shall be done' and there is no new thing under the sun." And with that she glared up defiantly; for into this sermon and indeed into the room, had walked her tall, tanned and healthy stepson.

"Did I interrupt something?" Paul asked, looking from Ward to Clara to Elizabeth.

Mrs. Darlinger continued to glare. Her wasted face had become extremely angular and, with her turban and glittering hazel eyes, she looked most ferocious as she read on: "I have seen all the works that are done under the sun; and behold, all is vanity and vexation of spirit. That which is crooked cannot be made straight, and that which is wanting cannot be numbered. For in much wisdom is much grief; and he that increaseth knowledge increaseth sorrow."

***

At thirty three Paul did not appear much different from the way he had seven years before. If anything he was, according to his stepmother, more addled than ever. To Clara he merely seemed more intolerably pleased with himself. Only his father found him utterly unchanged. Paul, in turn, was shocked by the transformation of Mrs. Darlinger. He alone at once grasped and fully believed the seriousness of her situation. He never said so to his father, but he knew Elizabeth would not survive the summer.

Having taken a leave from her job with Slava Aster, Clara spent most of her afternoons in the hospital, listening to Elizabeth's biblical readings. Paul came too, but frequently, to the unspeakable annoyance of his stepmother, was caught dozing in the midst of her scriptural discourses. Ward looked grayer by the day.

Weeks passed. Toward mid-July, Elizabeth rallied. Despite reservations, Dr. Smeltz agreed to let her go home for a few days. This produced such a terrific effect on her spirits that she was allowed to stay away from the hospital for a week, during which time, she lay around, "recuperating," as she put it, by the LaMarque's pool. By this time the now pregnant Mrs. Sunny Katz had returned to the East Coast to visit her parents. She came bearing tales of wild doings in Nevada.

"You mean you and Stanley and this shyster friend of his go to the racetrack every day?" Elizabeth demanded. She was lying on a lawn chair in a long blue and white striped robe.

Sunny nodded but said nothing. She had a popsicle in her mouth.

"In your condition?" Paul asked, staring at her swollen stomach from which he had seemed unable to remove his gaze since his arrival.

"Uh-hunh," Sunny slurped. "Mom, got any more popsicles?"

"God," Paul's blue eyes widened. He was still staring at her dramatically altered figure, "you've already had three."

"To say nothing of the Ring Dings. Whole boxes," Horace put in, as he bit into a large, raw onion. "Kid'll be born with a Ring Ding in his mouth."

"Better than an onion," Monica said without looking up from the latest issue of <u>Oui</u>

389

magazine. She was reading an article about sex and aging.

Clara came out carrying Hank, the Longhill's cat, in one hand and a glass of lemonade in the other. "Been an accident," she told Rita.

At this Monica, who was reading on her back, let the magazine fall on her face. "I knew it," she said from under the copy of <u>Oui</u>.

"Jeepers creepers child, can't you ever wear clothes?" Elizabeth said, regarding Clara's mauve bikini critically. "There's nothing there at all. You're indecent."

Clara put Hank and the lemonade down and walked over to the pool's edge. Rita asked where this accident had occurred. "On the hall carpet," Clara replied. "I was walking along, finishing the <u>Symposium</u>. Stepped right in it. Disgusting."

"Serves you right," Elizabeth said. "Walking and reading at the same time. Of all things, Plato."

"Great restaurant, I hear," Horace yukked.

"It's not a restaurant," Ray corrected. "It's a sex bar. Plato's Retreat."

"Poor little Hank," Rita cooed at her cat. "Wasums had a little accident, booboo? Wasums doesn't like Plato's."

"Philistines," Clara yawned and stuck her nose in the air. At this, Paul began studying her back.

"Plato wasn't a Philistine, was he Hank darling? He was a Greek." Hank meowed, which caused Sunny dog, digging up Monica's geraniums around the corner of the house to pause and prick up his ears.

"Yes pussy-poo. Booboo doesn't like Greeks."

"Quite a gal, my wife. Speaks her own language and everything."

"Boo boo boo boo boo."

"Baby talk!" Clara exclaimed, her nose still in the air.

"Meow, meow."

Paul rose stealthily to his feet.

"Mom. I said, do you have any more popsicles?"

"Woof, woof."

"Shut up Sunny, I mean Sunny dog. Never could tell the two of you apart."

Hank, his back arched and tail fluffed stalked to the edge of the pool.

"Goddamn dog's been digging up my geraniums. Look at him, covered with dirt."

"Next thing you know he'll go shit in the hall and Clara Darlinger, Chimes, whatever her name is, will go step in it."

"Woof, woof."

"Meow, meow," followed by a hiss and a spit.

"Oy vay," Clara exclaimed, her nose pointed at at the heavens. Paul grabbed her by the waist. Clara screamed. Hank hissed. Sunny dog leapt. Sunny the girl screamed. Clara was pulled over the edge of the pool. Rita shrieked. Paul did not let go in time.A mass of kicking, screaming, scratching cat and dog fur landed with a thud against his legs. Horace's jaw dropped open. Paul lurched forward, his head rather indecently entangled somewhere between Clara's flailing legs. The mass of cat and dog fur followed him over. Rita shrieked again and dove into the water with her glasses and high heels on. Everyone surfaced sputtering.

"You bastard!" Thus Clara, at which point Paul dunked her under the water.

"Get away," Rita coughed. "Get away from my precious, you horrible dog,"

"Woof, woof."

"Ray do something."

"Take your hands off me you shit."

"Paul Darlinger! Fairless I mean. You leave her alone."

"Ray!"

"Sweetheart," Ray replied, ambling over to the edge of the pool, a can of Coca Cola in hand. "Exactly what do you expect me to do?"

Meow," thus Hank as he was handed up. Ray reached down. Sunny dog had one paw on each of Rita's shoulders.

"Sunny, you cut that out," munch, munch on the onion, as Horace approached the pool. He was still holding Monica's designer robe over one arm. "That's no way to treat a guest." Unfortunately, at that moment, with Hank suspended in mid air, Sunny dog felt moved to respond to his master.

"Woof, woof."

Hank sprang. Ray lost his balance, grabbed his host, and in the two of them went.

"My Ann Klein bathing robe!" Monica, magazine in hand, leapt into the pool.

"Quite a circus we've got here," Elizabeth said to Sunny who was watching Paul dive between Clara's legs and then surface with her hanging from his shoulders.

Clara's vocabulary seemed to have failed her. "Oooh," she spluttered furiously, pulling him by the hair back into the water. "Oooh you shit."

"What a foul mouth that child has," Elizabeth remarked, observing her stepson tackle her niece, who in turn bit him on the arm. "Very unladylike."

"Christ!" Paul stared at the red mark on his arm.

"Him too," Elizabeth said. "A bunch of ill behaved brats."

By now Paul was staring furiously at his attacker who was backing away in a distinctly cowardly manner.

"Get away from me, you lunatic!"

"Ray do something!"

"My robe!"

"You little bitch! Now you're asking for it." And so it went.

That night at dinner Clara sat as far away from Paul as possible. "He's a complete barbarian," she said later to Sunny, while jumping up and down on one foot to get the remaining water out of her ear. "I don't know," Sunny replied and appeared for a moment to snicker.

"What's wrong with you?" Clara demanded. "Making faces at me."

"I don't know," Sunny repeated. "He's a good-looking barbarian though."

Clara had little time to be angry with Paul. No sooner did they return to New York, than Elizabeth began packing, on the very unrealistic assumption that she was "all better now," and so could go away to Maine. After several memorable disputes on the subject, Clara worked herself into a frenzy on the subject and phoned her uncle. Paul answered.

"She's gone completely berserk," Clara explained. "She's packing to go to Maine. She thinks she's recovered. I mean. granted, she's better —"

"She's not better," came his cool and definitive reply.

Clara was taken aback. "What do you mean? You have to admit, she's tremendously improved."

Paul said nothing.

"I mean those doctors are off the wall. No way Libby's going to die any day. She's got at least another year in her. Paul?"

"What?"

"You've got to admit she's better."

"She's not better. She's worse."

"I don't believe you."

Paul said nothing.

"I can't believe you're being so callous," Clara went on.

"Callous?"

"I call looking on the dark side, at a time like this, callous. Callous."

"Calm down, Clara."

"I am calm. Don't you tell me to be calm."

"You're not calm. You're hysterical. You need a vacation."

Clara held the receiver out at arm's length and looked at it. When she drew it back, she shouted, "How could you suggest such a thing? A vacation? At a time like this! She has to have somebody with her constantly. Sometimes I really think you're wacked out of your mind." This led to Paul's retort that if anyone in his family was crazy, it was Clara Chimes. But he said it in such a relaxed, placid tone that she became even more worked up and said a number of rather disconnected but evidently provocative things. Paul, however, was not drawn into an argument, which was somehow even more annoying. By the time Clara hung up the phone she was in a thoroughly sour mood and stalked off to the kitchen for a glass of lemonade. There was none left. So she put on her high-heeled sandals and sunglasses — which, combined with her rather tight black leather pants, "I'm okay, you're not" T-shirt and purple toe and fingernail polish, formed a quite remarkable outfit — and went down to the corner store. It was sold out of lemonade. Fuming, Clara went to the supermarket down the block. But it seemed that that day no one had any lemonade. Forty-five minutes later and most put out, she returned home with a jar of tomato juice. She was half way through her second glass of it and grimacing when it occurred to her that the apartment was unusually quiet. Then she realized that Elizabeth had not, as was her wont, shrieked out some random command, when she had reentered the apartment.Clara put her glass in the sink and listened to the silence with sudden foreboding.

She opened the door to Mrs. Darlinger's room, to see her aunt lying on the floor. "Oh brother," she said and turned away from a moment to pray that Elizabeth was still alive. At that instant she heard the lock turning in the front door and then the tall form of a brown-haired, blue-eyed man appeared at the end of the hall. At first she did not even recognize Paul.

"Skin tight leather pants," he remarked. "Not bad." But while he approached, saying that he had come over to talk Libby into going back in the hospital, he perceived that something was wrong. He stopped in front of Clara and looked at her.

"Paul, she's lying on the floor."

He flung the door open and leapt over to his prostrate step-mother. "Call the ambulance," he said after a second.

"Thank God."

"Hurry!" he shouted, pressing his ear to Elizabeth's chest.

That was the end of Elizabeth's plan to go to Maine. Indeed, Dr. Smeltz told her in no uncertain terms that she was going nowhere, not even down the hospital corridor and back.She was, in short, bedridden. And her doctor, furious with her and her entire family, refused even to allow her any visitors for the first few days. That very afternoon he told Paul and Clara not to come back until he said so. He lectured them at some length as to the irresponsibility of having let Elizabeth "run around."

"But she's impossible to stop," Clara said in a very low and evidently guilty voice. Paul just watched and listened.

"That's why," Dr.Smeltz concluded, "she is not even going to leave her bed."

They left the hospital rather glumly. Paul suggested they go get a drink.

"I don't think so," Clara said, standing on the corner, gazing disconsolately down the street. "I guess you were right. She's not better, she's worse. It's hard to believe."

"What?"

"That she could die," and Clara turned and started walking toward home. He watched her for a moment and then quickly strode up alongside her. "It's not good, you know, to be by yourself all the time," he said.

"I'm not."

"You'll turn into a manic depressive. If you haven't already."

Paul saw that behind her sunglasses, she blinked at him.

"Where'd you get that nail polish?" he went on.

"Elizabeth Arden," Clara replied, tossing her head. "Where else?"

"Go to punk clubs dressed like that?"

"I don't go to punk clubs." He glanced down curiously at the "I'm okay, you're not" T-shirt.

"What are you staring at?"

At this, Paul merely began whistling. They walked on for a while until they passed a bar that he liked. He took her by the arm, and, despite protests, steered her inside. They drank for quite some time. Then they went and had dinner and drank some more. In fact, they drank all night. At four in the morning, when Clara got into a cab to go home, it was only with the greatest difficulty that she could make out where she was.

"Where am I?" she asked.

"You're stepping into a cab to go home."

"Oh. Just checking."

Clara awoke the next afternoon quite hungover. The only reason she awoke at all was that her cat had just walked right over her face. Then she noticed that the telephone was ringing.

"I've been calling all day," Paul said.

"Yeah? Well I'll have you know the ceiling's on the floor, and the floor's not where it's supposed to be either."

"Eat lots of salt. Make yourself some scrambled eggs."

"I don't know how.Besides, I couldn't find my way to the kitchen if my life depended on it."

"Been sick?"

"If this is healthy, I'd rather be dead."

With much moaning and groaning, Clara made her way to the bathroom and took a bath. As she got out and dressed in her cutoffs and a Chase Manhattan T-shirt that Elizabeth had given her, she noticed that the walls were in orbit.

"Think I'll just lie down here on the carpet," she said to herself in the hall. She must have fallen asleep, for the next thing she knew two people were standing over her, gazing down at her with some amusement.

"Do this often?"Paul asked.

"It's your fault," Clara replied.

"Where'd you get that hideous T-shirt?" Sunny asked.She herself was gorgeously dressed in a Maremekko maternity jumper.

"David Rockefeller gave it to me."

"Cut it out Clara." Sunny did not like to be kidded.

"No, he did. He gave it to me."

"Really?" Sunny's green eyes widened.

"Sure," Clara said. The corners of her mouth began to twitch.

"Stanley thinks the Rockefellers are behind a plot to take over the country."

Paul glanced at Sunny rather coolly. "Stanley, your husband?"

Sunny nodded vigorously.

"Stanley always had it all over everyone when it came to politics," Clara put in. "Even back in Florida."

"Even back then!" Sunny exclaimed and then, looking at Paul, hastened to explain, "Clara used to go out with Stanley —"

One of Paul's eyebrows went up.

"—but she was too hard to get."

"As it were," Clara said.

Paul's eyebrow returned to its normal spot.

"He was her first boyfriend. Right Clara?"

"Hmm. More or less."

"He says even back then you were just the way you are now, aloof, cold, unapproachable and a complete banana."

Clara blinked. "I don't have to listen to this."

"Hey, I think I like this guy," Paul said.

Clara rolled over onto her stomach. "Goodbye."

Her visitors exhorted her to get up. Sunny said she had to eat something. Paul said maybe she should drink something. Clara said that all she wanted to do was sleep. So Paul picked her up, carried her into her room and dropped her on the bed. "Now you've done it," she said. "I'm really going to be sick." But she was not; and the day passed with Clara threatening to be ill and her guests insulting her and each other. At one point Paul stretched out on the carpet of Clara's bedroom floor. He was in the midst of a monologue on airplanes. When Clara looked down at him, sometime later, she saw that he was asleep.

***

Elizabeth meanwhile had made the transition from grouchiness to a certain haughty froideur about her circumstances. She scarcely deigned to acknowledge the existence of the nurses or members of the hospital staff. Seated on her bed nearly twenty four hours a day in her white gown and turban, Bible in hand and usually with cold cream all over her face, she had taken to referring to Dr. Smeltz as Dr. Smutz behind his back and, in his presence, always maintained the most offended and stoical silence. It was as if she regarded him and his entire hospital as part of a large conspiracy to ruin her life, but, being powerless to do anything about it, had resolved never for a minute to let them know that they were "getting to" her.

One day, to his immense surprise, she asked her physician in icy tones if he ever read the Bible.

"Can't say I do," the doctor replied, glancing at her chart.

"You should. It would improve your outlook on life. It puts things in their proper, miniature perspective." Whereupon, to his displeasure and her delight, she began reading to him from Proverbs.

"Never much cared for those bromides," he remarked.

"Be quiet. It's good for you."

Elizabeth thereafter insisted, every time she saw the luckless Dr. Smeltz, on reading him a few passages. "Woman's driving me crazy," he remarked one afternoon to a nurse. "Crazy as a hoot owl."

"Whole family is, if you ask me. You seen that daughter?"

"Niece. Nothing wrong with her. Good-looking girl."

"I don't know. She and her brother have a kind of odd relationship, don't you think?"

"Hmm. Never noticed."

The next time Dr. Smeltz saw Clara and Paul together, he observed what he thought a rather alarming look of desire in the young man's eyes.

"I see what you mean about those two," he later commented to the nurse, "something

409

downright incestuous about them, though I'm not sure if he's the brother or the nephew or the stepson."

The nurse nodded sagely. "Think she knows — Mrs. Darlinger? After all, it's right under her nose."

"She wouldn't know an elephant if it was right under her nose. Woman's wacked out of her gourd.Gonna be a born-again Christian at the rate she's going."

"Just like our last idiot president."

"What do you expect? Leader of the whole nation thought he was chased by a swimming rabbit. No wonder we're a country of crack pots."

Elizabeth, blithely aware that her physician detested her readings, continued to torture him. She had even taken to watching Billy Grahm's TV show and, after a great deal of nudging, had got her ex-husband to buy her a Beta Max, with which she taped the preacher's sermons, playing them back constantly and invariably when Dr. Smeltz checked in on her.

"The human heart is wicked, and infinitely deceitful," the preacher yelled from the television set as the doctor walked into the room one afternoon. He rolled his eyes. It was a habit he had lately picked up from Clara.

"Watch out Smeltz. Keep that up and they'll get stuck."

"Indeed."

"Happened to a friend of mine. Crossed 'em one day and kaboom, couldn't get 'em back. Had to have an operation. Wound up dumber than the village idiot. I won't tell you the conclusion of the story. It would upset you."

"Indeed."

"Don't believe me, hunh? Well, I'll spring it on you one day. Bet you five bucks you're not going to like it."

"Bet you ten you can't keep it to yourself for more than a week."

"Bet you twenty I can and twenty on top of that you're not going to like it."

Elizabeth "cleaned up on that bet," as she put it to her stepson. "Forty bucks.But I'll say this for him, old Smutzface forked over. You can't win with these doctors, though. He gave me an extra radiation treatment, just to get even." She was sitting bolt upright on her bed, her face covered with cold cream, her turban slightly askew, playing solitaire. "You know," she went on, "I don't think he likes me."

"Can't see why," Paul said. "Who else is going to read to him from the Bible?"

"Thinks I'm tooty fruity. Overheard him saying so to a nurse."

"Can't see why."

Elizabeth looked up and regarded her stepson sharply. Having just come from a business meeting on Wall Street, he was in a suit and tie.His light brown hair, she thought, needed cutting and the rather ironical look in his eyes annoyed her. He was smoking his second cigarette. "A little uninventive today," she snapped. "You sound like a broken record."

"Sorry," he grinned as if he were thinking of something he shouldn't, "my mind's kind of gone on vacation."

"Well bring it back. You need a hair cut, So does that fritterbug."

"Fritterbug?"

"Clara. Kid's got so she looks like she just escaped from a loony bin. Shaggy hair, purple finger nails, leather pants. When she bothers to wear clothes."

"Oh?"

"Runs around stark naked at every opportunity. You should have seen her in that apartment she had. Stayed in bed all weekend, eating green peppers, according to Sunny. Girl's got a cast iron stomach. Too bad she can't cook. When I go, she'll probably starve to death. Unless of course she marries a househusband."

"Not likely."

"Since when are you the big know-it-all?" He shrugged. "Just a surmise."

"I wouldn't make too many if I were you. In my experience with that fritterbug she never does what you think she will. Labor unions, tenant organizing. Gazing at the stars with that Martian. Bad enough her best friend's a two thousand year old man. Next thing you know she'll be voting Democratic. I shudder to think how she'll bring up her children. Then again, maybe she won't."

Paul looked surprised. "Why not?"

"Well, if I die — which is not at all a certain thing, mind you — if I die, somebody has to take over Darlinger-Fairless. Since you're out of the running, that leaves Clara. If she goes back into real estate, I doubt she'll have time to have children." Paul stared at his stepmother in disbelief. "Libby, she already left the company — left it for good."

"We'll see about that," Elizabeth snapped. "I'm going to have a talk with her. That girl has a real aptitude. A killer instinct. She may not have thought she was happy, but she was one of the most successful developers in town. Chance of a lifetime.She'd be a fool to throw it away. Besides, if she does, who'll run the company? Certainly you don't propose selling it off?"

"Maybe. Maybe not."

"Ungrateful child. The work of generations, generations! And you'd let it go right down the drain. Where is that fritterbug anyway?" Elizabeth reached over to the phone and dialed. "Clara? What are you doing? Yes I know. You're always drinking lemonade, something wrong with your system. Some deficiency. Surprised you haven't turned into a lemon. Don't tell me to be quiet. What else are you doing? Reading what? Oh God," Elizabeth put down the phone and stared at her stepson as if to say "she's

415

hopeless." Then she said "she's reading Einstein on relativity," and then, into the receiver, "you stop it, Clara, with that heathen stuff. It'll scramble your brains. If it hasn't already. Ask me, you're brain's a fried egg already. Why aren't you shopping or something? Well, get a boyfriend, then you'll want some new clothes. What? I know you don't like anybody. It runs in the family. Why aren't you visiting me? What do you mean you couldn't manage it? Your step cousin, or whatever he is, could, and he can barely tie his shoelaces. Good. Okay, good." Elizabeth hung up the phone and settled back to her solitaire. Paul watched her expectantly. At length he said, "well?"

"Oh, she's coming over."

He smiled and leaned back and loosened his tie.

Toward the end of that month and the beginning of the next, the East Coast underwent a heat wave. Day after day, and then week after week, the temperature stayed in the high nineties or higher. Even the nights were stifling and humid. Sunny proclaimed it "worse than Nevada," and departed for her ranch.Even the hospital, though air-conditioned, seemed warm, and Ward had bought Elizabeth several fans which whirred at top speed, day and night. Clara, in her summer clothes, perspired constantly and so laid for hours in the air-conditioned duplex, reading and drinking lemonade. Paul was busy completing the arrangements attendant upon his transfer to New York. Ward's doctor was anxious about his blood pressure in the suffocating heat; but Ward paid little attention to his own medical problems. He continued to work hard and to spend all his free time with his ex-wife.

Elizabeth, by this time, was doing quite poorly. All her hair had fallen out and, as a result, she now never removed the turban. They could give her no more radiation treatment and no more surgery. So she started on another bout of chemotherapy. She seemed to be losing weight by the minute. "I'll have to get an entirely new wardrobe," she said, looking with distaste at her wasted arms and legs. She had taken to referring to her medicine as rat poison and to Dr. Smeltz as Dr. Stinkpot. She was as cantankerous as ever. Indeed, one afternoon, Paul entered the room to find her in a truly ghastly mood.

"Just like a roach!" She shrieked over the drone of Billy Grahm's recorded voice. "They're killing me like a roach." She snapped off the TV set by remote control and snapped on the radio. It was tuned to a disco station. Elizabeth had only recently discovered this variety of music, and though she professed an abhorrence for it, listened to it constantly, "to remind me how much I hate it," she would explain.

"Why a roach?" Paul asked, taking off his jacket, loosening his tie and mopping his forehead with a handkerchief. "Why not a Japanese beetle?"

"And why not a caterpillar? Because I experimented. You are soaking with sweat."

"I know."

"Your shirt will be ruined."

"What experiment?"

Elizabeth sat up, her hazel eyes blazing. "I took some of the left-over chemicals, the one they're feeding me, see? And I made a paste and brushed in on the baseboard over there, in the corner, where I'd seen roaches. Look. Just look and tell me what you see."

Paul got up and walked over to the corner indicated. "Dead roaches," he said. "Hey Libby, you should patent the stuff. You'd make a mint as an exterminator."

"Ha, ha. I could die laughing. Aren't you going to do something? It's a scandal. They

419

might as well just spray me with Raid or put me in the roach motel."

"The what?"

"You know, roaches check in but they don't check out. It's on television. No. You're not going to do anything. What kind of a son are you?"

Paul sat down and regarded his stepmother. She looked, he realized, like someone about to die. After a moment she glanced at him and said, "what are you doing, staring at me with those cold blue eyes?"

"I didn't know they were cold."

"They are. They always have been. Like you think I'm a crank or you disapprove of me or you're judging me somehow."

"I'm not judging you."

"Then why are they so cold? Why have they always been like that?"

Paul went over and put his arms around her shoulders and kissed her on the forehead. And

III

then, for the first time since she had learned she had cancer, Elizabeth started to cry. She said she was terrified and that she didn't want to die and that he ought to use a deodorant.

During the heat wave, in the early part of August, Elizabeth began to fade very fast. Everyone knew it was the end, and so no one talked about it, since there was nothing to say. Her will was put in order, with all her money and possessions divided evenly between Clara and Paul. Dr. Smeltz, knowing there was nothing further to be done, became suddenly lenient in such matters as her diet. For her part, Mrs. Darlinger became more insistent than ever on reading to her assembled family from the Bible. She was especially keen on Proverbs.

"The light of the righteous rejoiceth," she read one evening to her ex-husband and his son," but the lamp of the wicked shall be put out. Wealth gotten by vanity shall be

421

diminished, but he that gathereth by labor shall increase. Hope deferred maketh the heart sick, but when the desire cometh, it is a tree of life."

"What's this about the tree of life?" Clara asked, walking into the room. She wore a rather tight and skimpy white cotton dress. Here and there damp patches of perspiration were visible. "It's an oven out there," she said, flinging herself into a chair. "It's enough to make you contemplate stripping off your clothes in the street."

"Oh, please. Feel free," Paul said.

"Shut up you two. Libby was reading."

Elizabeth looked at her ex-husband in surprise. "Ward, I didn't know you liked my reading."

"Anything that suits you, dear, suits me too."

"That's leaving the door kind of, ah, wide open, wouldn't you say?"

III

"Shut up you fritterbug. Where have you been?"

"On the roof of your apartment building. Perfecting my suntan."

"I hope you remembered to wear clothes. If you call that B-I-K-I-N-I clothes."

"No one can see me up there."

Elizabeth had a sort of spasm but then, in a considerably weaker voice, said "just everyone and their grandmother." She paused for a moment to regain her breath and then continued reading. The strange sound of her voice, however, made Paul sit up in alarm. Neither Ward nor Clara, he observed, had noticed it. She was still reading from Proverbs when she suddenly sat forward.

"This is it," were the words that passed through Paul's mind.

"And above all things," she read in that distant, alien voice, "keep the heart pure. For it is the starting point of life." And with that, the

423

Bible fell from her hands, and Elizabeth
Darlinger died.

At first Clara and Ward did not believe it
had happened. There were hysterics. Paul
fetched a doctor and then there was no question
about it. Elizabeth was gone.

"She was all I had," Ward said and walked
dazedly out into the hall.

That night no one knew exactly what to do.
Clara did not want to be alone, so she went
with the Fairlesses out to Long Island. Every
light in the house, she noted when they arrived,
was on. And far into the night, as she lay
awake in the bed in one of the guest rooms, she
heard Ward walking from room to room.

At Elizabeth's funeral it seemed to Paul that
the once athletic Mr. Fairless looked not merely
old, but ancient. Gone was the red in his
cheeks, the perennial tan on his nose. There
was more white in his hair than gray, and he
walked with a slight stoop. But though he may

have become more frail, he had also become stubborn. He refused to take his son's advice and go on vacation. In fact, he stayed in the office even later than before and went in on the weekends as well. Clara, who still had not gone back to work for Slava Aster, met him frequently for lunch. She had discussed his condition with his son and so also urged the prematurely old man to take a rest. But she went farther and begged him even to retire. He had reached retirement age anyway, she said, but with equally little effect.

Meanwhile Paul worked on Wall Street; and the heat did not abate. August, Clara said glumly to herself was "going to be a scorcher from beginning to end." The presidential campaign was in full swing, and Clara spent many hours lying on the roof in her bikini, several stories above what was now her duplex, and listening to the political coverage over the radio.By now a registered Democrat, she nonetheless found the thought of voting for Mondale somewhat distasteful. Otherwise she did little besides lie in the sun, listen to the radio and read. She was in what she called "a blue funk." Now and then acquaintances telephoned, asking her out or alerting her to various parties, but she rarely went.

She had made no changes in the apartment, except that she had moved into Elizabeth's room, which no longer bothered her. At night she lay on the bed for hours, reading science fiction novels and eating chocolate chip cookies. Her cat had appropriated the entire chaise longue, from which perch he regarded Clara with his green, unblinking eyes, hoping to catch her unawares in order to scratch the furniture. But this happened rarely. By means of a water pistol, she had her pet fairly well trained. It often lay on the night table, beside the framed photograph of her parents.

The days passed, long and sweltering, and still Clara did not want to do anything. She had become, for the first time in her life, utterly indolent. She slept until eleven o'clock every morning and had to wander around the apartment for twenty minutes in order to wake up. Breakfast consisted of cereal and orange juice, and then generally she consumed nothing aside from yogurt, and lemonade until dinner, whereupon she either heated up something from a can, sent out for Chinese food or went to a local restaurant. Thereafter the chocolate cookie regime took over, until she fell asleep. She smoked a pack of cigarettes a day and toward mid-August, occasionally drank in the evening. She generally preferred brandy.

It was on one such evening, as she lay on the bed in her underwear, the air conditioner off, the windows open, a copy of <u>Destination: Void</u> on her lap, and pouring her second cognac, that she answered the telephone to hear Paul's voice, oddly constricted, telling her that he had just arrived home, that every light in the house had been blazing, and that he had walked into the first floor study to find his father dead on the floor. Clara dressed, went down to the underground garage, got into what had once been Elizabeth's Mercedes, and drove out to Long Island.

***

After his father's death, Paul took a six week leave of absence from work. At first he stayed home "stewing," as Clara put it. She had met a number of his friends at Ward's funeral, but neither they nor she were able to cheer him up. She spent most of her time at the enormous house on Long Island, and most of it in silence. Her only living relation was in a taciturn mood. He did little besides drink beer, stare into space, watch television, smoke cigarettes and occasionally address her in what seemed to

Clara to be a growl. He appeared hardly aware of her presence. But when, after a week of these delightful activities, she told him that either they go out or she would return to Manhattan, he suddenly complied.

They joined a group of his Wall Street friends and their girlfriends at a club that evening to listen to music and dance. Clara generally liked his acquaintances, with the exception of one unctuous, blond fellow with a nose that seemed far too short for the rest of his face. She had met him at the funeral where he had, very inappropriately in her opinion, asked her out. She had declined but once again found him lurking around her.

"What do you mean, lurking?" Paul asked. "Drew doesn't lurk."

"Does too. Gives me the creeps."

Paul did not pursue the discussion. Ever since the day when Elizabeth had started weeping in his arms, he had been in a daze.

Scarcely aware of the people and things surrounding him, he seemed unable to hold a conversation for more than a few minutes. His mind was elsewhere; it was on scenes from his childhood, events, long forgotten, which had begun vividly and arrestingly to recur. He thought about nothing else, indeed he scarcely thought; he simply watched images from his memory, hold his attention, and then disappear. He gazed blankly at his scotch and soda. Clara sighed and accepted the invitation of one of his friends to dance.

"Quite a number," Paul heard. He became aware that someone had sat down beside him.

"Hunh?"

"That cousin of yours in the skimpy black and white dress." It was Drew.

"Oh, Clara."

"The aloof and snotty redhead."

"She's not a redhead," Paul corrected. "Her hair's auburn."

"Red, auburn, what's the difference? She's too good-looking and too loaded for her own good," Drew finished his drink. Evidently he had had a few too many.

"You're the one who's loaded."

"Not the way she is. Hope you don't mind — I asked her out."

Paul was suddenly alert. "And?"

"She said she was busy."

They sat in silence for a while, Paul gazing at his drink, Drew gazing at Clara. "You know," Drew finally said. "I think she's stuck on you. My luck."

Paul hardly heard him. He was thinking about an afternoon more than ten years ago, on a tennis court with his father. It had been a clear spring day, and his father had just won the game, but Paul, as he had told himself afterward, had "won the war." He had refused to go into the family business. Now he would have to get rid of that business — sell all the real estate, cancel the contracts, close the branch offices. Never for a second had he considered taking it over himself. He sighed aloud.

"It's nothing to be upset about, old pal. I wouldn't mind being in your shoes one bit."

Paul had no idea what his friend was talking about, then or even as Drew commenced a recitation of his woes, which centered mainly on the disparity between his salary and the style to which he had become accustomed to live. For his part Drew attributed his friend's inattention to intoxication. But the fact that Paul was not listening did not bother him in the least. He droned on about the overall unfairness of life, until the music group struck up a particularly lively tune. Then all at once he became silent, transfixed by something on the dance floor. Evidently Clara liked the music. She had unwound, or so it seemed to Drew, who thought he had never seen anyone dance so well before.

After a few moments Paul observed that his friend was not talking. "I say something wrong?" he asked.

"Shh. I'm busy"

"You don't look it."

"You know Paul, sometimes I think you have no appreciation of beauty."

"What beauty?"

Drew pointed.

Paul's vision moved in the direction of his friend's arm, settling on Clara. His melancholy thoughts about Darlinger-Fairless and its real estate vanished. He sat up. There came, his friend thought, a peculiar light into his eyes. And Clara, who danced well into the morning, noticed it too, when she finally came over to sit down. That night, she decided that she had better not go back to Long Island.

At noon the next day, Clara was happily snoozing under the covers in the room that had once been Elizabeth's. The shades were drawn. The cat slept on the chaise longue. All was silent in the duplex apartment except for the ticking of the grandfather clock in the the living room. Nothing stirred.The photograph of Elizabeth at age twenty two gazed down from the mantelpiece, the eyes still seeming to twinkle with a vibrant, feminine hypocrisy. Marilyn and Frank, laughing on the beach almost twenty five years ago, gazed out from their photograph on the night table at the tousled hair of their daughter on the white pillow case. The plants in the pantry gleamed in the strong August sunlight. The very modern blue and white couch in the living room seemed to wait expectantly for someone to sit on it. Upstairs, the rooms that had once belonged to Clara and Paul were exactly as they had been years ago. The window in Clara's old room, however, was a slight bit open, and the light green fabric of the curtain fluttered out in the morning breeze, like a flag from the thirteenth floor of the apartment building. Downstairs on the kitchen counter stood a pitcher of warm lemonade, left out the night before. All was quiet and somnolent. All was as it had been for years and years. The only difference was that, unlike the old days, none of the lights were on. The only abrupt sound was that of a key turning in the front door lock.

This was followed by footsteps that stopped outside of Clara's room. Then came the sound of her door opening. Then there was silence again, as Paul surveyed the scene of slumber before him.

"Wake up, sleepy head," he said at last and very loudly.

Clara raised her head suddenly, saw the man in the suit — for Paul had just come from a business meeting — in the doorway and then flopped back down on her pillow with a groan. "Whattimeizit?"

"Noon," he said and came over to the edge of the bed.

"Go away. I'm sleeping."

He yanked off the bedspread.

Clara sat up with a scream — "can't you see I'm sleeping?" — and then fell back down under the sheets.

Paul began to tickle her feet and, when she tried to kick him, took a sudden jump and landed on top of her.

"What, may I ask, are you doing?"

"Just a little familial affection. Boy, this is comfortable. I could do this all day."

"I couldn't. I can hardly breathe."

"Out of practice I see."

"Hunh? What's that supposed to mean. Get off me."

"Unh, unh."

"Get off you big bully. I want to get up."

436

Paul stepped off the bed and looked down at her. She didn't move. "Come on," he said. "I'm taking you to breakfast."

"All right, all right. Just go out of the room."

"So you can go back to sleep?"

"No. So I can get dressed."

He smiled and walked to the door smiling. "Not as if you're a sight I haven't seen before," he said, shutting the door in time not to be hit by a shoe.

Clara emerged in the hall in her purple corduroy slacks, high-heeled sandals and Hawaiian shirt. Paul, sitting in the living room, reading the newspaper, glanced up. For a moment they looked at each other. "Oh boy," Clara said at length.

"What do you mean," he grinned, "oh boy?"

"I can tell when you're in a mood," she said and marched to the front door. "Don't you ever wear anything besides suits?" she asked as they walked to the restaurant.

"You're hardly in a position to criticize," he replied, glancing with amusement at her outfit. "By the time you're forty you'll be wearing white shorts and knee socks, just like Libby. Even moved into her room, I see."

"I like the vibes. And you're in no position to criticize, living in that mansion on Long Island."

"I'm not," Paul said and began whistling.

"No? Then where are you living?"

"I'm moving in with you."

"We'll see about that."

"Oh yes. We will."

As they selected a place by the window at the restaurant, who should they see at a nearby table but Dr. Smeltz and a woman, evidently not his wife. It was the nurse who had originally remarked the unusual relationship between Paul and Clara.

"Read any Bibles lately?" Paul asked.

438

Dr. Smeltz smiled in an attempt to conceal a look of distaste.

"You know," Clara whispered after they had sat down, "that's not his wife."

Paul was busy scrutinizing the menu.

"I think it's a nurse from the hospital. She's looking at us kind of funny. She always did.Must be something wrong with her, maybe a nervous disorder. There'd have to be, to carry on an adulterous affair with old Smutzkopf."

Paul patted Clara's hand and continued reading the menu. "Anything you say, beautiful."

"What? You're not listening to me! You're patronizing me. How dare you!"

"Disgusting," Dr. Smeltz was muttering over at the other table, "an incestuous mess. Horrid family. Vile old religious fanatic and lunatic children." He glanced over at Paul and Clara and shuddered. "Can't keep his hands off her. Even in public."

"You don't suppose they're actually, I mean," the nurse said, "they always seemed very attached, but it's a big step from there to —"

"Not for those two. Besides, who's going to stop them?"

"Too bad," she sighed. "Looks are so deceiving. They look like two angels. I wonder if poor Mrs. Darlinger knew."

"That woman didn't know anything about anything. Stark raving mad, drove her husband into an early grave."

"Her ex-husband," the nurse corrected.

"That makes it worse."

Meanwhile Clara was carrying on a spirited monologue on the nurse's dreadful taste, evident from her attire and, of course, from keeping company with "Stinkpot." The waiter came over to their table and before Clara could say she was not ready to order, Paul had ordered for both of them. Clara gaped.

"What's wrong?" Paul asked, lighting a cigarette.

"You ordered for me! How do you know I want an omelette?"

"You always get omelettes when you go out for breakfast."

"What if I wanted eggs Benedict."

"An interesting hypothesis, but unlikely."

"Ooh," Clara flicked some water from her glass into Paul's face, "you annoy me."

"I think they're having a fight," the nurse said.

"Let's hope they kill each other."

"I think they're sweet. Two tiger cubs."

"Nauseating. They should both see a psychiatrist."

On their way out of the restaurant, Clara and Paul stopped by Dr. Smeltz's table. "It does my heart good," Dr. Smeltz lied "to see a brother and sister so obviously fond of each other."

441

Clara and Paul looked at each other. There was laughter in Paul's eyes. Clara decided not to enlighten the physician. "We're not," she said. "I hate him."

"So where are you off to now?" the nurse asked.

"Home."

"Live together?" Dr. Smeltz asked with excessive nonchalance.

Paul nodded.

Dr. Smeltz cleared his throat, sat back and surveyed them." Big apartment?"

"Fairly big," Clara chirped.

"But we only live in one room of it," Paul smiled.

Dr. Smeltz looked at his companion. "I see," he said after a second, and then," so what are you two doing these days?"

"Oh," Paul went on, still smiling. He put his arm around Clara's waist, "mostly just lying around."

"Lying around?"

"Unh hunh. In bed. A lot of deaths in the family — it takes a while to get over it." With that they strolled out of the restaurant, leaving the doctor and his companion wide-eyed and staring after them. Dr. Smeltz put his napkin on the table.

"What's wrong?" the nurse asked.

"Nothing, just lost my appetite."

"It is sort of shocking, you know, to have it thrust right under your nose like that."

The doctor said nothing. After a moment he called for the check.

"What are you doing?"

"Going back to work," he said sourly.

"Not coming over to my place? I took the day off."

He shook his head and, shortly thereafter, left the restaurant, mumbling something about a genetic nightmare.

Clara and Paul ambled down the street, pausing now and then to look into shop windows, or for Clara to critique the apparel of passers by. It was a bright, hot summer day. "Why'd you do that?" she finally asked.

"What?"

"Make old Stinkypoo think we're perverts?"

"Just came over me."

"Seems like a lot of things 'just come over' you."

"Hmm. So?"

"I think it's weird."

"I think you never stop talking."

"You should have seen her two years ago," a voice suddenly said, "she was quiet as a mouse." They turned and there, standing on the corner in a flood of sunlight, seeming to point at something with his cane, was Mr. Tannini. Beneath his brown felt hat and mane of white hair, his dark eyes sparkled at Clara.They seemed full of knowledge and meaning for her.

"This is certainly a day for running into people," Clara exclaimed and introduced Paul.

"Mrs. Darlinger's prodigal son," the old man smiled." Slava Aster told me she died, reading a proverb. My condolences." And then, after a moment, he asked, "What proverb was it?"

"Above all things keep the heart pure," Clara began.

"For it is the starting point of life," Mr. Tannini concluded.

"You know it."

He nodded. "Yes, and it brings back memories." He gazed up, sadly it seemed, at the blue and cloudless sky. "Come and visit me," he said after a moment. "My door is always open."

And with that he turned and headed off down the block, and soon became one of the many on the sidewalk, and then at last disappeared in the bright afternoon throng of strollers and shoppers and passers by.

When they arrived in the apartment, Clara made straight for the kitchen to inspect the lemonade. Finding it warm, she added ice, then went into her room and changed into her bikini. She emerged with a container of suntan lotion in one hand and a copy of <u>Star Travel 4000</u> in the other. Paul, his jacket off, tie undone and peering at the contents of the refrigerator in disgust, looked up. "That's nice," he said in reference to her attire.

"Want to join me?"

"Unh hunh, but not up there."

"Look here. You seem to be taking a number of things for granted," Clara took a step back.

"Going somewhere?"

Clara hurried into the living room for her cigarettes. Paul followed and sat down across from her in one of the Mies Van der Rohe chairs. "Well, darling, little one, at long last we have the place to ourselves," he said, lighting a cigarette.

"Don't imitate Libby. She's dead."

"It's Philistine, isn't it?" he made a gesture that was distinctly Clara's.

"You really are a fruitcake and you know," she said in sudden pique, "you haven't been the only man —"

"How many?" he interrupted, his eyes narrowing.

"Well, there was one who —"

"Only one?" Paul looked surprised and then pleased. Then his eyes narrowed again. "I don't want to know his name. I just want to know —"

"Who was better? I'm not telling," and she flounced off in the direction of the front hall. Paul stuck out his foot. Clara saw it in time and raced off in the direction of the staircase. Paul followed and was bombarded with items from the second floor. This game went on for some time, from room to room. It ended in the vestibule amid the clatter of the little antique side table, toppled by the also toppling

447

uncomfortable little chair, covered with antique needlework. This time, however, there was no Limoges vase to shatter on the floor. And Clara and Paul did not get up for quite a while.

Days passed. The sun shone brightly. People went to and from work and their vacations. The presidential campaign proceeded from state to state. Conventioneers gathered and departed. Young women roller skated down the avenues. The subways rumbled under the street. Out in Nevada Sunny Katz gave birth to a boy, and an indictment was dropped against her husband. Monica LaMarque, lying by the side of her pool, breathed a sigh of relief and dropped one of the several Nevada newspapers she had taken to reading. Horace, pausing in the driveway in the midst of a delightful daydream that involved his grandson and a future Republican presidential candidacy, did not notice Sunny dog, peeing on his motorcycle. Out on Long Island Slava Aster gazed at nebulas at night.

Ward Fairless's house was dark and empty, and its doors were locked. The grass on the front lawn had grown rather high and the neighbors thought it unsightly. Up in Maine an owl had made a nest under one of the eaves of Elizabeth's summer house. Raccoons came out on the lawn at night and right up the front steps. Ray and Rita Longhill threw a party at the Plaza for their son who had married a girl he met in EST.White flower petals wrinkled and turned brown in the long grass that had begun to grow over the two graves side by side on Long Island, and the wreathes around the headstones, engraved with the names Elizabeth Darlinger Fairless and Ward Cadbury Fairless, had withered. Parties were given at exclusive Park Avenue clubs where debutantes snubbed actresses. Gossip columnists reported that the Paraguayan Dr. Vittelini had been sighted at the dinner table of a well-known socialite, despite his impending trial. Dr. Smeltz had taken to Valium to cope with the fact that his wife had walked out on him. Downtown, not far from Gramercy Park, squirrels gamboled on the boughs of two locust trees entwined over the roof of a quiet old townhouse. Pigeons cooed under the eaves. And now and then from the street could be heard the faint and melodious sound of myriad chimes. In his twenty third floor office, Philip Angelica worked far into the night on behalf of Mrs. Shatzenkammer's tenants. Under her breath, when she was supposed to be listening to patients, Mrs. Shatzenkammer cursed the tireless attorney. Down in the Caribbean, Batter senior and Marty Stein clinked glasses and drank a toast to each other on a flagstone terrace that overlooked the dazzling aquamarine of the Gulf of Mexico. On Leonard street in Manhattan, down by the courts, prosecutors were still sifting through the thousands of pages of Judge Pepper's testimony. Judge Pepper having gone on to become a world champion golf player, stood on a rolling green in Scotland, contemplating his next putt. The days were hot and busy, but growing shorter. In the cool evenings, tourists and lovers and passers by strolled along the east wall of Central Park and now and then gazed up at the large and luxurious apartment houses across Fifth Avenue. Roberto Rodriguez, who had taken to blowing his whistle sometimes just for the hell of it, occasionally blew it at them. Everyone was occupied, going about their business. Everyone had appointments to keep, phone calls to make, shopping to be done, vacations to be enjoyed, work to be completed. But the shades on the bedroom windows of the twelfth floor duplex were always drawn.

Clara and Paul did not go out. They did not make telephone calls. They did not visit their friends. They did very little besides stay in bed, but there they were very busy. Somewhat embarrassed by all this amorous activity, Clara had turned the photograph of her parents away from the bed. Now and then, however, she was disturbed to spy her cat, perched on the night table, watching with its bright, inscrutable green eyes. At night she slept curled up halfway under Paul, dreaming of tropical oceans. Paul usually dreamt that he was flying upside down in his plane, with Clara beside him. It became, in fact, a delightful, recurring dream.

"What a limited imagination. Don't you ever dream about anything else? I mean, why not a helicopter?"

"Never flew a helicopter."

"That's immaterial. Paul?"

"Hmm."

"We've been here for weeks."

"So?"

"Don't you think we're taking a risk?"

"What risk?"

"Well, with my diaphragm lost. I should get a new one."

"Too late probably."

"That's very nonchalant of you."

"Hmm." Paul began to doze. He dreamt he was playing baseball and winning.

Weeks passed. Sunny began to wonder why Clara had not congratulated her and telephoned.

"Hi y'all."

"Who's this?" Paul said up, scratching his already tousled hair.

"Me. Sunny. That you Paul? What are you doing there?"

"Wouldn't be polite to describe it."

"Who is it?" Clara asked.

"Yeah?" Sunny went on with sudden interest. "You in bed?"

"Unh-hunh," Paul replied and then, "stop that Clara, it's Sunny."

"You in bed with Clara?"

"No. I just like to come over here and get in bed and talk to myself. That's my idea of kicks."

"You <u>are</u> in bed with Clara."

"Paul put his hand over the receiver. "You know, sometimes I think Sunny's a moron."

"Always said she had cement between her ears," Clara replied and rolled over onto her stomach.

Paul found this very distracting and for a moment sat silently gazing at her back while the little voice in the telephone said "What's this about a moron? What's this about cement? Paul are you there?"

He raised the receiver to his ear, still gazing at Clara's back. "Hi Sunny."

"Hey, we already went through that. What's Clara doing?"

"Uh, lying on her stomach with no clothes on."

"That's nice."

"Boy you said it."

"What are you two doing in bed at three o'clock in the afternoon?"

"Take a guess. A wild guess."

"I didn't interrupt anything?"

"Nothing that can't be resumed on short notice."

"Oh. Well, guess what?"

"What?"

"Guess."

Paul covered the receiver and leaned over and whispered in Clara's ear "a moron." She bit him and a bout of wrestling ensued. The receiver dropped to the carpet. The little voice was saying, "what's going on over there? Hey, this is long distance. I'm calling long distance! Paul, Clara, pick up the phone."

"Hi Sunny."

"That you Clara?"

"Who else?"

"You know, this is long distance."

"I figured as much. How's Stanley?"

"Fine. The indictment was dropped."

"Indictment? What indictment?"

"You know, that organized crime thing. I could never keep all the details straight. It was only six counts."

"What indictment?" Paul asked. He was doing something Clara found very distracting.

"Stop that. I don't know. Sunny doesn't even know. Bunch of birdbrains if you ask me. Amazing that boy isn't behind bars. May be the only safe place for him."

"What's that about bars Clara? You're going to bars?"

"Not exactly. I'm afraid we spend most of our time in bed."

"Oh yeah? Hot and heavy hunh?"

"Uh, you could say that."

"I hear wedding bells." Clara looked at Paul. "Sunny hears wedding bells."

"Sunny hears wedding bells. I see doctor's bills. Nine months of them."

"What's that?"

"You're pregnant." Paul said.

"How do you know?"

"I know."

"Sunny, Paul says I'm pregnant."

"What's he know about these things? Missed your period?"

"Just a few weeks."

"Well, guess what."

"What?"

"Guess."

"You had a baby."

"Yup. A boy."

"Oh boy, oh boy," Clara jumped up. "Paul!" she screamed. "Sunny had a boy. Sunny and Stanley had a boy!"

"Well, I figured it was Stanley. Then again, you can never be too sure about these things."

After Sunny had described her infant in great and, to tell the truth, rather tedious detail to Clara, Paul got on the phone and heard the same recitation of her child's charms. Then, of course, the proud father had to speak to both Clara and Paul. He seemed somewhat overcome by the whole situation and had little to say other than that Sunny was a real trooper and quite a gal. He seemed to regard his wife as a rather miraculous being. Then of course they had to listen to the baby, who slurped, gurgled and screeched into the phone.

"Poor kid," Clara said later. "He'll be demented. The combined intelligence of his parents won't get him through the first grade."

"You never know," Paul said, "sometimes stupid people have smart kids and vice versa. Life's full of surprises."

"Paul?"

"Clara?"

"We won't have stupid kids."

"Hmm."

"They'll be geniuses," Clara said. "Mighty, scientific geniuses."

"Right."

"Promise?"

Paul yawned, then gazed past her at the light around the edges of the window shades and smiled and said, "Anything you want, darling."